Carbon

Written by:
Carrie Yonge

2nd Ed. Copyright © 2015
CarbonBook Publications

Book Cover Design: Caitlin Hartigan

ISBN: 978-0-578-07588-4

Acknowledgements

Thanks to the many family members and friends for their prayers and encouragement, and a special thanks to J.D. Davis at Philips Chrysler Jeep Dodge for allowing me to test drive a beautiful black Challenger!

Dedication

This book is dedicated to my mother, who has seen me faithfully through my darkest moments, and taught me to never surrender even in the face of fear and discouragement. Her life is a tremendous example of seeking the Lord Jesus' heart and will throughout the twists of life, and I am indebted to her for teaching us commitment and love above all things.

Prologue

"Time is running out."

Sliding out from underneath a black car, a young man stood up and wiped his hands on a clean rag. Excited blue eyes met his father's gaze. He motioned toward the car, "We're almost ready here."

The older man barely suppressed a grimace, forearms leaning heavily on a workbench. "Let's hope it's fast enough."

"The Center for Disease Control has yet to categorize and examine the blood samples retrieved from Mesa Springs High," a woman's voice informed them. "According to sources, Irene was one of two-hundred students randomly selected to test for West Nile Virus."

"Nothing is random," the greying figure murmured.

"Either way," his son raked his fingers through blonde hair. "It won't take them long to figure out who she is, and where she is."

"I have set several diversions in place to maximize our window of opportunity," the woman intoned smoothly.

"What kind of time frame are we talking?" the older man asked.

"A minimum of three weeks, but it could be as long as several months. I will continue running as many distractions as possible."

"Good job, Carbon." Standing with a small stretch, thin outlines of a smile lit the father's face. "Keep up the good work."

He stepped toward his son and placed a hand on his shoulder. "Alex?"

The blonde man raised his eyebrows expectantly. "Mm-hm?"

"It's been a long time. Let's bring her home."

Chapter 1

"Hey Elise!" a voice shouted out the window of a passing car. "Where are you headed?"

A teenage girl, pedaling furiously on her bike, caught a brief glimpse of her friend Nia's old Jeep CJ as it tore down the dirt road, leaving rolling clouds of dust in its wake.

Elise rolled her eyes. No one ever knew where that girl was going, including herself.

She turned her bike to cut through some woods toward town, or at least what was called town. In this huge metropolis of Mesa Springs, the local grocer, a dollar general, and a thrift shop composed the heart of the city. It was not exactly the Big Apple. Some days it was okay, some days she hated it. Her foster family had made it clear she was nothing more than a paycheck from Uncle Sam, but they did provide a place to sleep at night and some sort of food on the table.

Crossing Main Street – one of the few paved roads out here – she got off and walked her bike inside the small thrift shop. The owners, Mike and Stacey Madill, had been very kind to her and given her a job as well as permission to come and hang out if she ever needed to.

"Hey, Mr. Mike," she said to the elderly man dozing behind the counter.

He slowly opened his eyes, "Why, hello Miss Elise! How was school?"

She shrugged, "Not too bad."

"Not too bad, eh?" He chuckled to himself, "Well, did you pick a career today?"

He asked her that question every day, and she still had no answer. "Mr. Mike, I'm only in high school, remember? I don't have to know yet."

He gave an understanding look and peered at her through thick wire-rimmed glasses, "When I was your age, I already knew what I was going to be. In fact...," he took a deep breath to begin a long story, but was mercifully interrupted by the bell at the door. Whoever that person was, she needed to thank them later.

Mr. Mike was one of those grandpa types who could probably talk forever about the world and the past. Normally she found it interesting or just tuned him out, but today she was too tired.

Moving to the back room to put her stuff down, she used the restroom before emerging into the store again to find Mr. Mike chatting happily with Mrs. George from down the street. Purchasing a new set of gardening gloves had led to discussions from weather to politics, but fifteen minutes later the talkative lady waved at them both and disappeared out the door.

Elise cringed inside as Mr. Mike turned back to her, hoping he had talked himself out already. "Ms. Elise, why don't you run on over to my house, and I'll hold things down at the shop awhile. Mrs. Mike is waiting for you."

She paused a moment. "For what? It's already almost four, and my shift has started."

"Don't worry about it," he cackled as he shooed her outside. "I think I can manage."

Allowing herself to be propelled out the screen door, she glanced back at him suspiciously, but he just smiled. This was strange.

It didn't take long to arrive at the Madill's home across the street. They lived in an old-fashioned wooden house that was a faded yellow. White shutters, an ancient picket fence, and a plethora of bright flowers added to the cozy feel. She reached the rickety gate when Mrs. Madill's voice rang out, "Elise! How are you today?"

She waved in response, "Fine, Mrs. Mike. How are you?"

2

Elise had been corrected long ago that while their last name was indeed Madill, she was to refer to them only as Mr. and Mrs. Mike. It was a point she failed to understand, but had decided to give up trying a while back.

"Oh, just peachy," Mrs. Mike hummed in her grandmotherly voice. "Come on in, I have a surprise!"

A surprise? Hopefully not that awful meatloaf again, Elise didn't know if she could survive another round.

The round cheerful woman nearly suffocated her in a huge hug before setting her back down in the living room. "Wait right here," she admonished, disappearing into the kitchen. When she emerged a few moments later, she was carrying a large gift wrapped package.

"I know you didn't want a big celebration for your birthday, but Mr. Mike and I wanted to get you something special for your sweet sixteen." She smiled warmly at her surprised guest, "Go on, open it!"

Elise was speechless. No one knew when her birthday was, except her foster parents, the Griswolds. She doubted they had even looked at the date since they signed the papers two years ago. How the Madills had gotten that information was beyond her.

"Thank you," she stammered, accepting the heavy box. She didn't want to offend the couple who had been so gracious to her, no matter how much she tried to forget that she even had a birthday. It brought back thoughts of her family; a family she didn't have.

Mrs. Mike's smile continually grew wider as Elise carefully removed the wrapping paper, finding the word "Dell" printed on the box.

She had mentioned weeks ago when a classmate started bringing her laptop to school. The computer lab was filled with decaying Macs, and the shiny new computer had been the envy of more than just Elise.

Opening the box further, she saw that it was indeed a brand-new laptop computer.

"Mr. Mike and I have done well with the shop this year, and we know how hard you've been working in school. This should help you with college and whatever you want to do."

Elise couldn't find anything to say. She had never been able to afford even a cell phone, and here was a beautiful new computer. The Madills lived at the edge of poverty themselves, how could they give her such a gift?

She was going to open her mouth to protest, but Mrs. Mike held up a hand to stop her. "You don't have to say anything, Elise. It's a gift, and we both really wanted you to have it." She enveloped Elise's slight frame in another bear hug. "And it's completely free, okay sweetie? We know you'll take good care of it."

The older woman regarded her with a sly smile. "Now you better get back to help with the shop. Come by and visit soon!"

Elise managed to stammer her thanks as she was propelled through the door, clutching her new possession in shock. No one had ever given her something like this before. Feeling guilty for taking such a valuable item, she was torn between going to give it back and clutching it closely.

Back at the shop, Mr. Mike only grinned and gave her a thumbs up. Excitement began to overcome initial guilt at taking such a huge gift.

She hugged the box first in unbridled enthusiasm. "Thank you so much, Mr. Mike! I can't wait to get home and set it up!"

He chuckled, "I'm glad you like it. Well," he eased himself off the stool behind the counter, "I guess I better head home. Remember to close up by eight."

"I will. Thanks again!" Elise gave him a gentle hug before helping him out the door.

Now she just had to survive hours of waiting to explore her new gift.

* * * *

It was the following day and Elise still had a good hour before the sun disappeared, but she wanted to get home to start her homework on her new computer. She told Mr. Mike goodbye, and sped off on her bike down Main Street.

She wasn't paying any particular amount of attention, lost in plans and daydreams, when she heard an odd whining noise behind her. Glancing back over her shoulder, she noticed a black car still a good distance off. She didn't recognize it and it was going pretty slow.

Slightly worried, because not much ever happened in Mesa Springs and visitors were as rare as snow, she pedaled faster and kept checking over her shoulder. The car seemed to stay the same distance behind, but once she turned onto another road she didn't see it anymore.

Someone was probably just lost, Elise rationalized to herself. She still kept up her speed, unsure if it had been following her or not. As she came up to an intersection with another obscure dirt road – there wasn't a lot of variation out here – the big sedan pulled up and stopped directly in her path.

It was an expensive looking car with a slick black paint job, now obscured by dust, with twin vents in the hood and an angled wing on the back. The engine reverberated through the ground at an idle, and the deep sound was accompanied by that strange whining she had noticed earlier. The deeply tinted windows made it impossible to see inside. This was certainly not a car that belonged in Mesa Springs.

Elise's heart pounded. She could go back down the road, in which case it might follow, or she could forsake her bike and run into the thick woods to her right. Something inside her found the prospect of her tearing through the forest a little silly. What would anyone want with her anyway? Maybe they just needed to ask for directions. Then again, maybe it was a creep looking for his next victim.

Frozen by indecision, she stared at the car with wide eyes. It hadn't moved, the engine rumbling menacingly. She couldn't see anyone inside, so she resolved to slip around it and race back to the house.

Fear gripped her chest, and she cautiously moved closer to the car. Nothing moved. She made her way around the front fender, careful to keep a safe distance while trying to nonchalantly slip a glance through the windshield at the driver. The silhouette was hard to see in the last rays of the setting sun, but she caught a glimpse of a black haired, professionally dressed woman probably in her thirties. She risked another glance and the woman's stony expression never changed, eyes concealed behind dark sunglasses. Who wore sunglasses at dusk?

Elise began to pedal further down the road, and when she turned to check on the car, it was still there. Elise wondered if the lady needed help, and she almost turned around before fear won out. Speeding quickly towards her foster family's house, she was relieved when the car faded into the distance.

Chapter 2

The next day Nia gave Elise a ride to school in her Jeep. It was six miles away, and the weather was threatening rain. Elise had spent the night wondering about the black car, and had trouble focusing on her Chemistry homework.

"Did you study for the vocab quiz in English today?" Nia turned to her at a stop sign.

Elise slapped her hand against her forehead, "Aw, I forgot."

"You always do well anyway," Nia gave her a sideways glance. "Is everything okay? You've been pretty quiet."

Elise paused. Why didn't she want to tell her best friend? With a sigh, she decided it was silly and maybe getting it off her chest would help. "Yesterday, on my way home from work, this weird car was following me."

Nia stared at her a moment, "One car got you all worked up?"

She recounted the rest of the story, and Nia looked thoughtful. "Hmm. I'll keep an eye out, maybe someone had a visitor from out of town?"

Elise sighed, "Yeah, I probably just overreacted. Hey, did you get the answers to that Chemistry homework?"

The two girls continued complaining about the cruelty of Chemistry, and the shadowy car faded into the back of Elise's memory. Once they reached Hawethorne High, school and gossip had replaced any suspicions.

Nia was a year older than Elise, and shared signature Braford curly dark brown hair with her father, the pastor of the Mesa Springs Baptist congregation. He was a little stiff, in Elise's mind, but the family in general had always been polite and shown her great hospitality. Nia made it her personal charge to take Elise under her protective wings. She could be a little crazy, especially when driving, but she was always loyal and a great friend.

Friends were extremely valuable to Elise, as she didn't have very many. She had moved around to different children's homes and foster families since she was a young child, and her two years in Mesa Springs were the most consistent and pleasurable of her life. She certainly wasn't rich, her new computer was by far her most valuable possession, but she was pretty much free here and accepted by the community.

Throwing her backpack on, she waved to Nia and headed to her first class.

* * * *

Several months passed, and the end of the school year was fast approaching. On her way back from the shop one day, a glimmer of something shiny caught Elise's eye on the dirt road's grassy shoulder. Pausing to investigate, she found it was a nearly-new cell phone. It looked expensive and didn't appear damaged, so she put it in her backpack to examine more at the house. The sun was setting fast, and she still had a few miles to go.

She pulled her bike into the driveway of the double wide mobile home and set it against a tree. "Good evening, Mrs. Griswold," she said cheerfully as she jumped up onto the porch.

"Evening, Elise," the plump, red-haired woman greeted her. She looked slightly cross today. "Remember to do the dishes and clean the floors before bed."

"Of course," Elise bounded into the house, excited by her discovery. Once in her room, she closed the door and retrieved the phone. It was already on, but as she began to search for a number to call, she found that the contact list was empty, as was the call history. That was strange. Maybe she would drop it off at the police station tomorrow. With a shrug, she tossed it on her bed and hurried to start on her chores. It was not fun to make Mrs. Griswold unhappy.

* * * *

Riiing!
A loud noise startled Elise awake. That didn't sound like her alarm, she thought as she groggily rubbed her eyes. 3:20? She blinked.
Riiing!
The sound continued, somewhere on the floor. The phone! She remembered with a start, curiosity taking hold. Sure enough, there it was under her bed, lighting up the dust bunnies with a blue hue.
Riiing!
She wondered if she should answer; it wasn't her phone after all. She flipped it open. Maybe the owner had just discovered their phone was missing and trying to find it. "Hello?" she whispered softly, trying not to wake the Griswolds.
"Elise?" a woman's voice asked for her by name.
She dropped the phone as if it had caught fire. It clanged noisily on the floor. Elise eyed the phone like it was a snake, afraid to pick it up.
"Elise?" the voice tried again.
Slowly she bent over and retrieved the offending item, holding it a good inch from her ear. "Yes?" she whispered.
"Go outside, I need to speak with you without disturbing the others."
Elise instinctively looked out the window. Was this person watching her? She felt cold inside. "Who are you?"
"Please go outside. I need to speak with you, and it would be better if the Griswolds were not disturbed." The voice was smooth and silky, but had a businesslike tone that emanated confidence and authority.
Against her better judgment, Elise moved toward the door. She froze once her hand met the rigid door handle.

"Elise," the even voice tried again, "I will not harm you. I just want to speak with you over the phone. I am not outside. No one is. You can check out the window."

Drawing back the curtains, she saw in the pale moonlight that everything appeared still and empty. She could hang up and turn the phone off, but afraid or not she wanted to find out what was going on. This woman seemed to know enough that Elise was probably no safer inside her house than out. Quietly, and jumping at every small shadow and noise, she made her way to the front door. It creaked eerily as she opened it and surveyed the front yard. Nothing seemed out of place.

After a brief moment, she stepped through and closed the door behind her.

"Good," the woman said, "but you should move farther from the house."

Glancing in every direction, Elise still saw nothing. She obediently moved toward the road. "Okay. What do you want?" she whispered, as if she might startle the night.

"Be careful who you trust, Elise. What I am about to tell you should not be repeated to anybody, even your friend Nia. Do not go to law enforcement. Do not tell anyone you know. This is both for your protection and theirs."

Elise's heart beat faster. "Who are you?" she asked again.

"My name is Carbon," the woman said.

"What do you want?" Elise whimpered into the phone. It was unlikely that this was a joke, it was way too elaborate for anyone in this town.

"Your father sent me."

Elise's heart stopped cold. "My father...," she stammered in disbelief.

The voice tried to sound gentle, but it wasn't very effective. "Yes, your father. He has sent me to protect you, Elise. I am sorry for frightening you, but you need to listen. In a few days, people will come from the foster system saying that they need to move you to a new home. Do not go with them. Hide anywhere you can. They plan to take you, and they will lie, steal and perhaps even kill

10

to achieve this. I would tell you to run now, except they will likely find you, and I am not yet close enough to help."

Her fingers felt like ice around the phone. Her father? He wasn't dead?

"I will try to stop them, but they will come eventually."

Elise's mind was spinning. Hide? Run? From whom? "Why?" she whispered.

The woman did not respond immediately. "I cannot answer that. You need to trust me." The statement did little to reassure her. "Go back in your room now. I will call you again if they come. If you need assistance, remove the battery and hold the send button down for five seconds. Then replace the battery and push send again. Do not try this unless it is an emergency. Do not, under any conditions, show this phone to anyone else. Continue life as normal, but be careful. Good-bye, Elise."

With a click, the voice was gone and a solemn silence took its place.

* * * *

The next morning, Elise felt terrible. She had spent most of the night trembling, questions shooting through her mind and fears racing through her heart. Her first instinct was to take the phone to the police, explain the whole story and forget it. She knew this was the proper course of action. But her heart would not allow it. What if the woman was telling the truth? There was no way she could dismiss the possibility that her father was involved, and hope intertwined with curiosity refused to be reasonable.

She slipped out of the house unnoticed and rode her bike into town where Nia always met her.

"Hey Elise!" her friend called cheerfully while she was still a distance away. As she drew closer, however, Nia frowned. "Elise? Are you okay?"

Elise only looked at the ground in silence. It was difficult to keep from spilling the entire conversation to Nia. The two usually shared everything. She was going to offer some excuse, but she was on the verge of a total breakdown, so she wordlessly lifted her bike into the CJ and climbed into the passenger seat.

"Hey, are you okay?" Nia asked again, staring at her with real worry in her eyes.

A small tear escaped, but Elise nodded. "Bad dream," she croaked, looking at her feet. She could feel her friend's eyes on her, unconvinced.

Starting the CJ's motor, Nia said quietly, "If you want to talk about it, I'm here, ok?" Elise nodded again, careful not to look her in the face. The trip was mostly silent, but Elise barely noticed the passage of time. She was confused and scared, her thoughts troubled. Nia tried to lighten things up by small talk and a few bad jokes, but Elise could only manage a weak smile.

Before she went to class, however, Nia gave her a quick hug and invited her to come by the church that night, suggesting Elise bring her worries to God if no one else. She only nodded slightly, and melted into her first class of the day.

Focusing in any of the subjects was nigh impossible, and she struggled just to keep nervous fidgeting to a minimum. She wondered if the call was a prank, a mistake, or even if it really happened. True, she had the phone, but she could have dreamed it all up.

The terror that had overshadowed her the entire day however, convinced her that the conversation had indeed happened. Which led to a new series of fears and questions: Was her real father alive? Was he actually looking for her? Was the woman trustworthy? Who was she? Who was named Carbon anyway? Was it a code name? Why would anyone come to 'take' her? Was she really in danger? What could she possibly do about it?

For the most part, her teachers ignored her lack of participation. During lunch, her friends were discussing boyfriends, grades and shopping, unaware of any danger. The desire to tell someone was nearly unbearable, but fear that had gnawed into Elise's stomach would not allow it. Besides, if she was going to believe the woman's story, she might as well believe all of it.

By the end of the day, the lack of sleep and constant worry had stretched her thin. She closed the shop early and pedaled home hurriedly, glancing around for anything suspicious.

She continued like this throughout the week, and when Sunday finally rolled around, she was awakened by Nia's prodding finger.

"All right, sleepyhead, I am taking you to church today whether you like it or not. You need a change of scenery."

Elise found herself dragged through the day, and though she complained quite a bit to Nia, she began relaxing a little and forgetting the nightmare. The sermon was slightly dull, but the pastor provincially spoke on not worrying, not leaning on your own understanding, and yada yada. At the end of the service, she prayed a brief prayer – although she wasn't sure that she ranked high enough in God's mind to merit a response – that He might protect the town, and even her life, if it wasn't too much to ask.

Afterward she enjoyed a pleasant lunch with the Madills and explored some nearby paths in the Jeep with Nia. By nightfall, she had all but discounted the disturbing warning. Grateful for the distraction and for friends, she fell into a deep sleep for the first time in days.

Chapter 3

Monday began mundanely enough, but several events at school raised glaring red flags. First, her English teacher received a call in the middle of class. She shot a surprised glance at Elise, but then was careful to not look at her for the rest of their lesson. When quiet time began, she asked the students to begin working on their homework assignments before motioning for Elise to join her outside the classroom.

Much to her relief, Elise found no suspicious men in the hallway. Her teacher looked at her, "That call was from the office. They asked for you to come down as soon as class was over." She hesitated as if deciding whether or not to say more.

"Why?" Elise asked, worried.

"Oh, you're not in trouble or anything," her teacher rushed. "No, nothing like that. They just said some people were here from the foster system, and they want to meet with you. That's it. Here," she handed her a small slip of paper, "take this hall pass."

Seeing her student's stricken expression, she placed a sympathetic hand on Elise's shoulder, "I'll get your things." She disappeared into the classroom, emerging seconds later with Elise's backpack. "You probably won't have time to come back before your next class. See you later." The English teacher vanished once more.

Elise stood for a moment, mind and heart racing. This couldn't really be happening.

Trying to remain calm, she walked into the girls' restroom and locked the door. It had to be the people Carbon warned her about. She ripped off her backpack, shaking fingers bumbling with the zippers until she forced herself to take a deep breath. She needed to hurry before they came looking for her.

After an eternal five seconds, she finally got the cell phone out of her pack. *Missed Call.*

Her heart beat several times faster. Quickly removing the battery, she pressed down the send button. Talking on the phone in the bathroom could be a problem, she realized as footsteps – probably the hall monitor – passed her position.

Trying to appear nonchalant, she made her way down the hallway and the stairwell. She was at the back of the building, and after a quick check to make sure no one was watching, she dove into the thick brush that separated the school from a small forest. She turned the phone back on and pushed send a second time. It only rang once before the woman answered.

"Elise." It was a statement this time, not a question.

She tried to keep her voice low to not be heard, but she was struggling against the fear rising in her throat. "They said people came to the office to talk to me. People from the foster system."

"Can you see the parking lot?" Carbon asked her.

"No, I'm behind Building four. I can barely see the office from here."

"Stay hidden. I am surveying the school right now. I will stay on the line, but make sure they do not hear you."

A few moments went by, and Elise retreated a little deeper into the woods, keeping her eyes glued to the school. She heard a commotion from somewhere inside.

"What do you mean, you don't know where she is?" Principal Baxley was grilling someone. "She was in your class, right?" A low murmur ensued, and soon she heard her name called out.

"Carbon?" she whispered into the phone.

"I am still here," came the instant reply. The woman sounded completely calm. "I see them by the end of the building. Hold still. I will tell you when they move on."

The line became silent again as Elise watched the scene in terror. She clung to the tree she was leaning against, desperate not to crunch any of the leaves beneath her feet.

A man came and scanned the perimeter, but another teacher, whom Elise only recognized from the lunch room, appeared and led him back into the classroom.

"Elise." Carbon's voice returned, "Prepare to run when I say. Head straight into the woods. It will lead out to 57th Street in one half of a mile. There will be a black Dodge Challenger waiting. Get in immediately. There is still one person nearby, but I will tell you when he moves."

Black Challenger? Was that the car she saw those months ago? Elise's concern over the implications was shoved aside as voices grew closer. She tried to calm herself as she waited for Carbon's word. It wasn't a long wait.

"Now, Elise. Run."

She tore off into the woods, running as fast as she could. Her cumbersome backpack was making it difficult, and when she heard shouts from behind, she shrugged it off and sprinted in open terror for the road. The cries became louder from the school, and soon she heard footsteps as several people took to the woods in pursuit. She had a good head start, but one man seemed to be gaining on her rapidly. Her lungs screamed for air and her legs seared with hot pain, but terror drove Elise with reserves she didn't know she had.

"Stop!" the man behind her yelled out between breaths. He was getting closer.

She kept running, ignoring the underbrush that clawed at her arms and legs. Her chest was on the verge of exploding, but she could now see a black car waiting on the road.

"Elise!" the man yelled again. "Do not get in that car!" He was way too close, and still gaining.

With a final gasp for air, she dove headlong into the open driver's door. She felt nothing as her head slammed against the other side of the car, and the last thing she remembered was the man leaping toward her as darkness swallowed her surroundings.

* * * *

16

Elise moaned as she cracked an eye open. Her body felt heavy and painfully resisting any attempt to move. Every fiber of her legs was screaming with sharp pain. When she tried to swallow, her throat stung like a dry pincushion. The dull aching in her head was nearly unbearable.

Forcing her unwilling arms to move, she touched her temple and was met with a new burst of fire in her eyes. "Ow," she hissed.

"Are you all right?" she heard a woman's voice ask.

What woman? Everything was foggy. Attempting again to open her eyes, bright light blinded her vision and seared into her aching skull. She hissed again at the pain as she shielded her eyes.

"Elise?" the voice asked.

Who *was* that? She fought to recall where she was, but the effort was met with no success, only pain. "Bright…" she croaked. Her voice sounded more like a creaking hinge, but the light diminished instantly.

"I apologize," the voice came again. "Is this more comfortable?"

Rubbing her eyes, Elise cracked them open with painstaking deliberation to find dim surroundings. Gingerly she opened them further. Before her was a black dashboard with silver trim.

She was in a car. The black car. The realization hit her as a painful knot formed in her stomach. She remembered being at school, running through the woods, the man chasing her…

"Elise?"

Carbon. That's who the woman was. More or less awake, Elise realized she was sprawled in the same position in which she had landed. Carefully she tried to bring her legs underneath her and sit upright in the seat. They had not appreciated her mad dash through the woods and stung with pain in response. She found herself gasping with the effort of the smallest movement.

Her head likewise did not appreciate the new vertical position, the faint surroundings momentarily swept away by sparkles of light in her vision. As the stars cleared, however, she took in her surroundings more fully. It was dark outside, and bluish lights from the dashboard softly illuminated the car's cab. The interior was all black, and as she glanced around her, it vaguely dawned upon her that something was wrong.

A little red flag began waving frantically in her mind, but in the fog that was still clearing, she didn't understand why until she surveyed the car again.

She was alone.

Her first instinct was to scream, but the air passing through her raw throat voiced as a squeak. She grabbed the door handle and jerked, fighting with the lock, but it stubbornly refused to open.

"We are traveling too fast to safely open the door," Carbon's voice intoned matter-of-factly.

"Wha...?" Elise swiveled back toward the voice, her hand grasping her throat as it stung anew. Did she hit her head too hard? Maybe she was still unconscious. But the pain in her body argued otherwise.

"There is water in the glove compartment if you are thirsty," Carbon stated in similar fashion. As if on cue, the glove compartment opened to reveal a plastic water bottle.

Elise suspiciously reached for it, snatching the icy bottle before the compartment could close. Pain overruled fear, and she quickly opened the cap and poured some cool water on her parched throat. It wasn't a complete fix, but at least now speaking was possible.

"Where are you?" she creaked, her voice sounding like a rusty hinge.

"I am here. I apologize for not explaining myself earlier. I am artificial intelligence, fully integrated into this car."

Artificial intelligence? Elise stared wide-eyed in disbelief somewhere near the steering wheel. "You're a *computer*?"

"Yes," Carbon replied simply.

"Carbon is a computer," Elise mumbled slowly to herself again. "A computer."

Carbon explained further, "Your father created me. As I told you, he sent me to protect you."

Elise wasn't sure how to take in this information. Her head already felt like it had been smacked by a two by four. "Why?"

"Your father programmed several video logs to help explain things. I need your fingerprint to access them." Instead of an ashtray, a small flat surface emerged from the dashboard. "Place your left thumb on the scanner."

Elise did as she was told, still trying to process what was happening. A thin blue light flashed on before scurrying up and down her thumb. Its course complete, it beeped with satisfaction and the tray retreated back into the dash.

"This is the first video log. It will appear on the screen in the center console." Elise looked toward what she had assumed was a GPS system as the top half of a middle-aged man appeared on the screen. He had light brown hair streaked with grey and wore a blue button down. But his face is what got to her. Light brown eyes brought up fuzzy memories and emotions Elise had all but forgotten.

Was this man really her father? Her piercing headache faded to the background as her eyes glued to the image.

"Hello Elise," he smiled. "If you are listening to this...," he trailed off, then laughed. "Okay, that sounds like a bad movie. Obviously you are already listening to this, and I'm sure many things have happened that you don't understand. But I am so proud you made it this far, and I am praying constantly that you remain strong and safe." He paused again, lowering his gaze. "I know it has been very difficult for you, and I cannot imagine what you are feeling right now. I am so sorry for everything you've been through."

He swallowed before looking back up. "I'm sure you have many, many questions, but I cannot answer them for you yet. Listen to Carbon and do what she says. Do not leave her; your life truly is in danger. I built her to keep you safe. That is all I can tell you now." He blinked back tears. "I'm so sorry, Elise. I love you so much." Then he reached forward, and the screen turned black.

Elise felt numb. Powerful emotions swirled under the surface and threatened break loose. Her father was not dead. He had not forgotten that she existed. But he had abandoned her. Anger and gratitude, hatred and love fought each other in her soul as a tear escaped and slid down her cheek. She wiped it away and tried to stop the aching sobs that began in her chest, but it was like clutching an umbrella in a tornado. Useless.

All the confusion, fear and chaos seemed to explode as she surrendered and wept. Carbon remained silent, but offered some tissues from the glove compartment. Eventually the sobs subsided, and the pain was replaced by fatigue and acceptance.

Elise leaned back against the seat and stared vacantly out the window. There weren't many lights near the ground, but the stars up above were beautiful, solemnly watching over the night as always.

The sniffling soon ceased, and they drove on in silence for what seemed like eternity. Emotional trauma or no, however, her body was still functioning and she asked Carbon to stop for a bathroom break. As there wasn't much civilization nearby, they only pulled over and Elise had to relive her camping days.

Stretching her sore muscles was a welcome relief, and when she got back in the car, she had gathered her thoughts somewhat. She spoke up, "Where are we going?"

"Elderidge, Montana."

"Montana? What's in Montana?"

"A ranch."

What else? "Why are we going there?"

"It is safe."

"Whose ranch is it? Will my dad be there?"

"The property belongs to a Mr. and Mrs. Allen. Their picture is on the screen." Sure enough, a photo of an older couple appeared on the display. The man looked rather severe, and the woman was also lean and withdrawn. They reminded her of that famous picture of the farmers holding a pitchfork.

"What about my dad?" Elise pressed. The car had conveniently avoided that question.

"I do not know."

Thousands of additional questions were falling in Elise's mind, but her headache made it difficult to reach even one of them. "Do you have a pain reliever or something?" she asked.

Much to her relief, Carbon said she did, and a pack of two tablets appeared in the glove compartment. She eagerly downed them with a gulp from the water bottle and hoped they kicked in quickly.

"You should get some rest, Elise. In a few hours it will be morning."

It was true; despite her earlier 'nap' – and she really wasn't sure how much unconsciousness counted for – she was exhausted in every respect. After a brief struggle to adjust the seat she managed to lay it back to a comfortable position.

She didn't even notice when sleep took her.

Chapter 4

The small wooden church was eerily dark, save a few candles burning inside. A lone girl knelt before the altar, her earnest prayers fading somewhat with fatigue, her cheeks stained with many tears.

"Nia," a soft voice spoke from the back pew. "Sweetie, you really should come home now." The preacher's wife walked up and placed a gentle hand on her daughter's shoulder. "We've all prayed for her. Elise is in the Lord's hands."

Fresh tears came to Nia's eyes, "But Mom, we don't even know what happened to her. I know what they said, but it just doesn't make sense. She never skipped class. Ever. Besides, something was really bothering her last week."

The official story had been printed on Mesa Spring's weekly newspaper, and the police claimed she was skipping class when she disappeared into a black sedan. They were not sure if she had run away or been kidnapped, but they had sent posters and alerts to all the neighboring towns and cities.

The two were silent for a moment before Mrs. Braford knelt beside her daughter with a heavy sigh. "I don't understand it either." She took her daughter's hand. "We'll pray a little longer, okay? Maybe we can get a group together tomorrow."

Nia sniffed, and nodded. Whatever the police said, she was convinced Elise was in danger.

* * * *

Elise didn't wake up until after nine. It took a moment to reorient herself, but at least her head was no longer pounding even if it remained a little tender.

"Good morning," Carbon's voice greeted her.

"Morning," she automatically replied with a yawn. They were on some country road with a rolling landscape and rounded hills in the distance. At this point, there was no sense clinging to the notion that this was only a bad dream.

"Where are we?"

"Missouri."

Elise considered her situation. She remained a little disbelieving that she was driving around in a talking car headed to a random ranch on the other side of the country. It seemed too good to hope for a father who would build something like this all for her. That he might want her back.

As the rural scenery passed by, Elise again tried to make sense of the past few weeks.

"Hey Carbon," she remembered, "That *was* you I saw on my bike, right? A few months ago?"

"Yes, I apologize if I startled you." Carbon responded. "It was necessary to positively identify you and your current place of residence."

"But I saw a lady driving. Who was she?"

"That was only a holographic projection. Your father thought a car without a driver would attract too much attention."

"That's for sure," Elise yawned despite the strange circumstances. "So, how long is this trip going to take?"

"Approximately thirty hours nonstop."

Thirty hours? Elise sighed. She wanted to talk to the people in Montana now. Maybe her dad would be waiting for her there.

Her stomach interrupted her thoughts. She wouldn't last that long without eating something.

"Do you have any food in here?"

"No." Carbon didn't waste words. "If you are hungry we can stop at the next town."

Elise felt in her pocket. All she had was a one dollar bill. Great.

Carbon continued, "Your father provided some money for you." The glove compartment opened again, revealing a ten dollar bill.

Elise was impressed. "How much do you have?"

"Enough," was all the car would say.

They stopped at an old mom and pop's diner, where Elise was able to refresh herself. After pestering Carbon, she managed to coax another twenty dollars out of the car, which she used to buy some food for the road, a pocket knife for good measure, and some sunglasses. She was both reluctant to get back in the car and in a hurry to get to Montana, but after stretching her sore legs she slipped back into the passenger side.

"Elise, would you please sit in the driver's seat?" Carbon asked. "There are several patrol cars around and it would be best to avoid law enforcement."

The request made sense, and Elise slid over into the left hand seat. This was her first full view of Carbon's instrument panel, and while it didn't appear to her much different from any other car, it was still pretty impressive. "Wow," Elise whispered under her breath as they pulled out into traffic and resumed their journey to Elderidge.

After watching the monotonous landscape roll past for a few minutes, her mind began to fill with questions and doubts. What she needed were answers. "Carbon," she asked, "you said earlier that my dad left several video messages. Can I watch more of them?"

"I am unable to access them at this time."

Unable to access? "Why?" Elise exclaimed.

"The files are locked."

Elise sighed in frustration. Why would her dad keep information from her? Was he doing something illegal? She needed some explanation, and the only clue she had was Carbon. "So, my dad built you to come and protect me?"

"We have already established that," the car responded evenly.

"Um, yes," Elise acknowledged. Apparently Carbon had a stiff learning curve. "Where is my dad now?"

"I do not know."

"When was the last time you saw him?"

"Two weeks ago. He gave me instructions to protect you and bring you to the ranch in Montana."

"But why?" Elise pressed. "Why then? What happened?"

"I cannot disclose that information."

"What? So you do know."

"Your father did not explain his actions to me; he only gave me instructions to keep you safe."

Why would her dad keep so much information from her?

She sat angrily for a while, her imagination running through all possible scenarios. Her father was some sort of government agent, and angry mobsters were looking for revenge. Or maybe he was a dangerous criminal, and she had run away from government officials. All the 'what ifs' and 'maybes' sent her mind into a downward spiral, and by the time she collected herself, she found that she had unconsciously chewed off half her nails.

Elise thought back to the video. Her father's kind eyes did not look dangerous.

Finally she reasoned that the best course of action was to be careful, but find out what was going on once they reached Elderidge. She hadn't done anything illegal, and if she wasn't satisfied, she could alert the police there.

Watching the countryside go by, it occurred to Elise that they were traveling exclusively on rural roads and a highway would probably be faster. When she brought this up to Carbon, however, the car said something about safety and not being found.

"Who is after me anyway?"

"Your father gave me a list of people he considered dangerous with instructions to monitor them. The goal was to keep them from finding you, and if that failed, to prevent them from reaching you. When I learned that some of them had discovered your location and planned to find you, I came to get you first."

"But who are they?" Elise pressed. "And why are they looking for me?"

But Carbon refused to share any more information after that, claiming she was not able. Frustrated, Elise asked if she could at least see her father's 'dangerous' list.

Carbon consented, "You may look through them if you want."

A face appeared on the screen in the center console, along with physical descriptions and personal facts. Carbon instructed her how to sift through the pictures on the touchscreen, but the faces were unfamiliar to her. One man could have been her pursuer back at the school, but she didn't recognize anyone else.

One profile stood out among the others. Dr. Geoffrey Rayford, an esteemed British chemist. He had received many prestigious awards, and looked like a classic gentleman, smiling in the photo while holding a large plaque.

There were about fifty people in total, with ratings of various degrees of danger beside them up to one-hundred percent. The only person that high was Dr. Rayford.

"I guess I'll avoid him," Elise muttered.

Despite her questions, Carbon refused to answer any further inquiries about her father, or pretty much anything that was going on. Elise dearly hoped that answers would be waiting for her in Montana. In the meantime, however, she realized why she had never been fond of long car trips.

After some liberal complaining about her boredom, Carbon showed her some games she could play on the screen, but in a few hours they were only giving her another headache and she resumed looking out the window.

They were passing through long stretches of cornfields and prairies, certainly not the most thrilling scenery. It took a while, but it finally occurred to her that there was one thing she could do to pass the time.

"Hey, Carbon?"

"Yes?"

Elise hesitated. She was kind of afraid to ask, but she went ahead anyway. "Can I drive?"

"I do not know." Carbon responded flatly. "Can you?"

Elise raised her eyebrows, "Was that a joke?"

"No. It was a question." The voice paused as if considering the idea. Or whatever it is computers do. "You do not have your driver's license. Have you driven a vehicle before?"

"How do you know that?" Elise was slightly offended. "And yes, I *can* drive. Nia always lets me drive her old Jeep in the woods."

"I am not an old Jeep."

"Obviously," Elise couldn't help a half-smile. This car had an attitude. "But the principle is the same, isn't it?"

Carbon didn't immediately respond, so she continued. "Besides, even if I can't drive well, you can teach me, right? And prevent me from hitting anything." She added the last part as an afterthought.

"Of course I would not allow you to hit anything," Carbon responded indignantly. To be fair, her voice was mostly monotone, but Elise was sure the car was offended by the notion it could run into something.

After another brief pause, Carbon relented. "You may drive."

Elise grinned as she cautiously put her hands on the wheel and her foot on the pedal. "Sweet."

Chapter 5

Back in Mesa Springs, Sergeant Bill Reyes flipped his notebook shut and slipped his sunglasses back into place. "Thanks for your help, Mrs. Madill. I can assure you we are doing our best to find Elise."

The older woman across from him wiped another tear from her wrinkled cheek and gave the balding officer a stern look. "She's a good girl, Sergeant. You bring her back safely."

Reyes nodded as he stood up from the small red table in the Madills' kitchen. "Thanks again," he repeated as he exited the small house and headed for his patrol car.

After thirty years of law enforcement, this case was not lining up like usual. Testimonies he had collected from previous foster parents, teachers, and acquaintances, together with the girl's history, painted a portrait of a model teen. She didn't drink or do drugs, had never been in trouble with the law, did well in school and her best friend was a preacher's kid.

The people from the foster system claimed she had been skipping class when she ran away from them in a black sports car, a car no one who knew Elise had even heard of. And since when did the foster system send four men to deal with a minimal to no-risk girl?

The officer scratched his receding hairline as he started his car. He had another appointment with the folks from the state and was hoping they could clear things up for him. There wasn't much happening in this town, and hopefully it would stay that way until he could get to the bottom of this.

As soon as he caught sight of the four black SUV's parked at the tiny Mesa Springs Police station, Sergeant Reyes knew he was about to get those answers. A dark skinned woman greeted him as he stepped out of his patrol car. Her black hair was pulled into a rather severe bun, but she offered a friendly smile along with an outstretched hand.

"Officer Reyes," her tone was as professional as her grey suit. "I'm Agent Liz Kerry with the FBI. Nice to meet you."

He shook her hand. He was always suspicious of feds, especially when they showed up someplace as sleepy as Mesa Springs. "What can I do for you?" He forced himself to return the smile.

"I hear you're the officer in charge of the incident involving an Elise Perry." She was still smiling, but the brightness didn't quite reach her eyes.

"You've heard correctly. Would you mind if we stepped inside?" The sun was hot, and he had been working a long shift.

"Of course." She turned and led him into his own office, which he found annoying, and even worse were the dozen or so agents already crowding inside.

"Wow. Ya'll about triple the population of this town," he remarked dryly. "What's going on?"

A blonde man who couldn't be more than thirty stepped out and offered another firm handshake. "Sergeant Reyes, right?"

The sergeant pointed to his name tag, "Yep. Anything I can do for you, Sherlock?"

The man gave a stiff grin at the title, "The name's Alan Stewart. I'm in charge of this investigation." He motioned to the stuffed chair behind the Sergeant's desk, "Please have a seat, I'm sure you have some questions and I believe I have some answers."

"Well, the first part is for certain," Reyes muttered as he slowly sank into his chair.

* * * *

Night was falling again, and Elise was nearly asleep. She had long since handed the driving back to Carbon, as it had ceased to be fun shortly after the second hour. They were still twelve hours away from Elderidge, due in part to several restroom and leg-stretching breaks Elise had insisted on. Now she just marveled at how tired a person could become from sheer boredom.

It was difficult to actually sleep in the car, but with the soft leather seat leaned all the way back it was at least possible. Reality had just faded to dreams when something jerked her back to consciousness. Elise noticed they had stopped and the engine was no longer running.

"What's going on?" she rubbed her eyes and tried to focus on their surroundings. Carbon had turned off all the lights, inside and out.

"Several cars have been following us at varying distances for the past day. I have tried to lose them, but have been unsuccessful. We cannot proceed until they are gone."

"Where are we?"

"Central Illinois. I turned down some service roads and have parked behind brush to avoid detection."

Elise squinted out the window at shapeless shadows. "And they're still following?"

"I am not certain. One car drove further along the main road, but the other seems to be attempting to follow me."

Several tense moments passed before Carbon spoke again. "It has turned down another road. I do not think they can find us."

Elise continued staring at the darkness as fear clenched her stomach. The noise of an approaching engine joined with the wind's blowing against the door. Headlights appeared over the horizon, a searchlight sweeping back and forth.

Elise realized she had stopped breathing. If they saw Carbon, she could make a run for it on foot, but her last run would not have ended well alone, and the dark woods were almost as foreboding as the nearing lights. Her chances were probably best with the car anyway.

As the vehicle grew closer, it slowed until rolling to a stop before reaching their position. Elise couldn't make out the type of car through the glaring headlights, and just as she was sure they would move on, the beam of light cut through the trees into her eyes. She squinted against the brightness, too afraid to close her eyes fully. The light moved a little past them, but then swung back in a gradual arc.

"Carbon," she whispered tensely. She hoped the car had a good plan. A cloaking device would be nice.

Elise was sure they had been spotted, but the vehicle moved forward again, searchlight swinging steadily away. What in the world was going on that people would be following them out here?

She waited breathlessly until they were out of sight. "Are they gone now?"

"Not far enough, and they have stopped near the main road. I will plot another route."

They sat in darkness for ten minutes before Carbon restarted her engine and pulled out into the night. She did not turn her headlights on until they had travelled a troubling distance, but assured a skeptical Elise that she did in fact know where she was going.

Sleep was more elusive after that. She tried deep breaths to get her heart rate back down, but the growing fear in her stomach refused to go away. She felt like she was trapped in a nightmare being chased by a faceless, unknown enemy and left to face it alone. True, the video from her dad offered some comfort and Carbon was on her side, but it was just a car. Elise felt another tear slip down her cheek. What she would give right now to see Nia, or the Madills, to explain everything that had happened and be comforted by their embrace and kind words.

The silence became suffocating, and she didn't want to collapse into a nervous wreck again. She offered up another desperate plea for God to help her, but it didn't help her feel any better, and she wasn't sure He was even listening. It certainly didn't seem like it. Nia's faith was so strong, sometimes Elise envied her. Her friend seemed so sure that God cared about her, and even that He spoke to her.

Elise wiped away another angry tear as she glared at the heavens. *Where are you now?* If there was a God, and He truly cared for her, she could sure use some help now. Feelings of hatred, despair and rejection welled up from somewhere deep within, and the torrent of pain that stirred inside threatened to overwhelm her.

But her thoughts shifted to her earthly father. How could he claim to love her when he had so clearly abandoned her? Why couldn't he even care enough to give her some sort of explanation of what was going on? Her very life was in danger, and all he could provide was a thirty second video of apology.

"Elise, are you okay?" Carbon's asked.

"Yes," Elise snapped. "I'm fine." Her father was dead wrong if he thought designing some advanced computer would erase what he had done to her.

"You're vital signs are erratic. You should rest."

She rolled her eyes. Now the car was giving her advice. She wanted to give that perfect voice a piece of her mind, but she feared that she might explode if she even opened her mouth.

"Would you like to listen to some music?" Carbon tried again.

"Whatever," Elise muttered.

"Do you have any preferences?"

When Elise didn't respond, soft music started in the background, and the blue letters on the radio read "Playlist3: Shuffle". She didn't recognize the artist, and while she clung desperately to the anger that surrounded her, the gentle melody began to erode her defenses. Instead of the dangerous fury she had felt, agonizing sorrow rose up from within her. Unlike her previous cries, which had been primarily of self-pity and fear, she now wept out of simple brokenness and a deeply aching heart.

As she listened to the lyrics in the next song, they might as well have come straight from her soul, and her whole being seemed to join with the tender harmonies as she cried.

> *I know this place well, for I have been here*
> *Many times before*
> *The tears I've cried here*
> *The prayers I've prayed here*
> *With darkness surrounding*
>
> *How I reach here, I reach for you here*

In this place of my need
And how I seek here, I seek your face here
To find you, to find me

How she longed for a deep assurance of love, to simply be safe, for someone trustworthy to come rescue her, just to not be alone. The following songs were also beautiful, but having exhausted her most vivid terror and hatred through tears, a dull numbness covered her as she drifted off to a restless sleep once more.

Chapter 6

The air inside the small Mesa Springs Police Station was hot and lethargic. All of the fans were running on high, but even with their help the air conditioner could not keep up with the fifteen or so people crowding the small building.

The noise level was also bothering Sergeant Reyes, but he suspected his foul mood was more accurately attributed to the 'debriefing' he had received from Agent Stewart about the Elise Perry case.

Not only had they taken him off the investigation, they gave him some condescending explanation of why this was a federal matter and his jurisdiction was null and void. Then there was the not so concealed threat that he should just forget the case. The implications, they stressed, reached to national security.

Reyes had kindly informed them that they should vacate his station if he had no concern in the case, but they just laughed and said their mobile command unit would be arriving shortly. Firmly clenching a fat cigar between his teeth, he watched them suspiciously from the station's front porch, eagerly awaiting the hour they would leave.

* * * *

Inside the building, federal agents were busy making phone calls, analyzing maps and discussing possible scenarios. Agent Stewart leaned over a young analyst's shoulder to scrutinize the fuzzy photo they had retrieved of the getaway car.

They were working to resolve the picture and find any defining characteristics of the vehicle, chiefly a license plate number. They had not met any luck so far.

The agent had identified the car as a new Dodge Challenger and managed to snap a brief photo with his iPhone as it sped away, but the vehicle had already covered significant ground and stirred up impenetrable clouds of dust that obscured everything but its color.

Agent Liz Kerry walked up with a sigh, "You know you're not going to get anything out of that picture."

The senior agent didn't even bother turning to face her, "Miracles do happen, Liz. Go do something useful."

With a sarcastic glance at Stewart's back, the lean woman moved on to fulfill her boss' demands. After all, *someone* needed to do something useful. They had a long standing warrant out for this girl's father, Dr. Samuel Mathis. The case involving him went cold eight years ago, but had recently flared up. The wild card here was the girl herself, as she was also their only current lead. It was only a few months ago because of a doctor's report that they realized she was even alive.

According to old files, Dr. Mathis had disappeared with his family over ten years ago after facing serious charges. The wife had turned up dead a few months later and he was implicated in the murder. He was never heard from again and it was presumed the two children had been killed as well.

This off-chance medical test was a miracle. Elise Perry had a blood sample taken at school during a West Nile Virus scare, and the results were categorized and filed by fingerprint. In a random twist, the results were automatically run through a missing children's database, and here they were. While it didn't appear that the girl had been in touch with Dr. Mathis, they had no idea how much she knew, and they needed to find out. Now it was looking like they might not get that chance.

"Stewart!" another analyst called excitedly from behind a computer, "We think we may have got something."

"Well, don't leave me in suspense, Gilroy," Stewart complained as he moved over toward the smaller man.

"Yes, sir," Gilroy stammered. "We just received a call from a convenience store in rural Illinois saying a black car and a young girl passed through a few hours ago. The employee just saw her picture on the news, and is sure it's the same girl."

"Illinois?" Stewart muttered to himself. "What in the world is she doing there? Did the clerk notice anyone else with her?"

"They didn't mention anyone, but I can check. They're sending the surveillance tape through now."

"Nice work," Stewart slapped the younger man on the back. "Get ready to analyze this tape and figure out what could be happening in Illinois. I want to know who owns that car."

* * * *

They had arrived in Montana. The sun was shining brightly and blue clouds drifted across the sky. Five people were resting on a checkered picnic cloth in the shade. Elise could smell the apple pie they had brought for dessert.

As she drew closer, she recognized the Madills, and beside them was Nia and another friend from four years ago in Cincinnati. Elise struggled to see the last woman's features. Her back was turned, but as she laughed she turned to glance beyond Elise, light curls bouncing over slender shoulders.

Elise gasped in shock. Her mom!? Joy filled her and desperately she wanted to call to them, to run over and join them, but she was firmly stuck and no sound would come from her mouth. The scene continued for a few minutes, and the love and joy in that place was so tantalizing Elise was sure she could have held it in her hand.

Then the peaceful scene began to shift. Another figure emerged from the distance, bringing with it looming shadows and angry storm clouds that moved closer with its every step. Horror and frustration overshadowed the carefree enjoyment, but the picnicking characters seemed unaware. Elise tried to scream and warn them, but she still couldn't speak. The dark figure only moved closer.

The face suddenly came into focus.

It was her father, but now his eyes looked evil. A wicked grin stretched across his face as he and the storm clouds drew nearer the happy scene. But then, with gruesome deliberation, his shadowy form stopped and his gaze stared directly at her.

"Elise," his fingers beckoned for her to join him with macabre movements. "Elise," the voice came again.

"Noooooo!" she screamed, desperately struggling to cut off the nightmare.

"Elise! Wake up!"

Elise opened her eyes with a start, panting.

"Are you all right?" The voice was only Carbon's.

Elise swallowed, trying to eradicate all memories of the horrible dream. The feeling of evil lessened, but she could not think of her father without seeing that awful face.

"I'm okay," she was breathing hard, but the stillness of reality was sinking in. Until she remembered that she was being hunted, and she had no real idea of what was going on. Just blind trust in a man who claimed to be her father.

Carbon interrupted her increasingly frustrated thoughts, "What happened?"

"Just a bad dream."

"Sleep is supposed to be a time of rest. Why were you so disturbed?"

"Well," Elise considered how to describe this to a computer, still trying to shake off the clinging fear from the nightmare. "When I'm asleep, my mind sorts through what has happened in the past day, and what I have been thinking about." She let out a deep sigh, "And my thoughts haven't been that great lately."

"How can it be fixed?"

Elise gave a short laugh. "Fixed? I have no idea. Maybe if random people weren't chasing me and I knew what was going on, things would look a little better."

"But you cannot change those things."

Brilliant observation, Carbon. "I know. Hence the nightmares."

"Oh."

The sun was just coming over the horizon, and despite the bad feeling that remained in the pit of her stomach, the sunrise *was* beautiful. "Where are we now?"

A siren from behind interrupted Carbon's reply. Elise swiveled around, staring at red and blue flashing lights. "The police?"

Maybe her dad was on the wrong side of the law. How could she presume to know a man she last saw ten years ago, at the ripe old age of six? Panic rose as she realized what she had done. For nothing but a silly hope of a good father she had become a fugitive. She should have known better. A man who would run away from his own daughter at age six was probably capable of anything.

"What are you doing?" she demanded as Carbon's engine roared and they sped down the road.

"I am evading the patrol car."

"I see that!" It was easy to be angry when fear was pushing the buttons. "It's a cop, Carbon. We should pull over and talk to him. If you don't we'll be in even worse trouble. Were you speeding or something?"

"Of course not," Carbon responded calmly as scenery flew by at terrifying speeds.

"Slow down!" Elise yelled. "You're going to hit something!"

The car was not listening.

"Pull over!" she commanded in desperation. She did not want to be the youngest person on the FBI's most wanted list. She could see the headline now, *Criminal Teen Girl Arrested After Dangerous Car Chase*. "Please!"

But Carbon's speed only increased as they all but flew down the open road. It was fairly straight, and nearly deserted, but they were approaching some type of town. "I cannot," the smooth voice stated.

"Why? We need to pull over!" Elise had seen enough police chases on TV to know that it never ended well for the criminal.

"I cannot verify that you would be safe, and it is unlikely they would allow you to continue on to Montana."

Elise stared in horror when she saw yet another patrol car up ahead in the distance. "Watch out!" she yelled. "There could be spike strips!"

"I know." The calm voice was extremely annoying considering the dire circumstances. "You do not need to yell," Carbon continued as she braked hard and spun off the road into the dirt, "I can hear you quite well." The force of the maneuver sent Elise flying into the dash, and she was subjected to violent jostling as the car's shocks dealt with the blows of unpaved ground. Her bones felt like they were being rearranged.

"Ow!" she yelled, more out of frustration and adrenaline than pain. She grabbed hold of the nearest solid objects and braced herself. "Are you trying to kill me?!"

"No. I am protecting you."

The car was crazy, Elise was now convinced, and clearly not listening to any advice. Glancing in the rearview mirror, their pursuer had long since faded into the distance, and they had bypassed the police blockade with Carbon's off-road adventures.

"Maybe you *should* be an old jeep," Elise muttered through rattling teeth. The car was still flying, even over this crazy terrain. The supporting police cars were joining their comrade in the background as they could not handle the abusive way Carbon was driving.

"Relax. I will get you to Montana safely."

"And if I'm a hunted fugitive when I get there, that's just no big deal, right? What is wrong with you? They'll probably send a helicopter, and have a huge force out looking for us. How do you plan to get away then?" She was hysterical. This stupid car nearly killed her, and then told her to relax?!

"They will not send a helicopter," Carbon retorted. "This area does not have an aviation unit."

"Oh, so it's okay then. What if they send in the National Guard or something?"

"That is unlikely. I have calculated the odds, Elise. This course of action has the highest chance of success."

"Define success." Elise demanded angrily. "As long as I don't die until *after* Montana, right?"

"No. The highest chance of you surviving at all."

The statement gave Elise momentary pause, "What do you mean?"

"I have calculated the best chance of your survival, and I am acting within that interest."

"Why would my life be in danger with the police? Didn't you calculate in due process and the right to a fair trial? I haven't done anything wrong!"

"The police will be inadequate protection."

"How did you decide that?"

"I am unable to disclose that information." Carbon stated firmly.

The constant lack of information was really beginning to annoy Elise. Why should she trust her 'father' when he couldn't even give a bare-bones explanation? Maybe he didn't trust her. Whatever the reason, how could he expect her to follow blindly when it went against everything she had ever known? How could he expect her to leave her whole life behind – friends, family, home – and risk everything without reassurance of a worthy cause, and even without assurance that it was truly her dad who sent the message?

They had crossed some sort of prairie, and now they entered a thin forest on a dirt road. Carbon was still speeding quite a bit, and Elise couldn't shake her fears over what just happened. The growing hope of finding her real father had been overshadowed by doubt and sinking despair over her newfound criminal status.

Maybe they didn't know it was her, she reasoned. After all, it wasn't actually her car. But something told her otherwise, and she couldn't dismiss the fact that there was no good reason to pull over a car that wasn't speeding.

"Are there any more cops around?" Elise had been straining her ears for any hint of sirens, but hadn't heard anything since they crossed the prairie.

"No. The majority of them went another way, and we have moved out of their jurisdiction. The state troopers have been alerted, but it is unlikely they will find us on these roads."

State troopers? Elise felt guilty for breaking the smallest of laws, and with shame and worry she began considering ways to talk to the police and explain the situation. Obviously a phone call wouldn't work, as Carbon would definitely not allow it.

She had nothing to be afraid of, despite Carbon's warnings, and the police could place her in protective custody once she explained the danger. If her dad had criminal connections that high, she wasn't sure she wanted to meet him.

Everything was backward in her mind. She should have known better than to blindly chase after a silly hope. She only hoped now that the police would believe her explanation that she really was innocent.

In normal Elise fashion, it took her nearly thirty minutes of mental debate and stressing before she resolved to run away to the police. The only possible time would be during a restroom break, and it couldn't be too hard to run away from a car, could it? Her mind made up, she waited and planned until the next stop.

Chapter 7

Agent Stewart slammed his fist on the desk in frustration. His team was careful to look busy and avoid eye contact as he stalked out the door to get some fresh air. Their lead had been a dead end. The clerk had looked back through the surveillance tape only to discover that the time he thought Elise was there, the tape had broken off into static.

Stewart could move his team into Illinois, but it was hard to justify on only one eyewitness report. If it turned up to be a rabbit trail, he could lose days of productivity for nothing. Even if the clerk had seen Elise, she could be anywhere by now. He swore under his breath in anger.

"Excuse you," a voice drawled. He turned to see the Mesa Springs Police Sergeant on a rocking chair.

"You're still here?"

The Sergeant gave him a hard look, one that would have made Clint Eastwood proud. "Son, this is my town and my office, and it is my job to look out for these people. Just where would you suggest I go?"

The man was strange, the FBI agent considered as he shook his head. "Just forget it."

But the grey haired police officer continued to stare with a hard gaze. Clearly no answers were to be found out here, and so Stewart turned back into the building to return to work and avoid the angry eyes of Sergeant Bill Reyes.

* * * *

Elise found herself waiting longer than usual for a restroom break. Carbon insisted that it would be wiser to not stop until Montana because of their run-in with the police. However, after a few hours of incessant begging by Elise, she agreed to stop at a small town restaurant somewhere in central Iowa. Elise couldn't help feeling a twinge of betrayal as she shut Carbon's door and glanced back. The shiny car was impressive, but not enough to draw her away from a normal non-criminal life.

"Lucy's Restaurant" was a small building with picnic-styled tables set up around the edges and a strange smell coming from the kitchen. The sign said to choose a place to sit, and so with nervous butterflies Elise selected the table nearest the back of the building. She was finding it difficult to work up the courage to make the call.

Her waitress was a pleasant looking girl not much older than Elise, and she immediately noticed her customer was having a hard day.

"I'm okay," Elise managed to respond weakly. "Do you have a phone I can use?" She had the cell phone Carbon had given her, but she suspected that the car would block any outgoing 911 calls.

"Sure," the girl responded sweetly. "Can I get you something to drink while you wait?"

"Just water." As the waitress disappeared, Elise wondered if Carbon could hear inside the building. Even so, what could she do? Smash through the wall? Elise considered it unlikely. Still, whatever she did probably needed to be quick. The girl returned after a few minutes with her water.

Elise summoned all her resolve and caught the girl's arm. "Um," she wasn't sure how to say this. "I need to talk to the police. Can you help me?"

The brown eyed waitress analyzed her face a brief moment before sitting down across from her at the table. "Of course. Are you okay?"

Elise nodded, "Yeah." Met with human compassion, she couldn't help the rising tears.

"Come with me," the girl gently took hold of her arm and led her into the kitchen. "I'm Amy," she gave Elise a sympathetic glance and pointed to an antique-looking phone hanging on the wall. "If you need anything, call my name. I'll be right back."

As Amy hurried back into the dining area, something inside Elise screamed not to make the call, but her fingers mechanically picked up the phone and dialed 911.

"This is 911, please state your emergency," the operator answered.

"Hello," she began shakily, "This is Elise Perry. I was just involved in a, um, a car chase and I need to speak with the police."

"Okay, Elise. How old are you?"

She actually had to think about it a moment, "Sixteen."

"Where are you?"

"I'm not sure," she glanced around the room for any clues. "Somewhere in Iowa, I think."

"Okay. I'm going to need more than that. Is there anyone else around?" the operator asked.

"Yeah," her voice was getting shakier, and fortunately Amy walked in at that moment followed by a plump black woman. Elise pointed to the phone, "Where are we?"

The black lady took the phone from her hands, "Honey, you sit down right here."

Amy helped her off unsteady feet and gave a hug of consolation before disappearing again.

Riing!

Elise jumped as the phone in her pocket sounded. She didn't need to look who it was. Carbon probably picked up the 911 call. Quickly silencing the phone, she wondered what the car would do to achieve its goals. Would it just allow her to leave?

The lady finished talking to the operator and turned to Elise. "They're sending a patrol car, and it should get here soon." She scrutinized Elise up and down. "What's goin' on, honey? Some boy got you in trouble?"

Elise shook her head and tried to answer, but now she found her voice momentarily paralyzed. What if she had done the wrong thing? Now she would never see her father. What if she really was safer with Carbon? How far would the car go to get her back? She hoped it wouldn't hurt anybody.

The round woman sat down beside her. "Don't worry, honey. I'll stay here until the police show up. You'll be safe."

She only nodded in response, fighting to think clearly and not bolt out the door. How she wished she was braver, stronger, smarter. She managed to collect herself somewhat and stifle the second guessing. Now committed to this course of action, she resolved to see it through.

* * * *

Sheriff deputy Shane Lawson got the call on his normal route. Some girl was claiming to be in trouble in Gad City. The operator said she sounded confused and didn't even know where she was. Probably a druggie, he thought as he turned his Crown Victoria around in a dusty driveway. He joined law enforcement to find some action, but in his two years so far, all he had dealt with were traffic citations and people wasted on drugs. With a sigh, he flipped his lights on and sped toward his target.

The trip wasn't long, and as he pulled into the parking lot he immediately noticed the big black Challenger. Sure, it was dusty, but he respectfully noted it probably had a lot of horses under that smooth hood. What would a car like that be doing here? At first he figured the girl had driven it, but then he glimpsed a dark figure sitting in the driver's seat. The hum of the powerful engine growled at him as he trotted into the small restaurant.

"She's in the back," a young waitress pointed to a door labeled 'kitchen'. Deputy Lawson nodded his thanks and headed in, putting on his serious cop face.

The teenage girl perched on a bench was not exactly what he was expecting. She lacked the distant and withdrawn look of drug users, and the eyes that met his were fully intelligent and resolved, but clearly scared.

"Hello, Miss Perry," he greeted the pale face. A big black lady sat next to her, but got up to leave when she saw him.

"If you need me, I'll be outside." With a last glance at the girl, she left the kitchen area.

"What can I do for you?" He watched her with slight suspicion. She didn't look like much of a threat, but neither did she seem to be in much danger. However, she did appear to pretty shaken, and probably wasn't playing a prank.

"I need to talk with you," she said hesitantly, almost as if the words stung in her mouth.

"Okay," he replied slowly. "I'm listening."

She gave a nervous glance toward the door. "Not here."

He attempted to follow her gaze, but nothing was there. "Why not? Is someone after you?"

The girl only shook her head in response, light colored hair falling over frail shoulders. "Please. Take me to the police station or something. But I can't talk here." Her eyes were pleading, and her nervous manner seemed thoroughly sincere.

Deputy Lawson stared at her a moment before he conceded. It wasn't like he was busy. It was probably an angry ex-boyfriend or something. He could just drive down to the station, listen to her story and reassure her enough to go home, maybe promise to talk to the boyfriend. "Okay. Well, let's go."

* * * *

Elise felt slightly more assured with the deputy sheriff present, but at the same time her apprehension built. He had undoubtedly parked in the small lot as Carbon. There weren't any other options. What would she do when they walked past?

She stood as he held the door open for her. He obviously didn't believe that she was in danger and was only humoring her. As they approached the exit sign, she had to push herself forward. The deputy turned and gave her a questioning look. "Is someone outside?"

She shook her head. How could she explain that a car was waiting for her? He stared at her another minute with something like pity, he probably thought she was crazy and paranoid. "All right," he switched to a cheerful tone, "We don't have all day."

When he pulled the door open, Elise saw his patrol car parked on the far side of Carbon. She swallowed hard and stepped through the door, trying not to look at the black car. The deputy started saying something, but she barely heard him, all her senses waiting in expectation of Carbon's move. She walked toward the car on wobbly legs, following her escort.

Directly in front of the big car, she couldn't help turning to look. The hologram was on, as was Carbon's engine, but Elise couldn't detect a single other noise or movement.

The cop had opened the back door to his cruiser and was now watching her. "Do you know that car?"

She ripped her gaze away and forced her legs to carry her into the back seat of the police car. "Na," she lied. "Just a sweet car."

He eyed her suspiciously, but closed the door without a word. He didn't seem to be buying her story, but he continued his silence as they backed out and drove off. Elise fought the urge to turn around and see if Carbon followed.

Glancing in the cop's rearview mirror, however, she saw that the black sedan hadn't moved at all. Was she giving up so easily? Relieved, Elise refocused her thoughts on what to tell the police as the town faded into the distance.

* * * *

Sergeant Reyes watched with satisfaction as the dozen or so federal agents piled their things into a mobile command unit. Agent Stewart was still inside the building, but soon they would all be gone. That woman agent walked past him with a stony face. She had dropped the friendly pretense shortly after kicking him out of his own office. Now it was his turn to be smug.

* * * *

Special Agent Elizabeth Kerry was not happy with the progression of this case. The locals were not helpful, and all the evidence seemed contradictory.

"Liz!" a voice called as she stepped back inside the humble police station. "Get over here now!"

Agent Kerry tapped her boss on the shoulder. "I'm right here, Stewart."

He was too excited to skip a beat, "We just received a call from a 911 operator that an Elise Perry called in trying to contact the police. She was in…," he turned to glance at the computer screen, "Gad City, Iowa."

"*She* called the police?" Liz was skeptical. "What did she say?"

Her boss motioned to the computer again, this time to the tech behind it. "Gerry, play the 911 recording again."

The faint voice of a frightened young woman came out of the speakers. Throughout the conversation, she sounded confused and uncertain, revealing no details about anything except her location, and that she had been in a car chase.

"What car chase?" she asked Stewart, but he only shook his head in response and shrugged.

"We haven't figured that out yet. But a deputy was called to pick her up, and she should be in custody now."

"Get me connected," Agent Kerry got out her cell phone. "We can't lose her again."

Chapter 8

Elise became increasingly convinced that her decision had been correct with every mile they drove. She would be safe with the police, and maybe they would explain more about her father. What puzzled her was her own reluctance to say anything about Carbon. She had lied to the deputy without even thinking about it. Her musings were cut off as they pulled up to a small sheriff station.

"Okay, Miss Perry." Deputy Lawson got out and opened her door. "Let's get this over with." He gave her a friendly smile, but his condescending manner was annoying.

They walked to a tiny room in the back, past the grumpy looking lady behind the front desk. After a brief explanation that everything would be recorded, they sat down at a bare table.

"So, what's going on?" The deputy leaned back in his foldable chair. This department must have a tiny budget.

Elise opened her mouth to begin, but the grouchy lady stuck her head in the door and made a telephone motion at Lawson.

"Excuse me," he left to take the call, leaving her alone with the angry woman. Elise was careful not to look at her, analyzing the linoleum flooring instead. It was pretty disgusting.

"Deputy Lawson," she heard him answer from the other room.

He said nothing for a long time, and then she only heard hushed tones and paper being moved around. When he returned he gave her quite a different look. In place of bored tolerance was excited determination as he pointed at her. "C'mon, we need to get back in the car."

"What's wrong?" she asked.

"We can talk in the car," he used her elbow to steer her out of the room and out of the building. He turned to the grouchy lady, "I left a number on my desk, please pass it on to the Sheriff."

Her permanent frown deepened, but she gave a slight nod and wave as they once again got into the patrol car. Elise had to stop herself from chewing her fingernails off as they backed out of the small drive in silence.

"Well, Miss Perry," her chauffeur seemed to be grinning. What had that phone call been about? "It seems someone else has an interest in talking to you first." He glanced at her in the rearview mirror to gauge her reaction.

She blinked, her expression blank. "Who?"

"That was the FBI. They have been searching for you for some time now. Said you ran away from home."

She stared at the back of his head in shock. The FBI? "Not exactly. What did they want?"

"Didn't say that much. Just that they wanted, excuse me, *needed* to speak with you ASAP. You have no idea why?"

She shook her head, wondering how much she should disclose. Even the FBI was involved? Had the people chasing her actually been agents?

The deputy seemed set on figuring this case out. "So, if you didn't run away from home, what happened?"

"It's a long story," she hoped he would let it go, and she could just explain this stuff to the FBI.

"Well, it's a pretty far drive, so we've got some time. What were you going to tell me at the station?"

The logical part of Elise chimed in. Why not share everything? She *had* just decided to inform the police. If she wanted to stay with Carbon, that time was past. She took a deep breath. "Okay. I guess I should start at the beginning."

"That would make sense," he interjected dryly.

Ignoring his comment, she began, "My parents died when I was six. Car accident. And so I've been in the foster system, moving around a lot but," she shrugged. "I guess that's expected. For the most part it's been pretty good. For the past two years I've been staying at a town called Mesa Springs, I doubt you've heard of it." His blank expression confirmed her guess. "Anyway, it's a town in South Carolina. The people are nice, it's quiet." She paused as a familiar homesickness returned.

Focusing back on her story, she realized the difficulty of explaining Carbon, considering that she had already lied to the deputy once. "A few months ago…"

"Yes?" he prodded. "A few months ago what?"

With a heavy sigh, she continued for better or worse. "I was on my way home from work on my bike, and I noticed a black car following me."

"The same car at the store?" He apparently didn't miss a thing.

She gave a brief glare. "I'm trying to explain."

He held up his hands in surrender, so she started again, explaining her first encounter with the car, only giving a vague description, then moving on to the months that passed and the mysterious phone call.

"You just found the phone in the dirt?"

"Yeah, I was going to take it to the police the next day. I figured someone had dropped it. Obviously after the phone call, I thought differently." She felt foolish for not taking the phone to the police earlier. Given his expression, he agreed.

At first she wanted to explain herself, but her face had flushed with embarrassment and she moved on to describe the following week and the people looking for her at school.

The deputy listened intently, occasionally asking for clarification, taking in every small detail. As she recounted her desperate dash through the woods and leap into the car, he gave her another hard look.

"You just jumped into a strange car? You didn't even know who the men were at the school. They were probably FBI."

"Well, the lady said they were after me. And they did chase me," she tried to explain. "Besides, why would all those people be looking for me? Wouldn't a phone call be enough? It just didn't add up."

"Whatever," he impatiently waved the hand that wasn't driving. "Who was in the car?"

At this question, Elise found herself answering without even knowing what she was saying. "The lady. She said my father had sent her to protect me, and I believed her until cops were chasing us. Then I decided to escape and call the police." She wondered why she was lying even as the words poured out of her mouth.

"What did she look like?"

"Black hair, professional suit, wore sunglasses," Elise trailed off. It was just easier to explain this way.

"So," he paused. "That *was* the woman back at the restaurant. In the black Dodge." It was a statement, not a question.

She nodded meekly.

Reaching for his radio, the deputy gave her an angry glare and swore under his breath. "This is Lawson requesting an APB on a black Dodge Challenger."

She listened with sinking dread as he communicated Carbon's description and last known location to dispatch. Again she attempted to wipe away any doubt and reaffirm that she *had* done the right thing, but the pit in her stomach refused to go away.

When he had finished, her turned cold eyes back to her. "So, you lied to me why?"

"I thought…" she began, but trailed off. Even the police were mad at her now, what had she expected? She kicked herself for telling them so much. "I didn't know what she would do," Elise was almost whispering. She didn't feel sure of anything anymore.

"And where was she taking you? On a tour of the continental U.S.?"

"I don't know!" she exclaimed, another lie spilling out of her lips. "She wouldn't tell me anything." At least that part was true.

Lawson's face softened slightly, but his tone was still tight. "No more lies, Miss Perry. You need to pick a side."

She dropped her gaze to the floor, then looked back at him defiantly. "I already have. I'm here, right?"

He didn't seem convinced, but let the conversation drop into oblivion. For the rest of the drive Elise was alone with her thoughts and worries.

It was an hour later when they arrived at a tall fence with barbed wire and a security gate.

"What is this place?" she asked apprehensively.

"A federal prison."

Elise's hopes drained as she considered the imposing perimeter.

The deputy continued, "It's the only secure place the FBI could find nearby."

The guard let them in after a brief chat with Lawson, and a knowing look at Elise. She hated being treated like a criminal. They were escorted into an ominous looking grey building where Elise was strip searched by female officers before being allowed admittance, not a process she enjoyed.

Personnel took her cell phone and pocket knife, items she had forgotten about. The guards were cool but not friendly, clearly regarding her as inferior. She was given her original clothes back, which she took as a good sign. At first she worried they would give her a black and white striped outfit and take her into custody.

Instead one of the officers led her to a dim room. It was a mansion compared to the sheriff's office she had just visited, though it contained only a steel grey table and several chairs.

"Wait here until someone arrives to talk to you. If you need anything, just push the intercom button and ask." The woman handed her a glass of water and turned to leave.

"What's going on?" Elise was worried. This felt like a detainment.

But the officer was not filled with comforting phrases, and merely shrugged and restated that people would come soon to speak with her. As the heavy door slammed and locked, Elise stared at the vacant room with mounting suspicion.

Maybe Carbon had been right after all.

* * * *

"Let's get this bird in the air," Agent Stewart yelled as he all but leapt up the steep stairs into the waiting Falcon jet. Liz Kerry and most of their team was already on board, and they looked up briefly at his declaration.

"Come on!" He yelled out the open door, "Get this ladder out of the way!" Several ground crew personnel bumbled slowly toward the stairs and slid them back. What was wrong with people? Before taking his seat, he poked his head in the cockpit. "We need to get moving. I want us going top speed, this flight needs priority."

The pilots exchanged glances and nodded, "Yes, sir." The first officer gave a little salute. What, were they mocking him now? With a sigh of disgust, he turned and sat down next to Agent Kerry.

She was regarding him with curiosity. "Boss, we don't exactly need to hurry. She's in a safe location. We have confirmed that they are holding her at a maximum security prison. What are you so worried about?"

"She's already slipped out of our grasp once, Liz. I'm not losing this lead again. It's the only one we have, remember?"

"Yeah, but what could possibly happen?"

"I don't know," he tried to settle back into his seat, but he was wound tight. "Obviously we're not the only people who want this girl."

The dark-haired woman just stared at her boss a moment. He had been getting a bit obsessive about this case. Then again, she had worked with him almost seven years now, and his hunches were usually correct. "Okay, boss. But try to get some sleep. I think you're going to need it."

* * * *

Deputy Lawson found himself face to face with Warden Tony Garrett of the LaDache Prison. "Thanks for your help, son. You can head back to your station now. I expect a copy of your report in the morning. Be sure to include everything she said. If you need anything else, let me know."

"Will do," Lawson nodded. The tall black man was just not the type easily refused. The warden waved and patted him on the back, but it felt more like a shove to get lost. Sometimes people were touchy about their districts, he reasoned as he headed towards his car.

Regardless, this had been the most interesting day of his career. He was sad to see it go.

* * * *

As Lawson's patrol car passed the security guard and headed back to Gad City, an unmarked car approached the entrance. Behind the wheel was a well-muscled Hispanic man accompanied by a red-haired woman. The guard waved them through after a brief conversation and analyzing their identification.

The two said nothing as they parked the maroon Chevy Impala and entered the building.

"Excuse me," another security guard held up his hand. "I need to see some ID."

"Of course," the Hispanic man said smoothly as he reached into his pocket. The guard scrutinized the card that was presented to him, and relaxed.

"Sorry, but you never know who's gonna try to bust in here."

"No worries," the woman smiled, showing a row of perfectly white teeth, "But I thought they usually tried to bust out of here."

They all laughed at her joke, and the pair moved on to the front desk.

"Hello," the man greeted the receptionist behind the counter, sliding his ID under the bulletproof glass. "We're here to see Elise Perry."

The receptionist peered at the IDs, then back at the two solemn figures in front of her. "Agent Garcia?"

He nodded, "That's me."

"And Agent Kelly."

The red-head only smiled in affirmation.

"One moment." The receptionist disappeared momentarily with the two cards. When she returned a large guard was with her. "This is Officer Forbes. He will show you the way."

He motioned for them to follow, buzzing them through the steel double security doors. They fell in suit wordlessly, weaving down hallways and passing through barred gates.

When they reached a door at the end of a long hallway, the guard slid his card through the electronic lock and pushed the handle down. "When you're done, just knock."

Chapter 9

Elise's tension had grown exponentially. Debate still raged in her mind, and despite firm attempts to block any doubts away, she couldn't fully suppress the regret that she had not stayed with Carbon.

The police hadn't exactly given her a red carpet welcome, and she was more than a little uncomfortable with their unveiled suspicion. She wanted to scream in their faces that she wasn't a criminal, that she was the victim here, but there wasn't even anyone to listen.

The empty room was almost mocking, a silent echo of her own doubts. Just as she considered knocking on the door to ask for a phone call, the door slowly swung open.

Two figures strode confidently through the door, and Elise's heart dropped to her knees. The man looked like he lived at the gym, but the red haired woman was the one that struck chords of fear inside. The attractive woman smiled broadly at Elise, but the effect was quite disconcerting. She had seen that smile before. That flawless face was on her dad's list.

The woman spoke, the joviality of her tone and expression not reaching her grey eyes, "Hello, Elise. I'm Agent Kelley with the FBI. I hope they've been kind to you here." She glanced around, "Sorry for this setting. Sometimes regulations are a little much."

The man stepped beside Kelley, "Truth is, we need to ask you some questions, and this room is just a security precaution." He took a seat across from her. "We have good reason to believe your life is in danger, Elise, and we're here to help you."

Maybe they were the good guys, she tried to convince herself. But as much as she wanted to believe them, something about their manner was uncaring and patronizing. Elise eyed them suspiciously. "You said you're with the FBI?"

Agent Kelley gave another bright smile. "You heard correctly."

Elise must have appeared wholly unconvinced, for the woman set two ID's on the table. "Here you are. This is my partner, Agent Garcia."

Why would her dad have an FBI agent listed as dangerous?

The man stared at her as if she was an alien specimen under a microscope. He leaned forward and she could smell a wintergreen breeze off his breath. "We need to know everything you know."

"Look," Elise tried to explain. "I don't know what's going on. I don't really have anything to do with this, I was just…"

"Relax." The woman set a reassuring hand on her shoulder. "We're not here to punish you. We just need to ask some questions."

Garcia cleared his throat, "Let's get to business. We have information suggesting that a man claiming to be your father has contacted you."

Elise tried to keep her expression blank, but the agent guessed her answer anyway.

"You should know that this same man is facing charges of treason, fraud, embezzlement, and is the chief suspect in a murder case." His eyes were hard, and she felt a deep impulse to hit his smug face.

It couldn't be true, she reasoned. Her father, a murderous thief? At the same time, she felt foolish for trying to defend a man she didn't even know.

"How do you know this?" she asked shakily.

Garcia eased back into his chair with a short laugh. "How do I know this? Believe me, Elise, if we didn't have good reason, we wouldn't be here."

Elise swallowed hard and refocused her gaze on the ground.

The woman spoke, "We want to help you Elise. If you …" but her voice broke off abruptly, replaced with the sound of faint taps on a cell phone followed by a curse. When Elise glanced back up, the man had repositioned himself behind her. With a swift motion he grabbed her right arm. Instinctively she jerked back with a scream.

"Stop it!" He commanded, pinning her hands to her side. She struggled against his grasp for a few moments, but quit after realizing the futility of her efforts. She was like a gnat against those muscles.

Keeping her firmly locked in his overly large arm, Garcia nodded to his partner. "Let's move."

Agent Kelley's friendly face had vanished as she returned his nod and knocked on the door.

"Cooperate, Elise," he whispered roughly into her ear. "We'll get you out of here." Considering that her options were nil, she only nodded.

The guard promptly opened the door, and Kelley flashed another graceful smile. His radio cackled, and he held out a finger motioning for her to wait as he answered it.

But before Elise could even blink, the woman launched herself toward the guard, snatching his gun as her pointed heel made contact with his face. He slammed into the opposing wall before crumpling to the floor. Kelley was right on top of him, and his expression was stunned as she forced him upright, twisting his arm and holding a gun to his back.

"Let's go, Forbes," she hissed into his ear. "Any trouble from you and it's over. We have more than one hostage. Remember you're not that valuable."

The big guard swallowed hard, clearly considering his options. It didn't appear that he had come up with any solutions as he flashed Elise a helpless glance. Eyes wide with horror, she could only stare in shock as her situation passed from bad to much, much worse.

Carbon's warning echoed in her mind. *The police will be inadequate protection.*

But here? In the middle of a federal prison?

Agent Garcia had materialized a knife from somewhere, and she could feel its sharp edge pressing against her skin. She bit back a scream.

"Cooperate, Elise," his breath was hot on her neck. "You don't want to kill your friend over there." Turning to the guard, he motioned toward the hallway. "All right, big guy. Let's open some doors."

When the guard didn't move at first, Garcia moved the knife to her throat. "Come on, Forbes. Let's not make things messy."

The man winced as Kelley twisted his arm further, "You heard him." Her eyes were hard, and Elise had no doubt she would carry through with her threats. "We would rather do this the clean way, okay? Let's move before someone gets hurt."

Forbes gave a last resigned look at Elise, then caved. "Nobody gets hurt."

"Nobody gets hurt," she repeated, pushing him down the hallway. "Now don't waste time."

They passed through several gates without resistance, and if Elise's memory served her well, they only had one more obstacle before the prison's outer doors. Forbes slid his card through the lock and pushed his finger into the slot, obviously dragging his feet to buy time.

Why hadn't the prison officials done something yet? Surely they had cameras in the hallways. Wasn't this place supposed to be secure? As the door slid open, there was a sickening thud as Kelley slammed the butt of the pistol into the back of Forbes' skull and the big man slid lifelessly to the floor. Elise screamed.

"Quiet!"

Her vision flashed with tiny suns as Garcia all but broke her wrist, yanking it cruelly behind her back. "Shut up, girl." He shoved her through the broad door as it slid shut and heavy locks clicked into place.

A whining pierced the air, and red lights flashed in the hallways. The prison had finally noticed.

Her two captors exchanged glances and quickened their pace. Elise found herself running toward the exit with the sharp knife still at her back. She dearly hoped that her captor didn't trip.

Their brief flight ended in front of the final set of doors. Garcia tossed a small square object to his partner who caught it and jumped over to the wall beside the door.

Elise was dragged back about twenty feet as the woman knelt beside the box she had just secured onto the wall. She likewise leapt out of range, clapping her hands over her ears.

Elise jumped as the box exploded into a fireball of cement shrapnel, barely noticing the prick Garcia's knife had made in her back as her ears rang and her vision blurred. She faintly registered several successive bangs and realized Kelley had disappeared into the smoke.

Garcia shoved her toward the doors as the buzzer sounded and they slid open, his partner dashing in behind them as the second door slammed shut.

Dozens of policemen had positioned themselves outside, but all of Elise's senses were still ringing from the explosion. Details were fuzzy, but she was aware of the knife again pressed against her throat.

Kelley jumped out in front, waving her gun at the policemen. "One move and she dies. Throw your weapons down," she commanded. "Now!" she pointed her pistol in Elise's face.

"Drop your weapons and we can talk!" one of the policemen tried.

A gunshot rang out and Elise wondered if she had died. But as she opened her eyes, she realized that the mad woman had only fired beside her head. "Don't talk to me about negotiations!" she yelled back. "Drop your weapons NOW!"

Perhaps because of the crazy fire in the redhead's eyes, they lowered their weapons in surrender.

"Thank you!" she shouted. "And if I even suspect being followed, I'll blow her head off!"

Elise was pulled backward by Garcia before he threw her into the back seat of a car. She screamed and beat the glass, the hopelessness of her situation momentarily muted by fierce survival instincts.

The policemen only watched as Kelley carefully maneuvered into the passenger seat, her gun firmly trained to Elise. "Not a move!" she reminded them before slamming her door.

Garcia had already started the Impala, and they shot backward as Kelley bent over to retrieve something from under her seat. Rolling her window down a crack, she lifted a large weapon and shot a smoking canister toward the policemen.

"Floor it," she muttered to Garcia, but the effort was wasted as they were already approaching the towering chain link fence at alarming speeds.

Kelley again stuck a weapon out the window. Elise couldn't tell what it was, but the fence seemed to melt before they slammed through it. Their velocity carried them over the thick dirt on the other side and onto the pavement.

Elise clung to her seat as they sped away. Her options spent, she screamed again.

"Stop it, girl!" Garcia yelled at her. "It won't do you any good now."

Frantic, Elise discovered that not only were there no door handles back here, but no window controls either. She was completely sealed in. Giving a final pound on the bulletproof glass that separated her from her two captors, she sank wearily back into the seat.

She would have cried, but she felt completely cried out with the past two day's events. What had she done? With a piteous moan, she stared out the window.

Kelley began to type into a laptop computer and spoke brief words into a cell phone. After a few moments she turned to face Elise. "Just relax, it will make it easier. We don't want to hurt you."

Somehow she doubted that.

"Are you hungry? Thirsty?"

Were they trying to play nice now? Elise shook her head. Her stomach was tied up in knots and the last thing she wanted to do now was eat. Some water would be nice, but she was far too upset with the red haired woman to even look at her.

She returned to staring defiantly out the window, despair and acceptance quickly taking over her remaining hopes of escape. What could they possibly want with her? Obviously her well-being was not of great concern to them. If her father's warning really was true, then she was in mortal danger.

Chapter 10

Elise began to wonder if the police would come to save her, but her reflections on their past performance only left her with bitter anger. Some police force. Apparently Carbon had been right.

Her father had gone to huge lengths to prevent this, and here she had waltzed directly into the enemy's hands. Guilt and anger at herself began to taunt her and threatened the mental dams she tried to construct. It *was* her fault. She had made a terrible mistake.

The two up front seemed to be in good spirits now, making comments about taking candy from a baby. Elise gave them an evil glare. It hadn't looked that easy to her. Maybe once they stopped somewhere she could escape, though she seriously doubted it would be as easy as running from Carbon.

They were traveling along a simple two-lane highway, barely having passed a single car – Elise guessed the prison wasn't a popular destination – and her eye caught a flash of motion a millisecond before impact.

Elise was thrown against her seat belt as they were launched into the air, the Impala violently flipping side over side before the smashing front first into a ditch beside the road. Steel snapped and twisted in an awful cacophony of chaos, but nearly as quickly as the terrifying flight had begun, all was still and silent.

Bang! Bang!

Two loud explosions sounded near Elise's head, and the momentarily dark crypt was invaded by rays of light. The car was upside down, Elise vaguely noted as she dropped to the floor – roof? – and painfully attempted to crawl into the daylight. She coughed with the dust and wondered how she was even alive.

Everything was spinning. The smell of gasoline assaulted her senses, but the whirlwind of scenery began to calm as she lay down on the solid earth, checking to make sure everything still worked. Her shoulder ached and her right arm was limp, but otherwise she seemed okay.

"Elise."

She twisted around, shocked to see a familiar black form waiting. Was she hallucinating?

"Carbon?" She asked tentatively. It was almost too good to be true.

"Yes. Please get inside. The man is still alive and the police are not far off."

Elise's heart lifted. She had never thought it possible to experience so much joy at the sight of a car. But the world refused to hold still, and as soon as she raised herself to her feet, she tumbled back over again.

Carbon pulled up beside her with the driver door open, inserting herself between the girl and the wreckage. Summoning her strength, Elise managed to grab hold of the running board and the door handle enough to drag her unwilling body into the cab. The door slammed behind her, and she lay trembling and dizzy on the seat a moment before she could sit up.

When she did manage to right herself, they were backing away from the heap of twisted metal that once was a car. It seemed impossible that she had walked away from the crash, or even stumbled away. The nose of the Impala was pushed into its cab, the engine block resting under the driver's seat. The rear end stuck out of the ground, roof and ground forming a near-perfect forty-five degree angle.

Elise closed her eyes and leaned back into the soft leather seat. Her senses had been stunned be the accident; she felt much like a bird who had flown into a window. A tear of gratitude and relief slid down her bruised cheek.

"I apologize, but there was not a better way to get you back alive. You have not sustained any permanent injuries."

Elise wiped the tear away and smiled. It was a very faint smile, but she was overcome with joy that she was no longer in the hands of Kelley and Garcia. "I'm fine." She gave a heavy sigh and glanced down with shame. "Thanks."

"I need to get you to Montana," Carbon reiterated.

Elise choked on a short laugh. The car was nothing if not persistent. "I know, I know." She turned around to give the gruesome wreckage a last glance as they drove away. "What exactly did you do?"

"I struck the Impala at a speed and angle that allowed a ninety–seven percent chance of rear passenger survival. The front passenger and driver were not expected to survive."

"Oh," was all Elise could think to say in response. She glanced out the windshield at the sleek hood. "Didn't you get a dent or something? That was a pretty serious crash."

"My frame and body panels are much stronger than the Impala's. I suffered no damage."

It was nice to know her ride was indestructible. "But how did you even find me?"

"I tracked your drive with the deputy using your cell phone. When you were admitted into the prison, I locked onto your vital signs and monitored your situation through the prison's communication system. I detected Agent Kelley's arrival and then the lockdown.

"It was necessary to intercept you quickly. If I had lost your signal, it would have been hard to locate you again. Furthermore, it has been difficult because of the APB out on me. We need to avoid all law enforcement, which will slow our progress considerably."

Elise was quiet for a moment. "I'm sorry." What else could she say? It was her fault. "Why didn't you stop me at the restaurant? Why did you let me get in the sheriff car?"

"Why did you decide to call 911?"

Elise had to pause to think of a decent response. The truth wasn't exactly glorious. "Well, I… I was afraid that my dad was a criminal, and with the police after me, I didn't want to be in trouble."

Defensiveness rose up from remorse. "How was I supposed to know that you were telling the truth? That I could trust you or my dad? I just made a mistake." But the justice of her reasoning seemed pretty pathetic in light of the weighty consequences. "I said I was sorry."

"I believe you. It was a reasonable course of action by many standards, and you acted within your own best interests."

"Yeah, but you could have forced me to stay. Aren't you programmed to protect me?"

"Yes. We have established that." Carbon's sympathy only went so far.

"You could have locked me inside, or run over the sheriff or something. Why did you just sit there?"

"Run over the sheriff? Elise," the car was almost patronizing now, as if she was explaining how to count to ten. Elise decided to overlook that, however, on the grounds that it had just saved her life. "Your father built me for the purpose of protecting you."

"I thought we established that." Elise couldn't help it; Carbon had walked right into that one.

"I am trying to make a point." The smooth voice paused dramatically. "As I said, your father built me to protect you. However, you still have the choice to refuse that protection. I cannot force you to accept it. If I had kept you inside by force or threat of force, you would have only become more determined to escape, and more susceptible to walking into the enemy's hands."

The concept made sense to Elise like oil mixes with water. "But I probably would've come around eventually. And why did you come back for me? Why not just let me make my own choice and walk off?"

"Elise…" If a computer was capable of sighing, Carbon probably would have.

"Stop calling me by name. I'm the only one here."

"Okay. Miss Perry,"

"No!" Elise interrupted. "Just start talking. You don't have to address me personally."

"My decision to allow you to leave was not because I was no longer pursuing the interest of your protection. On the contrary, it was within that interest."

The car was not making sense. Maybe it *had* been damaged by the accident.

"I continued to follow you, waiting for an opportunity when I was needed. When Agent Kelley, who is on your father's list, and an accomplice took you against your will, it was in the interest of your protection to provide you the opportunity to escape them."

Carbon's explanation reminded Elise of reading Shakespeare. "Can you just speak plainly?"

"I was."

"You weren't."

The car waited a moment before trying again. "I was continually making plans to bring you back to safety, but I was not able to act until you realized the danger. Even after escaping the Impala, you had to choose to come with me. I could not have forced you, only provided the chance."

"Oh." That was a good point, Elise realized. A car couldn't exactly make someone get inside.

"I will still get you to Montana. It is improbable you will leave again."

"That's for sure," she muttered.

"You should rest, Elise. Your body is recovering from the trauma of the accident."

The advice made sense as she realized the adrenaline rush had depleted her strength. At least they were headed to Montana again, and through the relief Elise's mind kept running over Carbon's strange theory of protection.

Chapter 11

A uniformed officer stood perched over his patrol car. His black hair was slicked back, blue eyes hidden beneath a pair of reflective sunglasses. The silver nametag on his shirt read "Hitchens", his pocket ID and badge further identifying a Matthew Hitchens. He scanned the horizon with a stony expression.

The highway had remained mostly empty, nothing out of the ordinary. Glancing at his watch, he saw that they had ten minutes remaining. His police scanner and a quick phone call had let him know they were successful, but he kept his eyes open.

A loud roaring broke the silence as a black Dodge sports car flew past his stealthy position along the road. Time inched past, and at the end of eight minutes only two other vehicles had passed. One beat up Ford truck headed south and a new Buick LeSabre heading north.

The dusty landscape was silent, and Hitchens checked the time impatiently. They should be here by now. Time was too valuable to risk, he considered as he climbed into his cruiser to find them himself. As he turned the key, he noted that the same Dodge made another pass, this time at speeds exceeding one-hundred and fifty miles an hour and pointed the other direction. An unlikely coincidence, he considered as he threw the unmarked Crown Victoria into drive and sped the opposite way.

There was no change in the police scanner, but he put the literal pedal to the metal as he raced toward the prison. Empty fields were on both sides of the deserted highway, not a single structure in sight. Hitchens' face drained of color and his grip became iron around the steering wheel as he noticed a heap about two-hundred feet off the roadway.

Idiots. He barely slammed his car in park before jumping out to check inside the mangled sedan. Police would be here any minute, and Hitchens forced deep breaths as he crawled into the exposed rear seat. The woman was dead, and her partner might as well have been. Unsurprisingly, the girl was nowhere to be found.

Hitchens reached his hand under the rear seats and withdrew a small object. His prize retrieved, the black haired man worked deftly to gather together some dry grass and brush. He struck a match and tossed it on the small pile near the Impala's ruptured tank. Why did he have to do everything?

The man inside moaned. Fortunately for him, it would all be over soon.

Hitchens jumped back into his cruiser and was driving away in seconds. Muttering angrily under his breath, he again floored the car despite the engine's protests, speeding away from the mangled wreck. There was only one possible suspect, and they had a good ten minute lead.

He reached into his pocket, only glancing in the rearview mirror as a fireball erupted behind him. At least now the incompetent fools wouldn't leave any evidence behind.

Retrieving the small silver box, Hitchens placed it carefully in the center console. It had not been difficult to remove the digital recording device from the vehicle; it had been hidden quite well. No one would never fully entrust such an important task to those two.

Amateurs. To them, it was nothing but a game. They were into gun-slinging and high speed chases, convinced that advanced weapons and the fastest equipment could win.

Hitchens' mind spun into high gear as he reached for his cell phone. He would have to move fast to sort this out.

* * * *

Deputy Lawson was halfway back to Gad City when he heard the announcement. Emergency at the LaDache Prison, backup requested. Could this be about that girl? After receiving permission from his precinct to head back, he called in to the prison.

"You say the name's Lawson?" the secretary answered.

"Yes, ma'am."

"Please hold." A brief segment of music played over his phone, and he could have sworn that same song was on the weather channel that morning. The thrilling tunes didn't last long, however, and Lawson recognized the voice of Warden Tony Garrett.

"Lawson?"

"Yes, sir."

"We have a situation, which I'm sure you are aware of. Get yourself over here and meet me in my office."

"Is this about the girl I dropped off?"

"You'll know when you get here, just make it soon." With a click, the rumbling voice was gone. Whatever happened, it had been enough to shake the prison's stony warden, a feat not easily accomplished. Lawson flipped his lights on and stepped on the gas pedal. Maybe this day wouldn't end so badly after all.

* * * *

Elise leaned back in the seat exhausted, but her eyes kept slipping back open. Carbon was driving erratically, pulling behind structures or shrubbery, slowly meandering down tiny streets, and occasionally blasting down a straight highway in the name of avoiding law enforcement. After about an hour, Elise had regained enough composure to complain.

"How long will it take at this rate?"

"It is impossible to predict."

"Can you at least try?"

"I estimate around thirty-four hours."

"Thirty-four hours!" Elise groaned and dropped her head on the dash. "That's longer than when we started!"

"Yes, and it may be slower, depending on the density of law enforcement and how hard they search. The search has been suspended now, due to the prison break and their discovery of the wreckage. When they find you missing, they will again increase efforts to locate you."

"What is the chance they will find us before we get there?"

"About sixty percent, as we have not moved far from the crash site. The likelihood will decrease as we get farther away."

That wasn't exactly comforting to Elise. "Shouldn't we just hide somewhere and wait for this to blow over?"

"No. I need to get you to Montana."

"I know," Elise reasoned, "but it would be better to be late than to never get there at all, right?"

"In the next few hours it will only be detrimental to wait. This is the window of opportunity to leave without their notice. Once they are fully mobilized, it will be much more difficult."

"But what if they do find us?"

"I will outrun them."

"Not all the way to Montana."

"No. But it should be far enough."

Carbon seemed overly confident. Elise stared at the window as an idea came to mind. "I have a plan."

The car was silent a moment. "Your last plan did not go very well."

Elise waved her hand dismissively. "That was different. I thought…" she trailed off. "Well, never mind. Maybe you should get a paint job." When Carbon didn't respond, she continued. "I know black looks great on you, but if you were another color, maybe we could avoid the cops." Still nothing. "Carbon?" she tried again. "Did you hear me?"

"Of course I heard you," came the level reply. "I was thinking."

"Thinking?" She wasn't aware computers could do that. "You were thinking?"

"Yes. I was analyzing the potential costs and benefits of your suggestion."

"Ah. And?"

"A proper paint job would take a considerable amount of time, and it would be suspicious. The police will probably investigate any recent paint jobs on black Challengers."

"Oh," Elise sighed and leaned back again. She was discovering that even hunted people could become extremely bored. Only it was a terrifying boredom that was wearing her thin.

"Do not worry, Elise. They will not find us."

She wished she shared Carbon's optimism. Practicing some deep breathing exercises, she tried to resign herself to thirty-some *more* hours sitting in a car.

* * * *

The Falcon Jet touched down a few minutes before FBI agent Alan Stewart was out of his seat and waiting not so patiently at the door.

"I'm sure they're doing all they can," Agent Liz Kerry reassured her boss.

"Oh, that makes me feel better," he returned sarcastically, pacing up and down the aisle.

Liz had the unfortunate experience of sitting next to Stewart when he had spoken with the warden of the LaDache Prison an hour ago. He had taken the information fairly well, considering his personality, but she knew he was boiling over inside.

The other agents were looking out the windows or staring down at the floor uncomfortably. This had been a blow to all of them, but Stewart was the one she worried about. He was too involved in this case.

As the plane came to a stop and stairs were rolled up to the door, the team began piling their equipment into the two black SUVs that were waiting. Stewart had excused himself to a few hundred feet away to talk on his cell phone. While Liz couldn't make out the words, she could hear him yelling and was glad she was not the person on the other side of the call. He returned just as they finished loading up and jumped into the driver door, muttering about incompetent dimwits and other words not fit to recall.

"I can drive if you'd like, boss."

"I'm fine," he snapped.

Liz sighed and leaned back against her seat. This wasn't likely to be a pleasant drive.

* * * *

The first thing Lawson noticed were the many uniforms milling around outside. The fence looked like it had lost a fight with a bulldozer, and deep skid marks in the sand were telltale signs that someone had made an unauthorized exit.

No one paid much attention as he walked toward the building, but one of the guards positioned himself across the entrance when he approached the outer doors.

"Excuse me," Lawson cleared his throat. He wasn't exactly small, but this guy was built like a tank. "I need to speak with Warden Garrett. Name's Lawson."

The guard eyed him a moment before motioning to his buddy. "Hey, clear him and take him to Admin. Garrett wants to see him."

Lawson's smile wasn't returned. The second guard appeared about as unhappy as his friend was ripped. He led Lawson through a brief security check, and after calling in to administration, pointed him to another steel door.

Lawson walked up and gave a knock on the door. It swung open to reveal about fifteen people crammed inside. They each seemed to be carrying on their own conversation, and it was safe to say none of them appeared very pleased.

The tall warden wasn't hard to find. "Lawson," Garrett shook his hand and introduced three other staff nearby, their names swallowed by the noisy chatter. "Let's find someplace quieter."

Lawson obediently followed him into a small conference room with a dark wooden table in the center. The three who had been introduced entered as well and took a seat, each appearing more than a little agitated.

"So, Lawson," to describe Garrett's expression as tense would be a massive understatement. "You were correct. This concerns the girl you brought to us, Elise Perry. She is no longer here."

The deputy's face didn't change. He had expected as much.

"Two individuals," the tall man presented him with several photos from security footage, "came in shortly after you left; Agents Sara Kelley and Carlos Garcia with the FBI." He pointed to a still shot of them in a hallway, the blond girl held in an arm lock by a bulky man, a redheaded woman shoving along a uniformed guard.

"The FBI had informed us they would be by soon to talk to the girl, and we didn't think much of it. They had valid ID's and repeated what we had been told on the phone earlier. Everything they said checked out and a guard escorted them to the room she was in.

"About five minutes later, we received a call from the agent leading this investigation. He was still an hour out by plane, and he was just making sure everything was in order. When we told him two of his team was already here and talking with the girl..." Garrett paused as if considering how to proceed.

"Let's just say he cleared up the misunderstanding. But the pair was already making for the exit, taking Elise and a guard hostage. We initiated lockdown, but they blew a hole into the operator room and overrode the system. They killed three personnel inside, and the guard is unconscious in the hospital." The warden's flashing eyes betrayed his cool tone. "Using the girl as cover, they managed to get to their car and drive off, warning us that she would be shot if we followed. They gassed the police forces on their way out and put some pretty impressive rounds in the fence. You probably noticed that."

Lawson's expression confirmed that he had. "You let them drive off with her?"

Garrett swallowed as if suppressing an immediate response. "Agent Stewart," he pronounced the word purposefully, angrily. "He's the man in charge of this case, and was quite adamant about one thing. Whatever happened, we could not risk the girl's life. If she was shot... well, let's just say he made some not-so subtle hints that my head would be on the chopping block.

"Anyway, of course we sent units behind them at a distance as an invisible tail, just surveillance for the time being. I received a call forty minutes ago from my guys. It seems the car they were driving crashed on the side of the roadway." The warden pulled up a photo on his Blackberry. "One officer sent me this."

Even on the tiny screen, Lawson could see firefighters spraying a smoldering crumpled frame.

"For the first few minutes, the blaze was too hot to approach. Later they pulled two bodies from the front of the car." The warden pocketed his phone, "but the girl was in the back."

"So?"

"The back seat was empty."

"You think she's alive?"

"I don't know. But if she's not, her body is still missing."

"Okay…" Lawson began cautiously. "What do I have to do with this?"

The warden looked up again. "If your district could spare you, I could use the manpower, but more importantly, you are the only one who talked to this girl. We need some more pieces of the puzzle and we need them fast.

"The FBI will be here in a few minutes." An unhappy face looked at Lawson. "Hopefully we will have more information for them. Checkers," he pointed at an Asian man across the table. What kind of name was that? "You take two officers and debrief the deputy. I want every piece of information. Anything she said, exactly as she said it. Got it?"

The man nodded violently and Lawson worried his head might bobble right off. He got up and motioned at the door, "Come with me."

Lawson glanced at the warden and excused himself, his mind wandering through endless possibilities. This case just kept getting better.

* * * *

An hour after landing in Iowa, two black SUVs pulled up to the LaDache Prison. The lead agent jumped out and addressed his team.

"All right, people." Stewart's rage had passed into focused determination. "Let's set up inside, I want a group ready to be on the road and one for some brainstorming. We need some answers, and we need them yesterday."

He stalked off toward the building, leaving Liz to delegate the appropriate tasks before following.

When she was done, she found him engaged in tight conversation with the warden. Neither acknowledged her presence as she stepped up from behind.

"They just walked in here and took her? No one was supposed to even see her until we got here!"

The warden's tone wasn't pleasant either. "They were FBI, and they were on your team. *Your* agents." He pointed an accusing finger in Stewart's face. "Now three of my people are dead, one is in the hospital, and my compound is compromised."

"*My* agents?" Stewart's voice was squeaking. This was not going anywhere good.

"Gentlemen," Liz inserted herself between the two glaring figures. "Let's calm down. We need to think. We can play the blame game later."

They continued to stare unflinchingly for a moment, and finally Stewart sighed in frustration. "Thank you, Agent Kerry. Now, I'm asking for a room to set up in for the time being, and access to your data."

Warden Garret stood with his arms across his chest. "We can give you a room, but sharing information goes both ways. I want to know as soon as you find something."

Stewart gave a curt nod. "Fine."

"Excuse me," another voice interrupted. Liz turned to find a uniformed officer standing next to them.

"Yes?" Garrett looked at the man expectantly, but the officer only glanced between the two agents and his boss in silence. "It's okay. They can hear it."

"We have an update from the crash site. The two bodies recovered were definitely the two agents. There is no sign of the girl."

Agent Stewart stared at the warden. "And you're sure she left with them?"

Garrett didn't even bother responding, dark eyes flashing.

Stewart held up his hand in surrender. "I just wanted to be sure."

"You can watch the security footage if you feel so inclined. For now, I need to attend to the security of this facility." He pointed to a small room in the back. "You can set up there. If you need information, just ask…" he paused, eyes scanning the room. "Hey Steve!" he yelled.

A short, balding man turned around.

"Get over here!" Warden Garrett turned back to them. "He will answer any questions you have. Now if you'll excuse me." The big man gave them a final glare and spun around to leave.

Stewart seemed to have just fully noticed Liz's presence, though his expression suggested that his thoughts were still elsewhere. "Elizabeth," he only used her full name when immersed in a case. "I want you to pick two others and take a car out to the wreckage. I don't trust these buffoons to notice details, and I want some eyes out there. The girl had to be in the car, and she had to have gone somewhere. I want to know what happened."

"Yes, sir," Liz replied. There wasn't much else to say to your boss when he gives orders like that.

Chapter 12

An hour had passed and Elise estimated they had made twenty miles of progress. Neither playing computer games nor shuffling through her father's playlists helped stave off her boredom, and the worry of being caught kept her edgy. Every time they stopped or pulled around small roads she watched out for a police car.

Carbon broke the silence. "I have been further considering your suggestion."

"Suggestion?"

"You suggested I get a paint job."

"Oh, yeah."

"It would be difficult to arrange without drawing suspicion. However, even considering the time to apply the paint, it could substantially decrease the time necessary to reach Montana."

"Did you figure out a way?"

"No. But if you come up with another idea, I will consider it."

Elise felt flattered that Carbon had not only found her idea worthy, but asked for another brilliant suggestion. "I will," she promised. The car seemed to have a weakness in developing original thoughts. Not bad for a computer, Elise reasoned. "Maybe we could find some paint in an old garage or shed?"

"That could bring police presence if we are caught, and leaves the problem of applying the paint job. If it is poorly done, it would be as suspect as black, if not more."

After a few more rejected plans and increasing frustration, Elise gave up. "Are there many police around?"

"Yes. I have been monitoring the police frequencies and they have steadily increased their search since finding the Impala. I am likely the only remaining lead they have."

Carbon didn't sugar coat things much. Elise gave a deep sigh, "And you're sure it wouldn't be better to just hide somewhere and wait?"

"That would only give them more time to find us, and it might take weeks before they give up searching."

There didn't seem to be a satisfactory solution, and Elise decided she needed a distraction from the worry. It wasn't like her anxiety was helping, and maybe she could clear her thoughts.

"Hey Carbon, can you play a game?"

"Why did you address me personally? There is no one else to hear you, and you instructed me not to address you by name."

"That was different. We were already in a conversation."

"We were also." The car wasn't letting this go.

"Well," Elise tried to find a good explanation. "We were talking, yes, but I was about to change the subject."

"And that is an appropriate moment to address a person by name?"

"Sometimes."

"That is not very specific."

Elise's first instinct was to yell "Carbon!" in frustration, but that would probably only complicate things. "Just forget it. If you want to call me by name, go ahead. It's not that important."

"Okay, Elise."

So the car preferred to use names. "Now, like I was saying, can you play games?"

"Games?"

"Yeah, like I say 'I'm thinking of something yellow' and you try to guess what it is."

This concept did not go over well with the car. "There are many things that are yellow. How will I know what you are referring to?"

"That's why it's a game," Elise said, trying to explain the point of a guessing game. Carbon eventually agreed to attempt a round, and

Elise's nervousness slowly slid to the background as Carbon's interest in the game increased. She was a worthy opponent, even if it took her a while to get going, and Elise found herself relaxing and even laughing – she thought she had forgotten how – as they continued weaving in a haphazard way toward Montana.

* * * *

The scene of the wreckage was cluttered with various police personnel: forensics, homicide detectives, and various officers that apparently had nothing else to be doing. An accident investigation specialist was being flown in and expected to arrive in a few hours.

Agent Kerry eyed the mangled car with grim curiosity. She was not an 'accident investigation specialist' but she could detect that this was a serious wreck, and probably not an accident. The forces required to toss the car nearly two-hundred feet from the roadway and smash the front end into oblivion were nigh impossible to create without an outside force. And yet, if another vehicle had been involved, it shouldn't be in much better shape than the Impala. So how could it drive away?

Then there was the problem of the missing girl. Clearly someone else had been present to take her, dead or alive.

"Liz," a brunette woman brushed the bangs from her eyes. Melanie Akers was the physicist of the group, and had been busy inspecting the demolished car since they arrived. "This wreckage is amazing." True excitement shone in the short woman's eyes. Always the scientist, Melanie's statements were usually void of human sensitivity. "Do you see that rear compartment?"

Liz glanced at the burnt shell.

"I know it doesn't look like much, but the rear structure is completely preserved. Amazing."

"What are you getting at?"

"I calculated a rough trajectory that suggests the car was traveling straight and normal, albeit above the speed limit, when it suddenly veered off."

"You think the driver just lost control?"

Melanie gave the wreckage another thoughtful look, then traced an imaginary path back to the road. "I seriously doubt it. This car was airborne to flip like that. That's a pretty violent maneuver to perform alone." She shook her head emphatically. "No. I'm positive the car was struck with something. And look," she turned around to point back at the highway.

"There aren't any brake marks on the road. Whatever hit this car, I don't think the driver had any time to react." Again she was submerged in an invisible realm where she traced the car's movements with her hand. "My rough guess is that something struck it from the opposite direction."

"Any idea what that something might be?"

The scientist paused and shook her head. "Obviously, a first glance implies some sort of missile or explosive projectile, but the metal doesn't have the right stress marks and nowhere is it blown apart. It's just smashed up. Maybe with some time and a computer I can find the amount of force, maybe the size and motion of the object."

Liz nodded. "Good work, Akers. Make sure the examiners record all the info you're going to need. Our camera is in the car."

"Yep." Melanie scooted toward their car, still pleased with the scene. Liz moved on to find Rico Guerrez, the other team member she had chosen to bring along. It didn't take long to find him scrutinizing the rear compartment from the other side.

"Hey Guerrez," she greeted him.

He jumped up when he heard his name.

"Gee, someone's tense, huh?"

He just looked at her sheepishly. Guerrez was about as tall as Melanie was short, and he was the newest addition to their team. He was supposed to be a brilliant critical thinker, the kind that solved ridiculous logic puzzles. So far his acclaimed skills had not been put to the test, but here was a golden opportunity. "You got this one figured out yet?"

A tense smile appeared on Guerrez's face, like he wasn't sure if he was allowed to smile at crime scenes. "This one's pretty complicated." His fingers nervously scratched his head. "If the girl was in the back of the car, it appears someone engineered this whole thing just to get her." He walked around to the side nearest the road, kneeling by the empty, upside-down door frame. "I think the preliminary exam missed this, but the door was shot off. Very precise shots." She leaned closer to inspect as he fingered the bullet holes. "Incredible, actually. I'm not sure what weapon did this."

"So, you're saying something hit the car so precisely that the front passengers were out of the way and the girl in the back could be retrieved, then shot out the door and left before anyone even noticed the wreck?"

The tall man nodded thoughtfully, considering her summation. "It's a guess, but I don't see any other possibility."

"But what about the fire? You think it exploded on impact?"

"It's impossible to tell yet, but... no. I think it caught fire later. Maybe whoever knocked them off the road got the girl out and then torched it to erase the evidence."

"There's no way it was just an accident?"

Guerrez glanced back to the car in response.

"Okay, I get it. Do you think the girl went willingly?"

"I doubt she was in a position to resist. Even with the rear end intact, those forces..." his voice trailed off.

"But she survived?"

"If the fire wasn't instant, it's likely. She was probably stunned and disoriented, to say nothing of injuries. All someone would have to do is pick her up and drive off."

Agent Kerry nodded. "Okay. Make sure you record any tire marks."

"I've tried looking, but the emergency vehicles obscured any tracks that were in the dirt."

"I don't suppose I could hope for any footprints?"

Guerrez stared at her blankly a moment, "Um..." His eyes turned to the soft dirt around the wreckage, now cluttered with prints from dozens of EMS, fire rescue, and police personnel.

She sighed in frustration. "Work with what you have. We need to know who, we need to know why. And keep working on the how." Liz slapped him on the shoulder. "Relax, Guerrez. It will get easier."

Clearly, the advice was not easy to apply.   With worry on his face, Guerrez nodded as she reached for her phone.

It was time to give the boss an update.

* * * *

"Are you thinking of a fruit?"

"No," Elise was growing tired of the guessing game, Carbon was too good.

"Are you thinking of a vehicle?"

"Vehicle? That's too broad."

"Are you thinking of a sedan?" Carbon tried again.   The car was incapable of tiring of the game.

"No."

They were driving through a small town and had come to a stop at the only traffic light in town; a light that seemed to stay red forever, regardless of the fact that no one was coming the other way. Elise had rolled the windows down to ease the pain of being locked in a car for hours on end, and a cool breeze blew through the cab.

She was berating Carbon again for a lack of specificity when the roar of an engine caught her attention. There was a brief moment of panic that it was the police, but when she turned to face the noise, it was just the opposite. Inside a shiny yellow Camaro with orange flames was a teenage guy who looked like he had just skipped out of jail. Tattoos covered most of his body, but an amused smirk covered his face.

"Hey baby," he taunted. "You *do* know there's no one else in that car, right?"

Elise glanced back at the light, hoping it had turned green. It stayed red. She cleared her throat. "Um, yeah. I just think better when I talk out loud."

The guy didn't seem impressed. "Whatever, baby doll." His look was making her quite uncomfortable, but she wasn't sure if he was eyeing her or Carbon. "Nice ride, but I got all the horses." He revved his engine ridiculously loud.

She tried to ignore him – how long could this light possibly be? – but he was not to be discouraged. "Wanna race?"

Trying not to look at him, or his flashy Camaro, she answered honestly, "No."

"Chicken," he leered, launching into obnoxious clucking noises.

The light turned green, and Elise was wondering why they weren't moving, and utterly shocked when she heard her own voice come out of Carbon's speakers. "Fine, I have a deal for you." Elise stared speechless at the dash.

The tattooed guy was thrilled. "Ooo, baby. You play hard, huh? What are you after?"

Elise turned her face the other way so it wasn't obvious her lips weren't moving. She had no idea what Carbon was thinking, but so far, the car had planned well. It was still weird to hear her voice though. "I need a new paint job."

The guy whistled. "You serious, doll? That's not cheap, and your custom job's pretty sick. Besides, what's in it for me if I win? I have some suggestions."

Horrified, Elise spoke before Carbon could answer, "No. Forget it." She glanced behind her, looking for an excuse to leave, but there were no other cars nearby.

"Come on, baby. Relax. I'll settle for a couple hundred."

"Okay." This time Carbon beat her to a response, "Where do you want to race? Here? Now?"

Dull looking blue eyes stared at her in excitement, "Whoa, baby. It's a little too dangerous in the light. Piggies, you know?"

"You mean the police?" Elise gave him a hard look.

"Duh. Just meet me at Nat's Diner at midnight. I'll bring some buddies and beer, we'll have some fun."

That did not sound like much fun to Elise.

"Catch you later, baby doll." With another rev of the Camaro's engine, he blasted off down the road.

Carbon casually pulled out and began to drive slowly down an obscure road.

"Carbon?"

"Yes. There is no one else here, remember?"

"I am saying your name for emphatic purposes," Elise explained through gritted teeth.

"Because you are angry?"

84

"I'm not angry."

Carbon said nothing in response.

"Okay, maybe I'm a little... frustrated. Why did you just set up an illegal race with that jerk?"

"May I ask how you know he is a jerk?"

"No." Elise did not care to disclose the art of instantly determining a person's character to a computer. "But you should tell me why you did that!"

"That 'jerk' is James Morgan. Using his license plate as well as facial and voice recognition, I found his identity and discovered that he operates an auto body and paint shop with his father. The Camaro's paint job was clearly custom, and their logo was also on his back window."

Elise tried not to look overly impressed. "You can do that?"

"Why would I lie? I also found that he has had five unpleasant encounters with law enforcement."

"Gee, that's a shocker," Elise muttered.

Carbon ignored her, "He is unlikely to side with the police, and is thus likely to help us evade them."

"Don't you think a street race will draw their attention?"

"Maybe, but the chances are low."

"Why can't we just *buy* a paint job from them? At least it would be legal."

"I do not have sufficient funds."

So there *was* a limit to Carbon's money stash.

They pulled onto a dirt road and parked behind a decrepit barn. "We will stay here until eleven. The police will not find us."

The situation was far from ideal to Elise, but she grudgingly admitted that Carbon's idea was pretty decent. After some further complaining about being a criminal, and Carbon's reassurance that she could actually *win* a race with the jerk in the Camaro, also known as James Morgan, Elise settled back into nervous boredom, hoping someday she could become a law-abiding citizen again.

Chapter 13

FBI Agent Alan Stewart was growing increasingly frustrated. Every minute that went by drastically decreased their chances of finding Elise Perry. He was sitting across from Deputy Lawson and giving the man a thorough debriefing of every word and syllable that had come from the girl's mouth.

"She said the woman was called Carbon?" Stewart asked, clicking his pen as he wrote down every detail.

"That's what she said. Described her as a dark haired, professionally dressed woman."

"That's it? No age, height, weight?"

Lawson shook his head. "I thought you guys wanted to interview her first. I was just asking basic questions."

"That *is* basic." Stewart flashed an exasperated look at the younger man. People around here were incompetent.

Lawson only held up his hands innocently.

"Okay, so she convinced Elise that she was actually saving her, but after a police chase the girl got suspicious and called the police?"

The deputy shrugged, "That's what it seemed like. But if this Carbon went to such great lengths to get Elise, why just let her call the police and walk away? She was sitting there in the black Dodge when we got in my patrol car."

"And you did nothing?"

"The girl said she didn't even know the car! I thought it was just a domestic violence case or something."

Stewart sighed in irritation. "Of course. So, the woman lets her go for whatever reason, you find out later and put an APB out on the car, drop the girl off at prison and head home?"

"Pretty much."

"And you mentioned a phone?"

"Yeah. It's how Carbon contacted the girl."

"So Carbon gave it to her?"

Lawson nodded.

"Where is it now?"

"I don't know."

"Did she have it with her in your car?" Stewart thought his question was direct, but Lawson only looked confused. "You never even asked?"

The deputy's face confirmed that he had not. Cursing under his breath, Stewart shot the man a hard look before leaving to locate Steve, their official prison guide. What was wrong with these people?

He found the short man waiting in the hallway. "What items did the girl bring into the prison? You searched her, right?"

Steve paused a moment. "Let me check up front."

"You don't know?" Stewart demanded.

But Steve seemed equally irritated with the day's events and only held up a stubby finger telling Stewart to wait. His bald head reflected the glare of the hallway's bright lighting as he radioed in to the front desk, inquiring about Miss Perry's personal belongings. The response sounded like garbled mumbo-jumbo to Stewart, but Steve nodded and turned to leave.

"Not so fast." Stewart was not about to leave another important task to these people. "I'm coming with you."

The little man looked uncomfortably down the hallway, but then shrugged in resignation and continued walking. His pace was unusually quick, and Stewart wondered how those short legs outstepped his own lumbering gait.

Hopefully the girl had brought the cell phone, though the enticement of such a solid lead seemed dangerous in light of all the dead ends they kept hitting.

"Hello, Martha."

A female guard wore a sour expression that did not change for the better at Steve's greeting. "The girl's belongings are in that bin," she pointed at a grey plastic container on a nearby shelf.

"Don't touch anything," Stewart jumped between the bin and the two officials. His eye caught the glimpse of a shiny metal object. "Gloves, please." He held out his hand toward Martha, who reluctantly retrieved a pair of plastic gloves from somewhere to their left and placed them in his outstretched hand. Her face said she would rather have flung them at him.

Stewart unconsciously noted that he disliked everyone from this compound as he eagerly slid on the gloves. There was also a pocketknife, and he snapped his fingers at Steve. "Come bag this as evidence. And put some gloves on." Without turning around to see the man's predictably angry glare, Stewart picked up the phone, careful not to smear any existing prints. It didn't appear to be anything special, just a simple flip phone.

He opened it cautiously and breathed a sigh of relief that it was on and functional. As he began to look through the menu to find missed calls, the smell of burning electronics wafted toward his nose.

"Ah, no...!" he shouted, frantically attempting to remove the battery, but it was too late. The phone burst apart, Stewart yelping as he withdrew his stinging hand. Plastic and metal shrapnel clattered to the floor, and all three stared in shock at the shards.

The shock didn't last very long on Stewart, however, and clamping his mouth shut to seal in the string of colorful expressions that came to mind, he jerked the door open and slammed it behind him. Some matters were best dealt with in private.

* * * *

Twilight was just beginning to seep across the dusty land. Tall mountains to the north were fading to black, the sun's daily disappearing act stirring anxiety in the sixteen year old girl alone in a sporty black sedan. This was the end of her third day on the road, the third day since someone flipped her life from ordinary to something dangerous and unknown.

Traveling several days in a car is immensely dull. Sitting for hours in a parked car is markedly worse. Elise's initial relief and joy of being rescued was fading, exposing questions and fears that had never been properly answered. Who was after her? Why would anyone go to such great lengths to steal her out of a federal prison?

After the pleasure of meeting Agent Kelley in person, Elise made a point to go over her father's list and memorize each person's name and face. It took some time, but Carbon helped drill her and eventually the list was as familiar as family. More familiar, actually.

She also watched her dad's video again, but didn't find any clues or hints that could be of value. What was he involved with?

Her fear reflex tried to kick in several times, but the past few days had drained her reserves and she was too tired to worry any more. It was like a never-ending nightmare where she was running blindly in terror. Unlike her nightmares, however, here she had an ally.

Carbon's voice interrupted her thoughts as if on cue. "Elise, I have a question."

"That's a change. What would you like to know?"

"When you were in Deputy Lawson's patrol car, he asked you several questions."

"Yeah, a lot of questions."

"When you walked to his car, he asked if you recognized me." Carbon replayed the exact conversation.

Elise heard her own voice say, '*Na, just a sweet car.*'

"When you were explaining your story, you described me as a woman, my hologram."

"It's partially true."

"You lied." Carbon sure had a delicate way of stating things. "Why?"

"I..." Elise began to explain, but realized she wasn't exactly sure of the answer. "I don't know. I just did."

"You just did? There needs to be a reason."

"Sometimes humans just do things without thinking."

"Decisions are still based on some brief thought or memory, even if unconsciously."

Who had made the car an expert on human psychology?

"You decided to call the police because you were afraid and did not believe me. You cooperated until you were abducted by Agents Kelley and Garcia, at which point you were willing to leave because what I told you had been validated. I can follow your reasoning. But why did you lie?"

Elise shrugged. Carbon was definitely over analyzing things. "I guess I still wasn't sure who to trust. It just kind flowed out of my mouth. I thought it was a good idea."

"It *was* a good idea. Thank you."

It's not like Elise was trying to do anyone a favor here, just protect herself. "You're welcome." The car was being weird. She changed the subject, "So, you're sure about this whole race thing?"

"No, but it greatly increases our chances of getting to Montana if my appearance is altered. Once we enter the mountains, it will be nearly impossible to avoid law enforcement."

"I know that, but street racing?"

"How do you know they were not referring to a real track?"

"Meeting at midnight? I don't think so. Are there any tracks around here?"

There was a pause. "No."

"My point exactly," Elise said, smug. "And don't you think this will draw the attention of police?"

"Perhaps, but I will ensure that none are nearby at the time of the race, and these people are already adept at evading law enforcement."

Sighing, Elise realized she was not going to get out of Carbon's plan. "So, you still want to meet this guy?"

"I do not *want* to. Do you have a better plan to get a paint job?"

The car did have a point here. "But that guy is creepy. And I bet his friends aren't much better." Just the thought of a streetside party with a bunch of criminals made her shudder.

"Are you worried they will harm you?"

Duh! Elise wanted to yell. But she knew its effects would be lost on Carbon, so she only answered, "Yes. One sixteen year old girl versus a bunch of drunk guys? Not a good combination."

"I see."

Elise doubted it. Some clicking noise sounded from inside the dash, and the glove compartment opened again.

"You can take this with you."

Elise glanced over at the opened compartment, but she couldn't see inside. She gingerly reached her hand in; fingers grasping cold steel. "A gun? You want me to shoot them?!"

"No. I do not *want* you to shoot them. It is for self-defense."

The logical part of Elise told her it was wise, the angry part whispered that it was great, and the scared part shrunk back. She eyed the weapon in her hands. It was a small handgun that could easily fit in a purse or pocket – kind of cute, she admitted reluctantly. But could she shoot someone? Another person? Even in self-defense, she wasn't sure she could pull the trigger. "I don't know, Carbon. I've never even shot a gun before."

"It is not difficult. I will show you an instructional video, but do not discharge the firearm inside my cab."

Elise rolled her eyes. She could figure that one out for herself. With a sigh, she placed the gun on the seat next to her. Outside the final rays of light were disappearing into shadows. She breathed another quick prayer for strength, and to do the right thing. Her black and white view of what was wrong and right was blurring together, and she wished for some divine guidance. The screen in the center console cackled as a smiling man appeared, welcoming her to his course on gun safety.

Chapter 14

Agent Liz Kerry studied her fingernails while lead Agent Alan Stewart stood silently at the podium waiting for each member to take a seat. He had called a group meeting to catch everyone up to speed and brainstorm about the case. Akers and Guerrez were sitting to her left, each trying to appear deep in thought, the latter hurriedly jotting notes on a small pad of paper.

"Okay, people," Stewart began. "Let's get started." The overhead projector flicked on, and he pulled up a graph. "Here is a timeline I have constructed. Some of the times are still rough; let me know if you have conflicting data. The girl has been missing six hours now, and we all know how important it is to find her within the next day. Let's deal with what we know first."

"Liz's team just returned from the crash site. Liz?"

Agent Kerry cleared her throat, "Um, according to our accident investigator, another vehicle was likely involved in the crash. The car was struck from the front left side, maybe oncoming traffic, and…"

Stewart interrupted her, "Where is the other car?"

"We don't know."

A picture of the mangled Impala appeared on the wall. "You're telling me another vehicle was involved, and drove away? Wouldn't it have been destroyed?"

Liz glanced at her boss evenly. She had learned to shake off his accusations and condescending remarks. "So far, we have not found any evidence of another vehicle, but the impact suggests another moving object was involved."

"No evidence of the other vehicle? What, was it a tank?"

Ignoring his sarcasm, she continued. "No, if it was slow-moving the driver would have swerved out of the way. It was traveling at speeds comparable to or faster than the Impala."

"It couldn't have been a projectile?" Someone suggested. "Like an RPG or something?"

Akers shook her head emphatically, "No way. The car is completely burned, yes, but we think it caught fire after the accident. The metal was bent and mangled, but not torn. There is no evidence of explosives."

There was a brief silence before another agent asked, "What about the dash cam? Wasn't it an official vehicle?"

Agent Kerry nodded, "We found it, but it was completely destroyed." She got up and walked around to the projector, "Akers pointed out a more baffling observation. You see the front of the car was completely obliterated," she pointed to the picture. "We think the woman was killed instantly, and the man died from the fire. Now notice the back compartment. The frame is structurally intact, and the door here," she used the laser light to point specifically, "was shot off to get the girl out."

She paused, allowing the information to sink in.

Gilroy, their top analyst, spoke first. "Even considering that the Impala caught fire after they got the girl out, do you realize how impossible it would be to hit a car that precisely? Especially if the other vehicle left without a scratch. There should be parts all over the place."

"Maybe the second car was towed away," someone else suggested. Several heads nodded in agreement.

Gilroy shook his head, "Even so, the driver should have sustained serious injuries. And the precision of the crash is implausible at best."

"So, you think it's just an accident? Luck? Fate?"

That drew several snickers; there weren't many believers in coincidences in this room.

"I don't know," the analyst responded. "How fast are armored cars?"

He received only blank looks.

Stewart nodded, "Okay Gilroy, it's your job to research into the armored car theory and try to find any located nearby. Go ahead and search towing and junkyards as well." He turned to Liz, "Anything else?" She shook her head.

"Akers, I want to know as much as possible about our mystery vehicle. Houston and Velasquez, find every person who drove on that highway between nine AM and ten PM yesterday. Maybe someone saw something. Let me know if you find *anything*. Immediately. Now, back to what we have."

He handed a stack of freshly printed paper to Liz to distribute. "Here is a copy of our interview with the deputy who drove Miss Perry here. He is the only one who has spoken with her.

"So far, we know she ran away from a woman who calls herself Carbon, driving the same black car she got into in Mesa Springs. Carbon told Elise she was working with her father, and trying to protect the girl. Now, maybe she or some other colleagues tried to get the girl back, and something went wrong, I don't know. But if we find that car, I think we'll have some answers."

"I want you," Stewart pointed at two analysts in the back, "to look for any information on Kelley and Garcia, and try to find any link with this Carbon, or the girl's father."

After assigning the search for the black Dodge to another analyst, Stewart adjusted his tie and exhaled slowly. "If anyone comes up with anything, find me immediately. Otherwise, plan on another meeting in three hours. Liz, you're with me."

* * * *

Elise had finished watching the gun safety video and felt fairly confident she could hit a target if it was standing next to her. Carbon wouldn't allow her to practice, but if the video was only half as informative as it was dull, she should be in good shape.

What she concerned her now was the assumption that Carbon could actually win this race. Sure, the car could definitely destroy things, but James looked like he knew what he was doing.

"What exactly is supposed to happen tonight?"

"I will obtain a new coat of paint to increase our chances and shorten our timeframe of reaching Montana."

Clearly the car did not share her concerns about winning. "Okay, but what are we supposed to do? What am I supposed to say?"

"What do you mean?"

"Like, if they ask what I'm doing out here or where I'm from."

"Oh, I understand. Do not give them any accurate information. Create a new name for yourself."

"An alias…" Elise liked the idea. She felt like one of those secret agents on television, only wishing that she too could leave the set at the end of the day. "How about Suzy Hammond?"

"That sounds flowery. Remember you are posing as a street racer."

Slightly offended, Elise gave the dash a menacing look. "What would *you* suggest?"

"Bonnie. She was a criminal in a movie."

"What, should I call you Clyde?" Elise returned snidely.

"If you want. But do not tell them I am anything more than a normal car."

"I know, I know." She sighed, "I will just pretend to be an amazing driver."

"Yes. Try to sound angry and tough. They will respect that."

Elise couldn't help a short laugh. Three days ago the thought of hanging out with a bunch of outlaws would have scared her to the core. Now she just rejoiced they weren't Kelley and Garcia.

"One more thing," Carbon continued. "Make James agree prior to the race to complete the paint job tonight. Just one coat, without sanding or priming my top coat. That is a protective layer; do not allow him to damage it."

"You really think he'll agree to all that?"

"It is highly probable. Show him the five hundred dollars ahead of time so he knows you are serious. I doubt he will back out, he seemed very confident."

"He's not the only one." Elise muttered under her breath.

"Perhaps not, but he is the only one who is wrong."

"Is there any chance you could lose?"

"No."

Gee, her ride really was quite cocky. The clock told her she had two more hours of waiting before showdown at Nat's Diner. Elise spent that time pondering what to say, and how to prevent things from heading south. She almost felt brave. With a brief smile, she even considered that this might be fun. She envisioned the look on James' face when he lost, spiffy Camaro and all. Maybe this wouldn't be so bad.

* * * *

"Is this how people run their departments?! We don't even know what our own people are doing!"

FBI Agent Liz Kerry only nodded in agreement. She and Agent Stewart had just finished an internet video meeting with the Bureau officials over Agents Sara Kelley and Carlos Garcia. He was fuming mad, his face worked up into deep shades of purple. Even deeper than normal stress. It didn't take much of an imagination to see the steam blowing from his ears.

"I just can't believe it." He was still muttering furiously as they walked down the hallway back to their makeshift office in the prison. The official had informed them the two agents in question had gone missing a few days ago, though it was considered normal and raised no alarm. They had no idea how or why the two agents were listed under Stewart's team.

Of course they were shocked to hear of Kelley and Garcia's role in the abduction of Elise Perry, questioning the evidence and denying any responsibility. The lady was hesitant to turn over classified documents about the agents, their history and assignments, but Liz felt confident they would surrender after Stewart finished yanking some chains. He was not a happy man right now.

As they rounded a corner, an anxious Velasquez collided with Stewart.

"What the…?!" her boss exploded as the other man shrank back in horror, apologizing profusely for the accident.

"Houston and I, we found something," Velasquez stammered. "I was just coming to find you."

"Well, what is it?!" Stewart roared.

Velasquez was actually taller than his boss, but he appeared downsized as he swallowed hard. "Um, a… the mother of an inmate signed out just one minute before the prison locked down. We called her up, and she said she remembered only a few cars passing her the other direction for like fifty miles."

Stewart had herded the man back into their makeshift office. "And?"

"She said she's not much of a car person, but would probably recognize the vehicles if she saw them."

"Bring her in, I want to talk to her."

Velasquez frowned, "I'm not sure we have enough reasonable cause to force her to come in."

Stewart only waved his hand dismissively, "Whatever. Make a deal with her, talk about her son's time, I don't care. Just get her in here. Immediately."

Without waiting for an answer, Stewart pushed past the man and disappeared into the conference room. Liz shot Velasquez a sympathetic glance before following her boss. This was how he always got when they were thick in a case. He wanted something, he pretty much got it. And many toes usually were trampled.

Chapter 15

There is a paradox hidden in the passage of time. What was there before Elise could blink had taken an eternity to reach. Carbon's engine started with a smooth growl, and they pulled out without a word. It amazed Elise that the courage she had discovered a few hours ago had diminished to a small stash, leaving her alone to deal with incessant fluttering in her stomach.

"Relax, Elise. I will get you to Montana."

It wasn't as if she didn't believe the car wouldn't try its best, she just wasn't sure how things would actually work out, especially the parts that depended on her.

Swallowing hard, Elise searched for that bravery to resurface. She could do this. Her fake story and identification had already been stitched together in her mind, and she had even practiced threatening looks in the mirror. This exercise, however, had been cut short with Carbon's inquiry into what she was doing and subsequent comment on her efforts. To say the least, the car had not been impressed.

"We are only a few minutes away. The money is in the glove compartment, and the firearm is still on the seat. Make sure the safety is on, and tuck it somewhere obscure."

Elise gingerly picked up the gun and slipped it into her waistband with a heavy sigh. Fortunately her father had supplied an extra-large jacket under the back seat, making it ideal for hiding weapons.

Unfortunately she was still more than a little uncomfortable with the idea of being armed.

She retrieved the money from the glove compartment; a various assortment of tens, twenties and one hundred dollar bills. The thick wad of cash should prove enticement enough. Elise briefly considered using the money for a bus ride to Elderidge, but after her last bright idea, she thought better of leaving Carbon. Besides, it's not like she knew what was waiting for her in Montana, and Carbon was the only real link she had to her dad.

The small building that was Nat's Diner appeared quiet from the street. The crisp air blew a small version of Old Glory around its pole in a lazy fashion, and the restaurant's neon sign flickered peacefully in the darkness. Behind the building, however, lay a different story.

There were six cars parked in some sort of line, several with their hoods opened and dark characters mulling around the front. Most of the vehicles were older, and clearly the crown jewel was the glimmering yellow Camaro in the middle. It was flanked by a green Dodge Neon and a boxy Mustang, both parked a conspicuous distance from James' baby.

Elise couldn't make out features in the shadows, but a figure near the Camaro pointed in her general direction, his remaining four fingers clutching a bottle. She doubted it was root beer. About a dozen heads swung to see where he was pointing, followed closely by catcalls and a few longing stares. Did she really think she could do this? She swallowed again, hoping to push down the tremors that shook her body. "Carbon, are you sure about this?"

"We have already discussed this. No, I am not sure. But it is our best chance of reaching Montana undetected."

Elise made a mental note not to count on Carbon for reassuring words. She took a deep breath.

"Remember to look like *you* are the one driving," Carbon reminded her.

Trying to put on her best 'criminal' face, she placed one arm on the top of the steering wheel like the gangsters do in movies. *Think bad thoughts*, she told herself. If only she had some bling.

They pulled up at the end of the line, where several suspicious looking guys had gathered to greet her. As she opened the driver door, being careful to step out with deliberate slowness, James sidled up close, reaching for her hand. "Hey baby." His pale blue eyes were still rather hazy and dull looking, but he clearly had enough respect for his Camaro not to drink before driving.

"I think I've got it." Elise's tone was ice as she removed her hand, hoping her jitters would go unnoticed. Fortunately the group was far more interested in Carbon, some trying to appear uninterested and reserved while others unashamedly cooed and whistled. "Nice wheels, baby."

She attempted a thankful smirk, placing a hand on the dusty hood. Just the knowledge of the big car behind her gave her courage. She wasn't completely alone. "We still got a deal?"

His grin told her yes even as he leaned back and said, "You got the money?"

She flashed enough out of her pocket that he was convinced. "Five hundred." He reached for the lump, but she pushed it back down. "You haven't won yet."

That ridiculous grin only widened as several of his 'colleagues' howled with laughter. They had obviously not restrained themselves from the bottle tonight. He winked at her. "Okay, baby. Want me to lay down the course for you?"

"Not just yet. What about my coat of paint?"

"I'm not worried." There was that smug little expression again.

Another guy whistled. "Hey, baby. You do know that Morgan hasn't lost a race in..." he scratched his head in confusion at the attempted counting.

"A long time!" another guy interjected, which set them all off into more laughter. Except James; he just remained smug.

Elise forced a calm smile. "I believe it. But in the off chance *I* win, let's get the deal straight, no?"

James motioned in the air. "All right, baby. Set us straight."

Ignoring yet another round of raucous laughter, she continued, "I need the paint job tonight. Nothing fancy, just another top coat without touching the current one." She rasped her knuckles on the front fender.

"Whoa," he jeered. "You runnin' from somebody?"

She gave no response, only stared at him blankly. "We got a deal?"

He nodded as his friends fell quiet. "Yep." The silence didn't last long as someone yelled an offer to help paint her ride if she won. More laughter; more offers to help. Clearly most of them were rooting for James. Not that she could blame them. If she was actually driving, he would be the clear winner. "You got a name, baby?"

"Bonnie," she said, sticking out her hand to shake. "So you can stop calling be baby." She motioned her head at Carbon. "That's Clyde."

James gave her a funny look before accepting her hand. Maybe he was having second thoughts. But then he shifted back into that effervescent smirk. "So you not only talk to your car, you name it. Whatever, *Bonnie*."

His friends moved on to place bets on the winner, and he opened the GPS on his phone to show her the map. She hoped Carbon was listening as he explained the route and the turns, finally pointing to the finish line behind the diner. "That's where you'll be chasing my bumper."

She tried to smile politely. Jerk. "You ready?"

"Sure thing, Bonnie." At his sly wink, she turned to slip back into Carbon. "You know the rules, right?"

That gave her brief pause. Rules? "Sure, are your rules special?"

"Nope. Just stay on course, and no cheating."

That probably included having your car drive. Elise made a face at him, "I think I've got it."

"Okay, baby. See you at the starting line."

She only glared, restraining herself from correcting him. Soon she would be far away from all these people. James continued, "My man Joey there will wave us to start. Good luck, you're gonna need it."

With that, he sauntered off towards his Camaro, some of his friends cheering him on, a few staring indecisively at Carbon. Clearly they were not all so sure of their great leader James Morgan.

Elise shut the door and the engine cooperatively growled to life, earning more respectful glances from the crowd. "Okay Carbon, I hope you're ready."

The car was silent, causing Elise momentary worry, but her attention shifted to the left as James gunned his engine, revving it ridiculously high. The response from his buddies was predictable, and she only shook her head at the scene. Men.

"Elise, place your hands loosely on the steering wheel, and shift into drive."

Relieved that Carbon had not forgotten her role in the whole thing, she did as she was instructed. It was not until they had pulled up beside the flashy Camaro that her heart began racing. She had never even dreamed of doing something like this. Ever.

But before she had a chance to further consider the implications, the chubby redhead identified as Joey began waving a black and white checkered flag. Fortunately no one could see Elise's petrified expression through the deeply tinted windows, as she had just realized that the practical application of racing involved dangerously high speeds and sharp turns. Never mind that this was illegal.

The flag dropped, and her thoughts were left in the dust as the two vehicles catapulted forward into the darkness. The force of acceleration threw her back into the seat, her system momentarily shocked by the rush of adrenaline. Between the deep roar of Carbon's engine and the higher squeal of the Camaro's, Elise was submerged in a surreal blast of noise and color. The soft lights of the instrument cluster bled into the night before she managed to adjust to the forces against her body and the contrast in her vision.

Her body slammed against the seat belt as Carbon braked hard, throwing herself into a sharp left turn. Tires were squealing somewhere, and she caught a glimpse of the Camaro close behind them. "Go, go!" she couldn't help screaming as Carbon's engine reverberated with the effort.

"Elise," the car's voice sounded patiently. "I am already going."

"Go faster!" she yelled again.

"It would be unwise to win by too great a margin, as that would raise suspicion and unwanted questions." As Carbon continued calmly, Elise felt like a ping-pong ball tossed between the center console and the driver door. They were now navigating winding roads, weaving smoothly through the loops and curves at well over sixty miles an hour. "And you do not need to yell, I can hear you very well."

The speed was doing strange things to Elise, and she felt an insane laughter forcing its way out as they flew down the road. Here she was, a shy, timid nobody now flying down the roadway in an illegal race with an ex-convict in an autonomous talking car. The craziness of it all and the surging adrenaline trounced fear and worry, and she indulged in a brief fit of laughter. She was brave, she was free, she was invincible, she was... "Hey!" she yelled as the Camaro screamed past them on a straightaway. "You're supposed to be winning!"

"Relax. I already said I would win, why do you not believe me?"

That was a dumb question. "Because you let him pass you! That's called losing, you know!"

"I am aware of the definition of losing. There is still sufficient time to pass him again, and he will accept losing easier in a close, competitive race." Elise let out an exasperated sigh, carefully monitoring the distance between them and the Camaro. "Remember the goal is a new coat of paint, not a large victory."

Elise begrudgingly admitted to herself that she *did* want to thoroughly pound the jerk, also known as James Morgan, into the dust, but a cautious win was the better option. "Okay, okay," she relented hurriedly. "I see the finish line!"

Nat's diner was just a speck in the distance, the neon from several other cars glowing like Christmas lights in the parking lot. The gap between Carbon and the Camaro steadily decreased as the distance to the finish line disappeared at alarming rates. "Carbon!" Elise screamed, unable to suppress the fear that the car wasn't paying enough attention.

She was again thrown back into the seat as Carbon pulled even with the Camaro, then a shot half a car length ahead only seconds before the two cars blazed across the finish line. A new rush of excitement and relief filled Elise.

"You did it! You did it!"

"Yes, I said I would." The car seemed offended at Elise's doubt.

103

She was still too overcome by joy and shock to stop from shaking, but she bobbed her head in agreement as they slowed down beside the Camaro. *Deep breaths*, Elise told herself, willing her body and mind to be calm as they returned to Nat's. Faces were hard to make out in the dim lighting, but most of them clearly registered shock, a few appearing torn between excitement and fear. The great Morgan had been defeated; she only hoped he would hold up to his side of the deal.

As they slowed to a stop, she slid out of the seat not sure what to expect. The yellow Camaro pulled up beside them, and James' head and torso popped into view. His face was not exactly what she had expected, but he appeared surprised and slightly awed. His friends quickly circled around them, their chatter hushing as he walked toward her. She stretched out a hand, "Good race."

Still looking baffled, he actually accepted her hand politely and shook it. "Yeah. That was some pretty nice racing." He scratched his head and motioned toward Carbon's hood, "What do you have under there?"

"Enough," she had no idea about engines. Or how Carbon would feel about disclosing such information. She changed the subject, "Thanks for the race. It was pretty close."

"That's for sure," he said with a short laugh. "You're a pretty good driver for a girl."

"Hey," she cautioned. Not that she had actually been driving at all.

"Just kidding," he held his hands up in surrender. Tallying the looks on their faces, Elise realized she had earned some respect. Yeah, it was coming from criminals, but it still felt good.

"So," she began coolly, "What about that paint job?"

James' attention shifted back away from the car, and he actually looked happy. "Hey Frank!"

A tall skinny boy who looked around fourteen saluted at James.

"You get a crew together, and let's get this lady's car painted."

The scrawny kid grinned and nodded and began collecting other people for labor. Elise wondered why they were excited about painting.

James tuned back to her, "So you just want a top coat?"

She nodded in response.

"I see we need a quick bath," he ran a finger along Carbon's front fender picking up an ungracious amount of dirt and grime. "And what color?"

Color? Carbon had never mentioned color. "Um," she glanced at the black car in hesitation. What if Carbon had something already in mind?

James raised his eyebrows at her questioningly, "You don't even know what color you want?" He looked at her with questions in his eyes, pausing to size up the situation. "Who are you running from?"

"Running?" She tried to laugh at the idea, but he didn't seem to buy the act. Hoping Carbon would take over, Elise bumped the front fender with her fist and turned her head away. Fortunately somebody was on top of things, and Elise's voice answered, "White."

James spun his head around in confusion, unsure where the sound had come from. Elise cleared her throat and verified, "White. I want white."

Squinting at her, he shook his head and decided to let it go. "Sure thing, Bonnie. Follow me, and we'll bring *Clyde* into the shop." She nodded in affirmation. "It will take a few hours to paint, and then you really should wait a day for it to dry."

"A whole day?"

"Yeah. Usually I would wait longer." Seeing the worry in her face, he continued, "You can hang in the back room if you want."

Elise's eyes only widened at the prospect.

"See you at the shop." James scooted back to his Camaro, pausing to coordinate with some of his painting pals.

A whole day? Elise stepped back into Carbon, wondering what she would do with herself for that amount of time. Hanging out with James was far from appealing, and she was already anxious enough to get to Montana. And quite frankly, James' cooperation and willingness to accept loss was suspicious. She had expected more resistance from the tattooed street racer. Unable to relax, she settled for chewing off more fingernails, watching and waiting for the yellow Camaro to move.

"You did well, Elise."

"Thanks, not that I did much. That was some pretty nice driving, by the way."

"Thank you."

James finally got into his car and pulled away, some of his buddies slowly moving back to their respective rides, others continuing to drink and indulge in what Elise could only assume was a good time.

They tailed the Camaro, and Elise asked, "Will it really take a whole day?"

"Are you referring to the coat of paint?"

"Mm-hm."

"No. We will have to wait several hours for it to dry, however, and it will probably take them five hours to wash off the dirt and apply the paint. Even a quick coat will require masking off windows and other trim."

"So, we won't be on the road again until tomorrow afternoon?" Elise asked.

"Possibly late morning."

"What am I supposed to do in that time?"

"Whatever you would like. Just be careful."

"What I would like," Elise replied, "is to be headed toward Elderidge, far away from these people."

"That is what we are trying to accomplish."

Elise sighed, "I know, I know."

"Maybe you can borrow a book or a magazine and relax."

Elise snorted at the idea. "Yeah, I might gain some new friends, too."

The car missed her humor. "Maybe. It would also be helpful if you could obtain another cell phone. I have no way to contact or find you if we are separated."

"Should I go buy one?"

"That would be risky."

"What should I do then? Steal one?" That way, she could really fit in with James and his friends.

"Whatever you think is best, just use caution."

Elise had that part down already, "Of course."

They had driven through the small town center into a dilapidated warehouse of sorts. Carbon's headlights illuminated several junk cars gathered within a chain-link fence, and the parking lot they pulled into had similar fencing around it with barbed wire on top. "Gee, this is a nice place." Elise remarked dryly.

"Why? It is old and decaying."

"I was being sarcastic."

"Oh."

James had parked his Camaro, and was motioning for her to drive Carbon inside a large garage. As they pulled in, the building seemed to grow, fluorescent lighting revealing a neat, clean workshop in contrast to the junk outside. "Remember to tell him not to touch my top coat. Try to stay close so I can help if you need me."

Elise only nodded, as James was watching her through the windshield. Maybe this wouldn't be so bad, she tried to tell herself, and to some degree she actually believed it.

Chapter 16

FBI Special Agent Alan Stewart glanced up from his desk. There were twenty minutes remaining until the second meeting, and they had yet to find any solid leads.

Velasquez's witness had turned out to be useless; the mother of an inmate had indeed been driving on the same highway in the right window of time, but the woman's vision was worse than a blind bat. Whoever had given her a license to drive was beyond him.

"Sir, I think I've got something." An excited looking Guerrez appeared in the open doorway. The man had only been assigned to their team a few weeks ago, and Stewart hoped his nervousness was being channeled into productivity.

"Well, let's take a look." Stewart motioned for him to step closer. Any bit of information could be helpful here, they were nearly empty.

Guerrez handed him a piece of paper, "I have put together the points of contact we have had with Ms. Perry to project a rough idea of where they were headed." He pointed to a rough sketch, "If I include only Mesa Springs and Gad City, where she called 911, all you can tell is that she was headed north. Maybe to a northwestern state, maybe to Canada."

Stewart looked up at his newest agent. "How does this help me?"

"It doesn't. But I added the unconfirmed sighting by the gas station clerk in northeastern Missouri, and it completely fits the timeline."

"So?"

The Hispanic man put up one hand, "Just hear me through. My guess is that Carbon was careful to avoid any freeways or interstates that might have cameras and more police traffic, and then here in Iowa, the girl gets suspicious and calls 911. Assuming Lawson is correct, and the woman he saw was this 'Carbon', then we have a problem. Why didn't she stop the girl?"

"We've been through this, Guerrez."

"Humor me," the man pleaded.

Stewart gave a deep sigh. "Okay. Maybe it would have raised too much attention, or she wasn't able."

"Maybe. But what if she let the girl go? What if she wanted to see what would happen and who would come after her?"

"Why would she do something like that? She went to great lengths just to get the girl."

Guerrez nodded, "Yes she did. And I think she went to great lengths to get her back. There are two parties looking for this girl. Three, including us."

Stewart leaned back in his chair and raised his eyebrows. "I'm listening."

"Sir, we've been working with the assumption that these FBI agents were operating in conjunction with Carbon to get the girl back. But Velasquez's witness identified one of the cars she passed as a black sedan."

"Yeah, but she couldn't tell a Mustang from a Cadillac. Her testimony would be thrown out in court."

"But let's say it's the same car. Either this Carbon came for a hand off of the girl and something went terribly wrong, or she came to get her back from those two."

"I'm with you Guerrez, but even if it was the same car, how does she get the girl out unscathed? How does she even know what's going on? Are we looking for a cop?"

Guerrez shrugged, "Maybe, I don't know. She probably had outside help, maybe a projectile fired nearby? And maybe she was

109

working with someone inside the prison. We could interview some of the officials."

"We don't have much time left. And what about the rest of Lawson's account? According to Elise, Carbon claimed to have been sent by her father to protect her."

"Well," Guerrez began thoughtfully, "Assuming Carbon was telling the truth, and that there are two sides here, the harder question is who is on the other side?"

Stewart stared back at the man, lost in his own thoughts. "I like where you're going, Guerrez. I'm calling a meeting in twenty minutes. Tell the team." But the man only blinked. "Go on." Stewart shooed him out the door. "Twenty minutes in the conference room. Send texts, whatever."

* * * *

It didn't take long to gather the weary group back into the conference room. As most of them had it figured, the quicker they produced something for Stewart, the sooner they could find a hotel and catch some sleep. That and the girl's twenty-four hour window of being found was dwindling.

Stewart had already started talking, and was just now reaching his main point. "What we are dealing with here is likely two separate sides. If the girl was telling the truth, Carbon was sent by her father to protect her. Other motives are unknown. Now, protect her from whom? We had assumed this meant from us, in our efforts to find the girl and her father. However, I no longer believe this is the case."

"The FBI agents were playing for another team." Stewart drew stick figures on the whiteboard to illustrate. "Let's say the black here is our Dr. Mathis, Carbon, and probably a larger team with them. Now," he drew a big VS. to the stick figure's left, "on the other side we have the pair from the prison break. It's doubtful they were working alone."

Houston, a usual wave-maker, interjected, "Where's the evidence with this theory? I mean, we don't have any proof that this Carbon had anything to do with the car accident."

His comment was only met with a blue-eyed icy glare from Stewart. "I'm explaining." He turned back to his stick figures, "Now, instead of a hand-off gone wrong or a simple accident, let's say Carbon is against these two, gets the girl back and heads off to wherever. And again, back at the school; the conflicting reports over how she initially got away.

"Both of these sides appear to have advanced capabilities and large manpower, and one of them even infiltrated into the Bureau." He motioned back to the board, "And where does this leave us?"

Gilroy raised his hand hesitantly, "Somewhere in the middle?"

"I wish. We've been in the dust, chasing our tails."

"What are you suggesting?" Agent Kerry asked. She was usually the practical one of the group.

"That we start running down the real trail," Stewart responded. "Guerrez has recreated the girl's known journey and plotted a likely trajectory," he held up a blown-up image. "I want you to start looking for any place she might be headed. Search the father's past, the family, whatever. Anything in the Northwestern U.S. and maybe Canada."

Houston wasn't finished, "Back to your theory, boss. No one else should know about the Mathis case or Elise's identity. Unless the information was leaked …"

The physicist, Melanie Akers, usually kept quiet at these meetings. But today she added, "Good point. All recent info on this case is kept completely confidential, only up the chain of command. But with the proximity of the other agents, maybe another department has some sort of investigation into …"

"Without our knowing?" Stewart didn't let the woman finish. "They said they were completely clueless, but I will check into the matter further. For now, continue your investigations. I want to know who this Carbon is, where she is taking the girl, and who is after them."

As the members began discussing among themselves, the chatter grew loudly until Stewart hushed them all, first with a recommendation, "People, let's bring it back." When that didn't work, he slammed a fist down on the table, "FOCUS!" Most people froze and stared at their boss. A few blinked. "Right now we need to find out what happened after she left the prison, and where she is now. Get to work."

* * * *

Elise found herself relaxing and immensely grateful to be seated on solid ground. James' family shop was much like any car repair place, and included a cozy waiting room complete with magazines and comfy chairs. Most importantly, stationary chairs.

James himself had been a perfect gentleman, showing her the room before disappearing to work on Carbon. She watched them for a while – there was a Plexiglas window in the waiting room – but soon was nodding off. It was nice to have walls around her instead of a car's cab.

They had asked for Carbon's keys to move it around, but Elise refused. Partly because she didn't trust them, but mostly because she didn't even know if Carbon had keys. Instead she told them to come get her if they needed to move the car. Through observation, she had realized why they were so happy to paint her car. Most of them spent a fair amount of time simply admiring Carbon, others excitedly speculating about it. James himself seemed quite impressed it had defeated his beloved Camaro.

Elise was almost asleep when a hand waved in front of her face. "Bonnie?"

"Mmm, what?" she replied groggily, rubbing her eyes and sitting upright. The figure that came into focus was not James, but one of his friends.

"They're just about finished with your coat of paint." It was Frank, the scrawny kid from the parking lot.

"That's good to hear," she answered. But the kid didn't budge, just stood and stared at the ground. She was still on guard, but Frank wasn't very intimidating, and in a fair match, Elise would probably win. His face was young, and he only appeared abashed.

"Do you need something?" she asked.

"Um," he tried, his voice trembling slightly. Elise was amused. He was actually afraid of her. Clearly she had earned more respect than she first thought.

"It's okay," she reassured him. "What do you want to say?"

"I just, well … I'm a huge Mopar and Hemi fan, and I wanted to know … um, I just wondered if …"

Elise raised her eyebrows at his freckled face. "Yes?"

"You don't have to, but could I maybe drive your car?" Without looking up at her, he rushed, "It's no big deal, I just … I'm sorry. I just love your car. *Clyde.*" He repeated the name in awe, his face beaming with reverence.

She couldn't help pitying him, he was so pathetic. "Well, I'm kind of in a hurry, maybe later?"

He nodded emphatically, "Of course, I don't want to cause trouble. Only if it's not a big deal," he paused, staring at oversized large hands awkwardly. He didn't even look old enough to drive, his body and voice still in that disproportionate gangly stage.

"Are you done working out there?" she pointed towards Carbon.

"Oh, yeah. It's my job to help mask, but they do the painting. James says soon I'll be able to help there too."

"I see. He's a good friend, huh?"

A big smile grew over Frank's thin face. "Oh, yes. He's my older brother," he gushed in admiration. Well, that was unexpected. She glanced back at the tattooed, bulky frame spraying Carbon. It was kinda sweet though. In the trying-to-make-your-little-brother-a-criminal sort of way.

"I bet you're proud," she managed to say, though the words were pretty hollow. "He drives very well."

Frank nodded more emphatically. "He teaches me."

"That's nice." What else could she say? This kid would probably die with excitement if he knew of Carbon's capabilities and AI. Another awkward silence followed before she tried, "So, you really like cars, huh?"

"Oh, I *love* them," he stressed.

From there, he must have spoken for at least thirty minutes, carrying on excitedly about their family's business with cars and then intricate details about his favorite years and models, going into depth about engines, transmissions and a zillion other words Elise couldn't decipher from Greek or Chinese. She only nodded occasionally.

113

Frank had just drawn another breath, about to go into the details of a Camaro vs. Challenger matchup and why the Camaro should normally win, when James burst into the room. He was partially painted white, but grinned as he announced, "It's done." He motioned for her to come over. "Check it out."

Clearly someone was pleased with their work. She checked the clock: 5:45am. She was amazed they hadn't fallen over. Stepping out, she was taken aback by the transformation. The menacing black had disappeared, but the white did have an allure of its own. She wondered how the car felt about its new image.

"See?" he continued excitedly. "You said not to touch the top coat, but it worked out pretty well. Oh, and I left the wing and some trim black. It just works better, you know?"

He glanced at her for affirmation, and she had to admit it was a nice touch.

"Technically you need a clear coat on top, but it'll probably be okay. Just don't touch it," James was cautioning her. "Give it a few hours to harden."

"Wow." She didn't have to fake her astonishment. The jerk had done a really good job. "Quite the artist, huh?"

James' chest puffed up slightly, and he grinned. "Yep. Runs in the family."

"Wow, dude! It looks awesome!" Elise turned to see Frank standing behind them. "You have to add the side stripes, though. Classic RT."

James nodded in agreement. "It's beautiful."

Well, it was good everyone was happy. Elise cleared her throat, "So, when can I drive it?"

The two blinked as if they had forgotten her, lost in their car admiration. "You really are in a hurry, huh baby?"

"It's *Bonnie*," she reminded him, bold with Carbon in the room.

"Oh, yeah," he waved his hands absentmindedly. "Whatever. But you probably should wait a day to drive it, at the very least like ten of hours."

"Are you sure?"

He gave her a blank look. "Duh, or I wouldn't have told you."

Frank nodded his head vehemently. "And my brother knows more than anybody about paint. Right, bro? And that time …"

"Hold it, little man." James grinned slyly at his brother. "I have an idea. I guess we could feed ya and show you the town. My mom's a mean cook. If…"

Elise raised an eyebrow. These guys really beat around the bush.

"You let Frank and I drive it."

She only stared at him.

"And we'll throw in the black stripes for free."

It could be a trick, but she didn't think James was capable of thinking that far ahead, and the guys just seemed honestly worshipful of the car. That was beside the point, however, and she probably shouldn't leave Carbon. "Thanks, guys, but I don't know…"

Frank jumped in, "Oh, please! We'll have the stripes done by two so you can be outta here by three. Please!"

"I just…" she looked back to Carbon, briefly imagining the car's opinion in the matter.

"Your car will be fine, I promise," James said with an earnest expression. "We always lock up the shop real good."

Sleeping on firm ground was tempting, and it was doubtful anything would happen overnight. Hopefully she wouldn't regret this, "Okay. Deal."

The two nearly exploded with excitement. James tried to look vaguely cool, but Frank leapt up into the air with a yelp.

"Just remember," she reminded them, "I need to be gone by three."

The older brother looked back at her. "Alright, we need to find a story to tell mom. Let's just say you're a friend from out of town. We met at a car show last December."

She nodded, wondering what the mother of such outstanding citizens would be like. No image came to mind.

"Come on," he motioned at her again, pausing to yell instructions to his remaining buddies to go home. "We'll show you a place to nap, and I'll give you the grand tour tomorrow."

She shot a worried glance at Carbon before turning to follow. Unsurprisingly, the car said nothing. It would be unable to track her without a cell phone, and she was a little hesitant to leave it. She finally shrugged in resignation and followed the two out the door. Maybe they wouldn't kill her, and she would even feel better after some real sleep. In a real bed. The thought was like heaven, and she stifled a yawn as they piled into the yellow Camaro.

Chapter 17

The sun had not yet risen to wake the morning, but Hitchens was hard at work. It had been difficult to locate the black Dodge, but with some outside assistance, satellite tracking, and his own ingenuity, he had traced it somewhere in the modest town of Cavalier.

The car had fallen off the radar a few hours ago, but Hitchens considered it unlikely they would continue driving with the volume of law enforcement searching for them. No, he figured they might ditch the car, but given the damage it had inflicted on the Impala, he had another lead to consider.

Hidden inside a dimly lit motel room, Hitchens was seated in front of an impressive array of tools and computers. Precise fingers twisted a final wire into place. He cautiously connected the small silver object to one of the laptops, grinning in triumph as an image lit the screen.

The small recorder had been placed carefully in the Impala. He learned to never trust his employees completely, disloyalty and incompetence among the main reasons. Today his precautions had paid off.

Hitchens leaned back in his chair, watching and listening as the video played. The audio reception was actually pretty good, even if the image was a little lacking. He sighed. It was hard to find good quality, durable equipment.

A derisive laugh escaped as he watched the dashing escape from the prison. Amateurs. The conversation between the girl and her two captors was only slightly more interesting, and his colleagues' performance was embarrassing. It's a wonder they managed to escape at all.

As two voices began hushed argument, Hitchens glued his eyes to the wide open road on the screen. He barely noticed a flash in the distance before the camera's angle went haywire, the image flipping over until it jerked to a stop upside down.

The video cut to black, but the audio continued recording two successive shots. He heard scraping and crawling, and then the girl's voice asking something that sounded like Carmen. Another female voice responded, telling her to get inside, followed by a few more minutes of silence and then the sound of his car arriving.

It wasn't perfect, but was plenty to start with. He took about thirty minutes to refine some imagery, then moved work some voice identification.

The latter revealed nothing, but the image soon cleared to a recognizable vehicle and Hitchens allowed a stiff grin of pleasure. He definitely had the right car, now he just needed to find where it had disappeared to.

* * * *

The ride to James' house would have been awkward if not for Frank's unnatural ability to talk. And talk and talk and talk. She missed most of what he said, but watched his animated account of the race between James and Carbon with amazement. Surely the kid should be tired by now, or at least a little winded, but nope. Maybe he would grow up to be like Mr. Mike.

The thought of her old friend brought a slight smile and tears to her eyes. Hopefully she would see him again soon, as well as Nia and the others in Mesa Springs. She wondered what they were doing now, if they had forgotten about her yet.

"This is it," James interrupted his brother's steady flow of words as they pulled into a short driveway. The house was surprisingly cozy looking, situated in a nice part of town. It wasn't the country

118

club, but it was far from the slum she had been expecting. It was a white, two-story block house with nice landscaping and a fenced in yard. After parking the Camaro under a Sam's cover, James motioned for them to be quiet as they got out.

"We don't want to wake the dog, so walk carefully," he whispered. He turned to Frank and made a zipping motion at his lips. "Okay, come on."

Frank disappeared into a side door, and James held it open for her. They went down carpeted steps into a basement of sorts, where James flicked on a dull lamp. "The bed's all yours, someone will probably wake you up in the morning."

Probably?

"If you need anything, Frank and I have the rooms on the second floor." With that, he closed the door and disappeared.

Elise considered a more careful analysis of the house and her surroundings, but the beige bed beckoned to her with more force than her tired limbs could resist. She only took time to flip the door's lock and stuff the gun under her pillow before climbing between the soft sheets.

Within moments she was sound asleep.

* * * *

A warm, wet surface met her cheek. What was that? It moved to her forehead and then mouth. Elise lifted an arm to wipe it off, but her hand was met instead with warm fuzz.

"What the…" she jerked awake, completely disoriented by the figure that obscured her vision. Pulling herself upright, the form moved backward and she blinked.

A medium sized mutt sat before her, short tail swinging with joy, drool running out of its whiskered mouth. "Ew," she complained, attempting to wipe the slobber off her face with a sheet. "That is nasty." She glared at the dog. "What did you do that for?"

But the tail only wagged faster, and the dog licked the air making the clear statement it would do it all again. There was not a hint of remorse in those brown eyes. Still offended by the messy kiss, she sighed in annoyance before swinging her legs over the bedside.

The dog jumped off and sat at her feet. "What do you want?" she snapped, still groggy and tired. It only whined pathetically and rolled over. "You expect me to pet you after what you did?" Its expression said yes, it did indeed. After a brief staring contest, she caved to the hopeful brown face and scratched its belly, finding it to be a girl dog. "Okay, girlie. But don't read too much into this," she warned. "You still slobbered me."

Glancing around, she saw there were no windows in this basement – maybe not such a brilliant observation – and she couldn't even find a clock to tell time. There was a door, however, and the doggy door at the bottom told how her visitor had appeared. So much for locks. Regardless, her body informed her it was time to find a bathroom. Stretching with a yawn, she again tucked the gun into her waistband, carefully obscuring it by her jacket. She doubted it would be needed, but better safe than sorry.

As she stood, the dog leapt in joy around her feet, and she had to stumble around it up the stairs. "Hey, calm down," she commanded to no avail.

She would have preferred a quiet entrance to the rest of the house, but the dog began yelping and whining, begging to be played with and petted. Sunlight streamed into a simple living room revealing video games and movies scattered over the floor. Clanking sounds were coming from the kitchen, but paused with the dog's racket.

A freckled face appeared around the wall. "Oh, you must be James' friend. I'm sorry, come here Muffin!"

The brown mutt took off towards the tiny blond woman, zooming around the corner and then back at Elise.

"Muffin!" the woman yelled again. "I'm sorry, she doesn't listen too good. Come on in, you must be hungry."

Elise was beckoned into the kitchen and met with some delicious smells. Oh, she was hungry.

"So you're Bonnie?" The petite woman offered her hand, which Elise accepted with a small nod. She had the look of a wild past life, a couple of old tattoos evident on her legs and one on her neck. The smell of smoke was thick, an ashtray on the table containing several charred ends.

"I'm Mrs. Morgan, It's a nice to meet you. James said you just happened to be passing by last night. I'm sorry about your dad."

Elise froze. How did this lady know?

"James said it was a freak accident, I'm sure it's tough." Freak accident? James did say he would invent a story. Trying to go along, Elise feigned some tears and sniffed.

"Just come sit down, sweetie, I've got some biscuits and gravy already cooked up."

"Thank you," Elise croaked. "Could you please point me toward the bathroom first?"

"Oh, of course. Right this way."

After relieving herself and quickly washing up – a real sink was such a treat – she sat down to her first delicious warm meal in days. Muffin settled on curling up by her legs, and James' mother went on about her sons, her husband, and the weather, giving Elise a clue as to the origin of Frank's incessant speech.

James burst in with a wide grin just as she was finishing up. Surely this wasn't all over a chance to drive Carbon.

His mother gushed about how nice Elise was, and how James needed more friends like her. The fact that Elise had barely spoken a word was apparently beside the point. James only nodded and responded that his mom should check out Elise's ride, it was the sweetest car he'd ever seen a girl drive. Mrs. Morgan rolled her eyes and winked at Elise.

"Dad wants Frank and I at the shop till two, so can you bring Bonnie by later to get her car?"

She looked thrilled at the prospect, "Sure, that gives us four hours. Don't keep your dad waiting." With that, she shooed James back out the door. "I'll show you the town, Bonnie. After all this talk I've heard, I'll have to see this car of yours for myself."

Elise offered to help with the dishes, but Mrs. Morgan wouldn't hear of it, laughing and going on about finally getting some girl time.

It didn't take long before they were driving off in a white Honda Civic, and Elise realized very quickly where James' driving habits came from. Screeching around corners and slamming to stops, it was also reminiscent of Nia's driving.

The town was actually quite charming, and she enjoyed relaxing and visiting several historic landmarks including an old school house and the town square. It was a quaint little place, and Mrs. Morgan proved easy to get along with, despite her rough appearance. The woman appeared truly ecstatic just to have another female for company.

They had just been seated at Nat's Diner as Mrs. Morgan insisted they had absolutely the best hamburgers, when the woman leaned back and looked at Elise.

"So, where are you from?"

"Florida." It was partially true, she had lived in Tampa for six months.

"Oh, I bet it's nice there, huh?"

Elise only nodded and took a big gulp of her Coke.

"How did you end up here?"

"Well," Elise tried to recall her fake story, hoping it went along with James' fabricated tale. "I'm headed to my uncle's house in Seattle, after my dad's accident and all."

Mrs. Morgan nodded, having no reason not to accept her story. "That must be tough, I remember when my dad passed on. I hope everything works out."

The woman's compassion pulled strings of guilt inside Elise for lying. An uncomfortable silence hung between them before Mrs. Morgan changed the subject. "Where'd you get your car? James was sure impressed."

"My dad gave it to me," she answered honestly.

"I bet that makes it really special to you."

Elise couldn't look the woman in the eyes, careful not to disturb the ocean of emotion lying under the calm surface. She swallowed hard.

Mrs. Morgan sighed in sympathy, "I'm sorry, sweetie." The lady moved over to give her a hug, "If you need anything, you let me know."

The waitress was just rounding the corner with their hamburgers, and Elise was still hungry enough to override any awkward feelings. James' mother moved on to talk about recent movies, music, and the weather, and by the end of lunch Elise realized how much she missed human companionship.

As they got back into the Civic and headed home, she thanked Mrs. Morgan for the meal and asked if they could stop somewhere to buy some new clothes and a cell phone. She made up another story about losing her last phone and failing to pack well for the trip.

The petite woman's eyes lit up at the prospect of shopping, even if it was just the dollar store. "Of course," she glanced at her watch. "We'll need to make it fast, though. It's already one and I bet you're anxious to get on the road again."

Not exactly. Elise looked out the window as they flew down the streets of this quiet city. It was so peaceful. Why wasn't she born into a nice, albeit rough, family like this?

"How long have you lived here?" Elise asked, unhappy with where the silence was taking her.

"Oh, Pete and I got married in Texas, and we both wanted to get away a little. We found this town, he set up his shop and we never left. That was twenty-three years ago." Mrs. Morgan smiled at Elise, "It's a good little place."

"Yeah, it's lovely," Elise agreed as they pulled into the Dollar General's parking lot. More lovely than she would have thought a week ago.

* * * *

Frank was sitting in the driver's seat of the newly whitened Challenger, big brown eyes lovingly taking in every detail of the dash. This was his dream car. Not only that, but it had beaten his brother in a race, and that was worth more than money could buy.

"I wish you were mine," he whispered, watching his brother pace on the phone outside. James was calling his friend Steve – almost as big a Mopar fan as Frank himself – to see if he had some RT stripes in the warehouse.

"What the...?" Frank began as the car's dashboard lit up and the engine rumbled to life. He stared at the steering wheel in shock for a moment, trying to locate the ignition. Had he accidently turned it on?

"Frank!" James was yelling from outside. "Cut it out! You better turn that off, it's not a toy! Or you're gonna be dead!"

The threats were followed by cursing as the engine failed to shut off.

"I can't!" Frank wailed back to his brother. "I don't know what happened!" He continued to search for a key or button, ducking his head under the steering column.

"Please remain calm, I require your assistance." A woman's voice sounded from inside the car.

"Ah…!" Frank screamed, jerking his head to see who had spoken, but his skull met the bottom of the steering wheel quite solidly. He yelped again, this time in pain, leaping out of the car as he touched his stinging head with his hand.

"What's wrong with you, freak?" James glared at him angrily and moved to get inside the car. His younger brother only stared, gaping at the empty cab.

"Didn't you… I mean…" Frank stuttered, unable to grasp what just happened. "Did you hear that?" He glanced around the shop, but there was no one else nearby except for his brother, who continued to stare at him, halfway inside the Challenger.

"Dude, chill. What happened?" James slid the rest of the way into the driver's seat, also searching for the ignition. "How'd you turn it on?"

"He did not." The woman's smooth voice sounded again.

"See!" Frank burst, pointing at his now speechless brother.

"Who is that?" James was glancing around the cab, processing.

"I apologize for startling you, my name is…" the voice paused. "Clyde. I need your help."

Jame's mind was slowly grasping the facts as he stared at the dashboard. "You… you…"

Frank was a few steps ahead, still gaping at the side of the big white Dodge. "You're the *car*?"

"Yes. I need to find Bonnie immediately. Where is she?"

James had not recovered from the shock, but Frank answered, "She's with Mom."

"Do you know where they are?"

"Uh, no. But I can call Mom. You're really the car?" Frank asked again.

"Yes. Please call, I need to find her immediately."

"Whoa," James had just finished sorting through the past minute, nodding approvingly. "You're Bonnie's ride."

"Yes. Please hurry. Call your mother."

The older brother pulled his cell phone back out of his pocket and handed it to Frank. "So, you wanna go find Bonnie?"

"Yes."

"Right now?"

"Yes." The smooth voice never changed inflection.

"Whoa," James breathed again. "I guess we should unmask your lights then."

"Please do. Hurry."

He seemed to snap out of his stupor, quickly snatching the paper covering Carbon's headlights and mirrors. Frank was talking to his mom, pausing to ask, "You just want to know where she is?"

"Yes."

He turned back to the phone, then flipped it shut, proudly pronouncing, "Dollar General. They're at the Dollar General."

"Thank you." The car began to back up, "Good-bye."

"No, wait!" James yelled. "I gotta get another piece off." He scurried to the car's other side.

Frank wasted no time, jumping inside the driver's seat as the door was closing.

"What are you doing?" the smooth voice asked.

"I'm coming with you."

"Frank, get back here!" James shouted as he tore off the last piece of masking paper.

"That is unwise."

"I'm not leaving." The boy stubbornly stuck his chin in the air. "Besides, what if you need me to call my mom again?"

James had made his way over to the side of the car, "Get out of there now, Frank! I'm not kidding."

"There is a car approaching." The car's voice informed them. "I must leave before it arrives."

The tattooed form only scratched his head, "Hold on. Who is it?"

"There is one man in the vehicle and he is a serious threat to both Bonnie and your entire family if he finds me here."

"Wow, cool!" Frank exclaimed. "It's just like a movie!"

"This is not a game. I need to leave, now please get out." The driver's door opened in suggestion.

"Wait," the older brother leaned inside. "What are we supposed to tell this dude?"

Before the car could respond, Frank interjected, "Duh! We tell him to get lost!"

"That is acceptable," the voice agreed. "Just be sure he does not know I was here."

Understanding was finally dawning on James, and he gave crooked grin. "Sure thing, Clyde. C'mon Frank, get outta there."

But before his younger brother could comply, the car spoke again. "Wait."

The two brothers stared at the car in suspense.

"What is it!?" Frank blurted impatiently.

"The man is too close. Do not let him in the shop."

"What'd you want me to do?" James asked, clearly baffled by the overwhelming events.

"Try to stop him from coming inside."

"Oh," he rubbed his chin thoughtfully. "I get it. You're trying to hide." It was like a revelation.

"Yes. Now hurry, he will be here in fifteen seconds."

James nodded and winked, "I gotcha. Hang tight." With those reassuring words, he headed outside to see a dark blue Crown Victoria pulling into the shabby parking lot. A tall, black haired police officer got out, smiling broadly. "Hello, son. How are you today?"

James squinted his flat blue eyes at the officer. "Fine," he responded curtly, standing guard in front of the shop door. "This is private property, you know."

The tall man only laughed, "Yes, yes, I know. I just need a second of your time."

"Maybe." James instinctively didn't like anyone wearing a uniform, and this jovial man was no exception. "Don't come any further," he warned, "unless you have a warrant."

126

The officer paused a few feet from James, holding up his hands in surrender. "Sure thing, son. I'm not here to stir up trouble, I'm just looking for an endangered runaway."

"So?" James shifted his weight, eyes not leaving the man's face.

"We have reason to suspect she might have tried to get her car painted..." he paused, glancing around the nonexistent yard. "Can we step inside and talk?"

"No."

The officer paused as if debating his next move. "Okay, son. If you see a black Dodge Challenger, one of the newer models, you let me know." The man reached forward as if to hand James a card, eyes never leaving the younger man's stony face. "I'm sure a law-abiding citizen such as yourself would only be too happy to help, no?"

James' expression never changed.

"Just as I thought."

"Hey!" James protested as the officer pushed past him. "You can't go in there!" He tried to stop the man, but was shoved aside easily as the officer strode inside.

"Bingo." The tall man turned to James, putting a strong hand on a tattooed shoulder. "I think we need to chat."

Frank watched from inside the car's cab, ducking down instinctively. The man was a police officer?

He froze as the car shifted itself into drive and risked a glance upward.

"Turn the car off now!" The officer had positioned himself directly in front of the car, gun pointed at Frank's head.

The car had no intentions of obeying. In a tremendous thunder, its engine roared to life, sending them smashing through the closed garage door. The man leapt out of the way and sent a spray of bullets after them as they sped out into the sunlight.

Frank screamed, turning toward the back window to see his brother standing in shock and the policeman dashing for his car. "Wow, this is sweet!"

"No," the car corrected him, "This is unfortunate. Fasten your seat belt."

Frank obeyed, staring out the window in awe as they skidded around corners, madly accelerating on short straightaways. His jaw dropped as he watched the speedometer bounce up to one hundred and back down just in time to make a sharp turn.

The car flew down another straightaway before screeching to a halt, pulling into a random garage and remotely closing the door.

"Wow!" Frank was quite impressed. "How'd you do that?"

The car ignored his question. "You should get out."

"What?! No way! I'm in some random person's garage!"

"It is too dangerous for you to remain with me. I need to get to Bonnie as soon as possible."

"I'll leave at the Dollar General," the boy offered.

There was no response, and Frank took the silence as affirmation. "Now, who was that guy?"

"An extremely dangerous man. He may try to get information from you and your family. I strongly recommend leaving town, you are all in danger."

Frank puffed up his chest. "It's just one guy, I think we can take him."

"That is unlikely. Staying in your house is unsafe."

"He's a police officer!"

"He was dressed like a police officer," the car corrected him. "And he is identified as a Matthew Hitchens of a police department in Colorado, but his facial structure and voice print matches that of Larry Thompson, a convicted murderer and ex-Marine."

"How do you know that?"

"Just be careful."

The garage door opened again and Carbon backed out.

"Are you sure he's gone?" Frank asked worriedly.

"If we wait much longer, he will find out where Bonnie is from James, and then it will be too late."

The boy kept a watchful eye out the window. "Too late for what? What's going on?"

"It is better that you do not know," the smooth voice informed him.

Chapter 18

Elise was enjoying her last hour of freedom, grateful to Mrs. Morgan for her kindness. They were standing in the checkout line waiting to purchase another pair of jeans and a t-shirt as well as a pay-as-you-go standard cell phone.

The girl behind the counter looked young, probably a good friend of James' with an attractive nose ring and tattoos covering her right arm. Regardless, the girl was certainly not in a hurry as she slowly rung up item after item with painstaking deliberation.

Mrs. Morgan was flipping through a magazine, and Elise sighed. She wanted to get to Montana and find her dad, but she was tired of road trips and running away from everybody. She couldn't help envying the Morgans' family and kept wishing she was back in Mesa Springs, waking up to find this had all been a crazy dream.

The line had finally moved up one person, but a commotion at the sliding glass doors turned everyone's attention forward. Mrs. Morgan's younger son burst in and collided head on with an elderly woman.

"Frank?!" Mrs. Morgan stared in disbelief, running to help the stunned lady to her feet.

"Mom, I..." Frank started breathlessly, but his mother wasn't about to let him off.

"You apologize right now, young man." She turned to the elderly woman, "I'm so sorry, Ms. Linda. I don't know what's gotten into my son." Mrs. Morgan turned to give him another meaningful glare, but he had just spotted Elise at the end of the line.

"Bonnie!" He ran over to her, pointing outside. "You gotta come, you gotta come now!" He was speaking too rapidly to form full sentences. "There was this guy, and… and…your car… Clyde, she needs you now! Hurry!"

Elise blinked a few times before comprehending Frank's lightning speech. He stood staring at her, mouth hanging open with one arm pointing at the parking lot. The whole store, in fact, was staring at her in similar fashion.

She crammed the fifty-dollar bill she was holding into the checkout girl's hand, "Here, keep the change. I've got to go."

Dashing out of the store, she paused to yell thanks to a flabbergasted Mrs. Morgan. Unprepared for the drastic shift into daylight, she squinted to locate Carbon. The brightly white car was right in front of her waiting with open door.

As she moved to get inside, James' yellow Camaro squealed to a stop beside her, its owner jumping out with a baffled expression.

"What's going on?" he shouted to Elise, his eyes flickering between the girl and her car.

"I'm sorry, James, I don't have time to explain. I…"

"Elise, hurry." Carbon's voice came loudly.

"I've got to go," she said apologetically, moving closer toward the car. "Thanks for everything."

Several shoppers had come outside to watch, and James just stared in bewilderment. Feeling slightly guilty, she grabbed some bills from her pocket and stuck them in his hand. "Here, thanks for the paint job." She offered a strained smile before slipping into Carbon, the door slamming shut behind her.

Carbon's tires squealed as she catapulted them out of the parking lot.

Every head turned to watch as the white car disappeared around the corner and a dark blue Crown Victoria materialized in pursuit.

Frank broke the silence. "Wow."

* * * *

"What's going on?" Elise swiveled around, trying to look at who was chasing them.

"The man driving that car came to James' shop looking for you. I do not know how he found us."

"Who is he?"

"A highly dangerous convict wanted by the FBI. He was posing as a police officer, but more alarmingly, he was waiting to rendezvous with the FBI agents who kidnapped you. His patrol car was parked along the roadway several miles from where I intercepted the Impala, and I picked up phone calls between him and Agent Kelley."

She could now see the sedan following them. "What should we do?"

"I need to lose him, but that is proving difficult."

"Are there more?"

"I do not know," Carbon answered. "But it is unlikely he is working alone. You are fortunate the Morgans were of assistance, I would not have been able to locate you on my own."

Elise swallowed as they continued fleeing down tiny roads. "Let's talk about this later. Right now we need to get away."

"We will."

The Iowa countryside was flat and barren, although Elise spied some hilly land off in the distance. "We need some trees or something."

"Agreed," Carbon responded. They turned onto an empty, straight road and Carbon's engine roared as they shot down the pavement, the speedometer pegged at one-hundred and eighty miles an hour, the force holding her firmly against her seat.

Elise listened curiously to the sound of the engine. It was like an odd combination between a train, a semi, and a jet plane. She smiled as the pursuing car became a dot in the distance.

"Nice work."

"We are not safe yet, Elise. He knows where we are."

"Yeah, but not where we're going."

Carbon said nothing in response, but as they reached the hilly landscape, it was clear they had lost their tail. At least for now.

"Do you think the Morgans will be okay?" Elise had failed to previously consider the implications to those who helped her.

"I do not know. I informed Frank that they should leave the area."

The thought was unsettling. She hoped she had not brought trouble to the family that had been so kind to her.

"Oh," she remembered. "Here is a cell phone I picked up at the store."

Carbon seemed pleased at that, and talked Elise through the process of reprogramming. When they finished, the car insisted she put it in her pocket immediately. Elise didn't need much encouragement, and she complied as they again headed toward their destination with about fourteen hours remaining.

* * * *

Elise had observed the landscape shift from slight hills to pancake flat many hours ago. Carbon provided her with a map of their journey on the screen, placing them somewhere in eastern South Dakota. She had not seen any sign of the blue Crown Victoria, and after her desperate pleadings, Carbon agreed to call the Morgans to warn them again. Nevertheless, it had bothered her for most of the trip, and she felt dirty for lying to the family.

Carbon had become extra cautious, insisting that she stay within fifty feet at all times. Bathroom breaks were extremely short now, but Elise required no further persuasion that her life was in danger.

On the bright side, Carbon's white paint job seemed to have worked as they passed multiple law enforcement vehicles, none of them very concerned.

She had finally found a better way to pass the time, however, as Carbon had downloaded some audio books. They took her mind off the present and provided a welcome relief from fear, her new constant companion.

"Hey," Elise complained as the audio broke off. "It was just getting interesting!"

"I apologize, but I have gained access to another of your father's video logs."

"The video logs?" she was incredulous, having given up on those more than a few miles back. "How?"

"One of the files was unlocked."

"All by itself?"

"Perhaps it was remotely accessed or previously set to unlock at a certain time. Shall I play it for you?"

Elise gave a short laugh, "No. I'm just going to wait here and not watch it."

"Oh. I thought you…"

"I'm kidding, Carbon. Of course I want to watch it."

"You were being sarcastic again."

Elise wasn't sure if it was a question or a statement. "Yes. Sorry. Just play the video."

The screen immediately flickered on, her father's upper torso again appearing in some sort of garage or shed. He smiled, "Hello, Elise."

"I'm sure at this point you're getting pretty tired." He gave a small laugh and she wondered how he could be cheerful under the circumstances. "And I'm sure you've got a bunch of questions, but I'm afraid you won't understand most of the answers."

Elise narrowed her eyes. How would *he* know what she could or couldn't understand? He continued, still looking quite jolly, "You should know this." A finger pointed at her, paused in midair, "Don't listen to what they may tell you. I *am* your father. You." His smile deepened, curving with grace and love. "That fancy car did not grab the wrong kid."

She gave a questioning glance at the dashboard. Yes, the car had trouble grasping irony and levity, but it did seem pretty trustworthy.

Her eyes moved back to the screen as her father's face darkened. "They will probably tell you all sorts of things." He blinked as if the thoughts were painful, "About me, about your family, even yourself. Always check with Carbon." The same finger was now wagging at her. "Always. She knows what really happened."

The lean figure closed his eyes and sighed, "My little girl."

Her throat closed up with emotion, tears instantly ready to pour down her cheeks. Elise fought them back.

"Just hang on. You will learn more, be patient. Carbon should have everything you need now, and remember I pray every day that you will make it here. I can't tell you anymore, okay?"

His tone said he wished he could, and Elise desperately wished he would. She felt that she was ready to hear an explanation, a good reason for all of this. But with a smile and a somber 'I love you', her father's face faded to black, leaving her to ponder and struggle in silence.

* * * *

Only an hour had passed, but Elise was becoming truly frustrated. She had decided upon Carbon's rescue that agents Kelley and Garcia were kidnapping criminals and thus liars as well. But she was still following this man – father or no – blindly. And try as she might to believe he was innocent, his lack of explanations was beginning to poke holes in the trust she had given him.

"Carbon, my dad said you know everything I need. Can't you just tell me?"

"What would you like to know?"

Maybe it was like twenty-questions and eventually some useful info would come out. "Let's start with who is trying to kidnap me and why."

"Sara Kelley and Carlos Garcia were agents of the Federal Bureau of Investigation. I do not know what they intended to do with you."

"But the lady was on my dad's dangerous list! Why was she there?"

"Your father considered her dangerous."

"That is not an answer!"

The car fell silent.

"Why do they want me?"

"You are your father's child."

"Thanks, Carbon. That was deep, and extremely helpful." Elise switched subjects to her latest pursuer. "What about the blue car? The one who was after me?"

"As I said, the Crown Victoria was licensed to a police officer named Matthew Hitchens. But further searches reveal that the man driving it matched facial and voice recognition and other characteristics with a wanted fugitive named Larry Thompson who has eluded the law for fourteen years. He is an ex-marine and highly dangerous."

Elise sighed deeply. "I remember. But why is he after me?"

"I do not know. Perhaps he was hired."

"By whom? Why?" Elise was tired of half-answers, she wanted to get to the bottom of this.

Carbon paused. "I am unable to disclose that information at this time."

Elise threw her hands up, "What?!" She groaned in frustration. "I thought you were supposed to help me. I need to know!"

The smooth voice responded, unperturbed, "If you needed to know, I would tell you."

"Oh, I see. And you decide when I need to know?"

"Yes."

"But you're just a stupid car!" Elise burst out. "If you're on my side, you should tell me what I ask you." What kind of dumb computer made its own decisions?

Elise sat angrily in silence for a few moments; it would seem Carbon had no answer to her outburst. But she wasn't quite done with her tirade yet and heck, they still had a lot of time before Montana.

"You and my dad are the same. '*Oh, you won't understand*' '*No, you can't know that yet*'. I'm sixteen, okay? What will I not get? I'm supposed to trust you guys, but you can't trust me at all? This isn't fair!"

"Elise, if..."

"No," she interrupted, unwilling to step off her newfound soap box. Maybe complaining wasn't productive, but it *was* making her feel better. "I'm not done. If you guys are on my side, then you should at least let me know what's going on. At least. So I can be free to make my own decisions."

"You are free to make your own decisions."

"Not without the necessary information!" she fumed. "I don't want to walk into a death trap! Doesn't my dad care? If you would just tell me what's going on, we can figure a way out of this mess, and I can go back home, like nothing happened."

She paused as it dawned on her that things were probably changing permanently. Mesa Springs might never be 'home' again. Was this blind running and traveling a new way of life? The thought was too horrible to consider, so Elise pushed it to the back of her mind.

"Anyway…" she paused, as the thought of home had derailed her angry diatribe and sucked the wind from her sails. Truth was, she had no home. Not a real one, anyway.

Carbon spoke, "Elise, there are many things you cannot know at this point. I *will* tell you when it becomes advantageous or necessary. For now, it would only hinder you."

Elise mimicked the car's even tone, "Sure. *'When it becomes advantageous or necessary'*." She resumed staring out the window, still off-track by her thoughts of home.

"I *am* on your side," the car stated firmly.

"Yeah, whatever." She was not in much of a mood to argue anymore.

"What you know or want to know is irrelevant," Carbon continued. "I *am* on your side."

Elise slumped down with another sigh. Dusk was falling and the sky was lit up a brilliant orange. This wasn't what she wanted – to be traveling across the country alone and ignorant, with people chasing her to boot – but a tiny voice argued it might turn out okay. Carbon had at least kept her alive and provided some link to her dad, whatever it was worth. Maybe she just needed to hear a friendly voice.

"Carbon?" She fully expected a negative answer, but gave it a shot anyway.

"Yes, Elise?"

"Can I… uh, maybe call Nia?"

The car was silent a moment. "They have likely bugged her phones and will track your call. It could endanger you both."

Elise looked down at her hands, "I just want to talk to a friend or something. It's hard, you know? Weren't you citing human psychology earlier?"

"I could scramble the call," Carbon offered, "so they could not track us. But it might place Nia at risk."

"What if I don't say anything important? Just tell her I'm okay?"

"I will not stop you from calling, but I advise against it."

"That's it? You won't stop me?" Maybe she had more freedom than she realized.

"No."

Elise grabbed the phone. She doubted Nia could be in much danger. Besides, if they listened to the phone call, what would they need Nia for? She flipped it open and dialed her friend's cell. It rang twice.

"Hello?"

Just the sound of Nia's voice was like a blanket against the cold. "Nia! It's Elise!" Tears sprung up as she thought of her friend.

There was a brief silence. "Elise?" Nia responded, her tone incredulous. "It's really you?"

"Yes, it's really me! I'm so sorry for leaving like that, I can explain later."

"It *is* you!" Nia cried joyfully. "Are you okay? They said you ran off, but I didn't believe it!"

"Ran off? No! It's just... complicated. And yes, I'm fine. Just... don't tell anyone about this call okay? I just wanted to talk to you." Elise choked on the words.

"What's going on? Are you sure you're okay?"

"I..." she gathered her resolve, resisting the tears. "Yeah. I can't explain. Tell me about town. How's everyone doing?"

They chatted for about ten minutes, Elise careful not to say anything about the past few days, Nia explaining all that happened in Mesa Springs. When they finally hung up, Elise wished they could talk longer, but took heart that she still had a friend.

She glanced out the window and leaned back against her seat. In the dim light of dusk, she could see the flat earth had been replaced by rolling hills, tall mountains stoically guarding the horizon.

"Wow," she breathed. The sight was truly stunning.

"That is the Absaroka Mountain range, a sub-range of the Rocky Mountains." Carbon informed her. "We should arrive in Elderidge in approximately eight hours."

A knot twisted in Elise's stomach at the thought. Who knew what would be waiting there? Given her father's latest warning, she had doubts that he would be there, but obstinate hope remained that he would be waiting with open arms and full explanations.

Ha! Her mind scoffed at the idea, but it was a flame not easily snuffed.

"Restart the audio book, please?" she asked, wishing her mind would lift to higher thoughts.

Chapter 19

The LaDache Prison had grown considerably quieter. Most of the employees had gone home, though security was still heightened. The FBI agents had cornered themselves off in makeshift offices after receiving permission to stay for another day.

While they did their best to exclude him from any real knowledge, Deputy Lawson had managed to pick up on scant details of the case. It seemed that the girl's father, someone named Mathis, was the real target. He couldn't tell if it was something the man had developed or stolen, but the FBI considered it a threat to national security.

But this didn't explain why they were so bent on finding the girl, who was thought to not have had any contact with Mathis since at least age six.

For his part, Lawson had grown extremely restless. He was tired, and while the FBI insisted he stay nearby, they weren't actively involving him in any of the investigation. To pass the time he had chatted with some of the corrections officers, wandered the halls, and occasionally received permission to get a bite to eat.

He had been asked a thousand times about his conversation with Elise, and the more he recalled it the less it made any sense. It was like a puzzle with no solution.

He was walking aimlessly down a monotonous hallway when the voice of one of the FBI agents caught his attention.

"So you have no idea?" the woman's voice wasn't happy sounding.

Lawson paused before he reached the open door. Technically, it was none of his business, but they were the ones who wanted him here and if a conversation was supposed to be private, they should take it somewhere else.

"Look. We're doing all we can on this end, but the car's a mess and I don't know how much we can get from it."

Phone conversation, he brilliantly deduced from the quiet pauses.

"Of course. I sent you the approximate trajectory, but you'll have to act fast."

Another pause.

"You're sure about that? Okay. Thanks."

The woman stepped out of the room, and Lawson smiled innocently.

She frowned, "What are you doing here?"

"Whatever you guys want, I guess. Who were you talking to?"

"Deputy, this is a federal investigation and it does not concern you."

This lady was really defensive. Something about making a phone call in a back closet was just inherently suspicious.

"In fact," the lady continued, "why don't you head back now? If we need you, we'll call."

"Don't I need to talk to Agent Stewart about that?"

"I speak for Agent Stewart. Good-bye."

Flashing a smile that definitely could be categorized as a smirk, she strode past him down the hallway. He considered reporting the strange conversation to Stewart, but quite honestly had no desire to deal with the angry man and besides, the woman hadn't done anything wrong. The FBI was just weird, maybe they held all important phone conversations in back closets.

With a sigh, Lawson headed after her toward the exit. At least he got to go home.

* * * *

Elise hadn't even realized she had drifted off to sleep when something jerked her back to consciousness. Focusing on the clock's softly glowing numbers, she saw that she had only been asleep two hours.

Stifling a yawn, she asked, "Where are we?"

"Four hours from Elderidge."

Elise blinked against the dark, straining to see the scenery. "We're in the mountains?"

"Yes."

They drove in silence a few minutes, Elise trying to glimpse the stars above. They were on a windy two lane road bordered by a cliff face to her right and only a foot of ground past the pavement on the other side. She couldn't tell if it went straight down, but for all purposes it might as well. For reasons of comfort, she preferred not to think about it at all.

The steady hum of Carbon's engine began lulling her to sleep once more when her body was flung violently forward like a rag doll and her head smashed into the steering wheel.

"Ow...!" she exclaimed as her world went dark. "What are you...?" But her words stopped in her throat as she refocused on the road ahead. Carbon's headlight beams illuminated a large truck and several SUVs blocking the roadway.

"Carbon?" Elise asked uneasily. "Can we go around them?"

"No, there is no room. I could not see them. I should have noticed them miles back."

Elise's mind blurred as she tried to weigh the implications with their options. They had stopped about twenty feet from the solid obstruction and were now backing away quickly.

Carbon's tires squealed loudly, skidding across the pavement as she again slammed on the brakes. Elise turned to see several dots of light emerging around the curve behind them. There were at least three vehicles.

Adrenaline and fear flooded her system. "What do we do now?"

"I cannot pick up sufficient speed to safely penetrate either obstruction."

"What? We're stuck?" Her voice trembled. Were all those cars really after *her*?

"Yes. The cliff is too high to drive off. My infrastructure would survive, but you most likely would not."

A dull shock gripped Elise's being, "What are you saying?"

"We are trapped."

A vehicle stopped only ten feet from Carbon's rear bumper and men's voices pierced the silent night. Several dark forms materialized in front of them.

"What do I do?" Elise was panicking. "What's going on?" She jerked her head around, trying to see what the people were doing, but the bright headlights from behind glared off her mirrors and the cars in front, blinding her.

"I am calculating our options."

"Hurry!" Elise cried. A harsh banging sounded on her window.

"Get out of the car now!" A voice yelled. "Out of the car!!"

The headlight beams bounced into the cab at strange angles, and in the sickening lighting Elise noticed the barrel of not one, but three guns staring her in the face. With a scream, she jumped into the passenger seat, ducking down as the banging continued and someone yanked on Carbon's door handle.

More voices were yelling and shouting, and the next time Elise glanced up, they had been boxed in on both sides by the caravan of heavy vehicles with about eight guys surrounding the car. Heavier pounding rained down as an electrical tool whined to life.

"Elise," Carbon's smooth voice contrasted the chaos outside. "If we attempt to proceed, you will likely be killed. There is not enough room to maneuver on this cliff."

"What?" Elise whimpered.

"Keep the cell phone with you, although they may take it." The dash opened revealing a tiny pill. "Swallow this quickly."

Elise did as she was told, trying to control the shaking. She stared in horror and disbelief as crowbars and saws were brought out.

"Listen to me carefully, Elise."

She fought to focus on Carbon's voice over the commotion outside.

"Go with them. I will come back for you. Be careful and do not believe what they tell you."

Terror swallowed Elise like a towering wave dragging her under. "Wait," her throat was suddenly parched. "What do I do?"

"Survive," Carbon didn't hesitate to reply. "Do not be afraid. I *will* get you back. Now you need to go. I am sorry."

Just like that, the door swung open and greedy hands grabbed her. It occurred to Elise to scream, but in the surreal shock her body was completely frozen.

"Don't move!" Someone shouted, slamming her face against sharp pavement. A strange feeling of aloofness shadowed her, and her mind slipped mercifully into unconsciousness.

* * * *

"Don't hurt her!" Hitchens glared at the men dragging the girl's unconscious body toward the waiting Denali. These people were such idiots. A few good ones, but mostly idiots. "Pick her up, and put her *gently* in the backseat."

Swearing, he turned back to the white car. They had briefly searched the vehicle to confirm that no one else was inside, which left several troubling suspicions.

"Lad and Henry!" he yelled at the two men openly admiring the Dodge. Lad was usually a competent thinker; Henry was just a towering hulk. Hitchens directed his instructions at the former. "Tow this car behind you. We'll search it when we get back, okay?"

The two exchanged glances with a shrug.

"Drive back together, but don't make it obvious."

Lad waved him off. "Yeah. We remember the plan."

Imbeciles they may be, but they were still mildly competent and this was an easy job. With a final glance at the white car, Hitchens jumped into the Denali beside the girl's limp form.

"Be quick about it!" he yelled as he slammed the door shut. "Let's go."

* * * *

The silver SUV executed a quick three-point turn and disappeared down the road as Lad and Henry exchanged glances. No one liked that man, but the wise were careful to follow his orders. "You heard him, let's get moving."

The other heavy vehicles also departed; they were just 'local help' according to Hitchens and headed back to wherever they came from. One other man remained, his older Jeep Grand Cherokee blocking the roadway and providing light as Henry maneuvered the tow truck into place.

"Hey Lad!" he shouted. "Why don't you drive it? That ride's pretty sweet! Hitchens will never know."

The thought was honestly tempting, however foolish. "Yeah, sure. You drive it, and I'll watch when he puts a bullet through your head."

"Aw, come on man. You're no fun."

Lad shook his head and turned back to his work. "Henry!" he signaled for his companion to stop the truck. "Just stop there!"

The truck hissed as the parking brake was set. Henry's burly form appeared and the man began to lower the ramp into place.

Lad cocked his head. He thought he heard an odd whine through the loud diesel engine. One glance at Henry said the big man heard it as well, his eyebrows furrowed as he stared at the electric ramp motor.

A sharp crack split the air. Henry slammed into the back of the truck before crumpling to the ground. Lad had been in enough gunfights that his body instinctively dropped flat against the pavement, using the truck as a shield. But his reflexes weren't fast enough, and a deep black swallowed his thoughts before he could register the pain searing through his chest.

The man standing by the Jeep was dead a split second later, the truck's engine rumbling on as if nothing had happened. Pulling alongside the idling vehicle, the white car carefully pushed the vehicle toward the road's precarious edge. The heavy truck groaned and creaked before finally disappearing over the side with a final shudder.

Shoving the Jeep off the cliff side in similar fashion, the white car wasted no time falling in pursuit of the silver Denali.

Chapter 20

Shane Lawson sat molded into an overly overstuffed chair in his living room. The TV had not provided the relief he wanted from this Elise Perry Case. The FBI's reluctance to share information, the strange phone call; something was just plain wrong. A voice of reason echoed that there was undoubtedly a good reason for the FBI to be secretive, they were the FBI after all, and that his heroic dreams had slipped him into overdrive.

The young sheriff deputy set his jaw and flicked his television off. His right hand was wrapped around a now-empty can of Coca-cola, and with a violent squeeze it became as squashed as those annoying rationalizations. Granted, he didn't have much to go on, but he did have a phone number and that was good enough for now.

* * * *

Sergeant Bill Reyes rolled away from his sleeping wife with a moan. Where was that dern phone? The first time it rang, he tried to ignore Pachelbel's Canon in D, but Alice was beginning to stir and facing her past midnight could be plain frightening.

His bare feet swung around to hard wooden floors as he flipped open his cell, "Reyes here." This had better be good.

"Sergeant Reyes," an unfamiliar male voice greeted him. "I'm sorry to call you at this time."

"Yeah," Reyes grunted into the mouthpiece as his toes located his slippers. "Can't this wait till morning?"

"I'm afraid not, sir."

The bald police sergeant let out an irritated sigh. "Okay. Give me a sec."

After collecting and donning his bathrobe, he moved quietly toward the kitchen. Alice was used to him leaving at odd hours, but she never wasted an opportunity to complain about the loudness of his exit. "Go ahead."

"Yes, sir. My name in Shane Lawson, I'm a deputy in Gad City."

"Never heard of it."

"It's in Iowa."

Why would someone call him from Iowa? "What can I do for you, son? It's late and I'd like some rest."

"Yes, sir. I just have a few questions about an Elise Perry."

Sergeant Reyes gripped the phone a little tighter, "Elise? What did you say your name was?"

"Lawson. I'm not sure how much I can tell you, with the FBI's involvement in the case and all."

Reyes let out a derisive snort. "Listen, son. This call is off the record."

The other man hesitated. "So you're not a big fan of the feds yourself?"

"You could say that."

"I see. This phone's clean?"

"As a whistle. Believe me, Lawson, I value my privacy."

"Yes, sir. This is supposedly public info, so it shouldn't be a problem." The deputy sounded hesitant.

"Go on son. We just want to see Elise safe here. That's it."

"Elise made a 911 call about a day ago." Lawson paused, then continued. "I was the one who responded to her call. I picked her up in a restaurant in town. She was scared, so I took her to the station for whatever might be necessary. She seemed to think someone was out to get her."

Reyes listened silently.

"Anyway, the FBI called before I could talk with her. They practically chewed my ear off demanding that they speak to her before anyone else and that she be taken somewhere secure. But she was kidnapped again, right under their noses," Lawson broke off. "I'm sorry, I can't go into more details."

"How can I help?"

"Something is strange about this case. I'm looking into it, and I just wanted to know everything you know about this girl and her disappearance."

"You working with those feds?"

Lawson gave his own derisive laugh. "No sir. Just seeking justice."

"Ha. The real Kemo Sabe, no?"

"Excuse me?"

"You know, the Lone Ranger?" Slience. "Nevermind. You better be tellin' the truth, son." Reyes sighed. They all wanted Elise back. This deputy was right, things just weren't adding up here. "All right, I'll share what we know. But it isn't much."

"Anything will help, sir."

* * * *

Having just finished his conversation with the Mesa Springs Police Sergeant, Lawson leaned back in his cushy chair. He stared at his phone with a frown. The sergeant had been correct about how little they knew. If one thing was for certain, it was that the facts just didn't line up. His phone startled him with a ring. *Unknown Caller,* the face of his beloved Droid proclaimed. His frown deepened as he answered the call.

"Lawson here."

"Deputy Lawson?" A young boy's voice asked.

"Who is this?"

"No matter," the teen spoke quickly, fearfully. "I have... uh, information."

"Information? I'm listening."

"About that girl in the news? Elise Perry?"

Lawson's mind raced through possibilities. "How did you get this number?"

"Sh!" The voice sounded frightened. "I have to go."

"Wait!" he tried to keep from yelling. "It's okay. What did you need to tell me?" He grabbed a pen from the table.

"I know where she is. I saw... I saw who's got her."

"Okay, can you be more specific?"

"Um, meet me here. Don't talk to anyone else, or she'll die. And hurry!"

"What? Wait..."

But the small voice interrupted him, "Archer, Montana. CR45, there's an old gas station south of town." It fell to a whisper, "Hurry."

"Wait! Hello?" Lawson glanced at his phone to verify that the call was over, sinking further into the fluff of his favorite chair. He knew the right course of action: report the call immediately, turn in his phone, forget about it. Could he really hope to sail his career on a highly suspicious call? An image of the Titanic came to mind.

On the bright side, he had been looking for a one in a million lead.

Deputy Lawson made himself a fresh pot of coffee, grabbed his emergency stash of cash, which certainly was no fortune, his trusty Taurus .45, extra ammunition, a change of clothes, his laptop and several other tools that might be useful. Preparations finished, he stood before his garage door, keys in hand. A stern smile plastered itself on his face as his excitement grew.

Worst case scenario, he would take a scenic drive of the northern United States in his beloved new Mustang GT. Not bad, he chuckled to himself. In the morning he would call in sick, but in the meantime...

He smoothly shifted the dark red car into reverse, exiting his garage as inconspicuously as possible. He kept the headlights off until down the road a few blocks; you never knew who was watching.

Enjoying the feel of the powerful engine, he shifted up through the gears rapidly. Direction: North. Gypsy, his faithful GPS, was his guide. Just like James Bond. Almost.

* * * *

After a night of driving and more coffee than Lawson could remember, the young deputy found himself approaching the town of Archer. The land was a mixture of flat grasslands and rolling hills, and CR45 didn't appear to be in much better shape than the old gas station.

The caller hadn't been kidding about old. The place could have popped out of a World War II movie. It had definitely seen better days. If there was any pavement in front of the decaying building, it had been long obscured by layers of dirt and growth.

Surveying the grounds carefully, Lawson searched for any clues of recent activity or movement. Everything appeared still, and once he was satisfied, he got out of his car and walked cautiously toward the dilapidated structure.

The person had sounded young and frightened. Maybe they were hiding inside. But the door didn't even appear capable of opening, and the building looked ready to collapse with the gentlest touch.

"Hello?" he called out.

Only the wind replied, shaking the building's thin metal roof. Lawson glanced around and noticed a small shed that was hidden from the road. It appeared newer than its surroundings with beige sides and modern shingles. Upon investigation, however, it was equally quiet and vacant.

Slightly disappointed with the empty setting, Lawson walked around the structure for a last check before giving up. It was possible that the person would wait to see who came before revealing themselves.

He was trying to carefully place each foot so as not to make a sound when music clicked on from somewhere inside the station. Lawson froze. Some sort of Bluegrass floated out from the boarded windows, cackling with static. What the heck was going on in there? He squinted to see through the cracks, but it was no good. But if someone was inside, there had to be a way in.

Lawson prided himself in being tough, but the creepy tunes and the eerie ghost-town surroundings were getting to him. Finding a small back door, he pushed it slowly, cringing as the hinges squealed in protest. Shafts of light broke in, an occurrence that seemed foreign to the dismal interior. Pushing the door about two feet further, he saw a small back room with another door leading to the main part of the building. Coughing with the dust he tried again, his voice quieter than he intended, "Hello? Is anyone here?"

The music slipped to commercial, and the sound indicated that the radio must be in the main room. Straining his ears, a strange whining buzzed through the air. He paused to listen, wondering if it was his imagination, but the sound was definitely getting louder. And fast.

Lawson could only place the strange hum as something between a freight train and a fighter jet, and it occurred to him for the first time that he hadn't yet heard a single other vehicle. There must be a railroad track nearby, he reassured himself, but the deep pitched sound only screamed louder. He jogged around to see the road, wishing he'd parked his car behind the building. His beautiful red Mustang didn't exactly fit in with the decrepit lot.

He had just turned his head left to look when a plume of dust and a flash of a car rocketed past. A cataclysmic impact shook the ground, punctuating the stillness with a sickening crunch and the smashing of pliable metal.

Lawson blinked. And blinked again, his heart having stopped at the sound.

His mind refused to accept what had just happened. As the dust cleared over an empty parking lot, a white Dodge Challenger backed away from a heap of smoldering metal a few hundred yards off. He tried to swallow and realized his mouth was hanging open.

There was a considerable space of time when no words would come, no thoughts, no feelings.

It was gone. His car was gone.

The white Challenger executed a neat 180° to forward and pulled up five feet from where he stood.

The first coherent thought that ran through Lawson's mind was Yoda's warning that anger was of the dark side. Somehow, that didn't count for much as he had just witnessed the sudden, unprovoked destruction of his baby. Carbon. That evil woman. So she had gotten a new paint job, but the custom spoiler and rims left no doubt that this was the same car she had been driving at the diner just days ago. This had been a trick all along.

He was clearly stuck now, so a brief bout of fear didn't even register as rage boiled up inside. Sure enough, there was the same woman sitting inside the deeply tinted car, and she didn't even move. Some nerve.

"Hey!" Lawson yelled, smashing his fists down on the white hood. It wasn't even scratched. "What do you think you're doing? What was that!? What!?"

No discernible movement from inside. The reason that told him she was most likely well-armed was dismissed as he marched furiously to the door, banging on her window. "Answer me!"

The woman vanished. He blinked once before stumbling backward. That wasn't possible; she was really gone.

Without warning the car's door swung open, knocking an already unstable Lawson into the dust.

"Deputy Lawson, please relax. I am not here to hurt you." A woman's smooth voice came.

Jumping back to his feet, he stared into the empty car. "What..? Who are you?"

"My name is Carbon."

His mind was not connecting the dots. "You're... the woman who abducted Elise Perry."

"No. Please get in, there is not much time."

"You're... where are you?"

"I am sitting in front of you. Please get in."

Lawson didn't know what was going on, and had yet to decide upon a course of action, but he was pretty sure that getting in that car was not in his future. "Um, no. I think I'll pass." The cop in him was beginning to take hold again and he commanded authoritatively, "Stop playing games. Where are you and what's going on?"

"I will explain once you get inside."

"No," he snapped. "You will explain now and then *maybe* we'll talk." Having just watched the joy of his life completely destroyed, he was in no mood to comply.

He expected more resistance from the mysterious voice. "Okay. I am artificial intelligence, fully integrated into this vehicle. The woman you saw was merely a hologram."

Oh, well duh. Why didn't he think of that?

"I made that call last night because I need your help to get Elise back. She is in grave danger."

For a moment, he said nothing, just stared at the white car suspiciously before glancing back to what remained of his own car. He felt a fresh surge of anger and adrenaline, "Why did you destroy my car?"

"It was necessary. I need you to come with me; your car provided you with a means of escape."

Lawson glared at the empty vehicle. It was not as fulfilling as staring down a person; there was no discernible change in the car and it didn't melt like he had hoped. He tried to speak calmly, but his efforts were to no avail as his face maintained a purplish-red color. "But you didn't have to... to do that!"

"I am sorry. Elise needs your help."

The young deputy tried to breathe deeply and think. But his exhale resembled a dragon's hissing more than anything. Closing his eyes, he held up a shaking hand toward the car, willing it to disappear. He *had* been awake all night. Maybe this was just a side effect of too much coffee and not enough shut eye.

Clearing his mind, he went through the past twenty-four hours of his life, and decided it must all be a dream; a horrible, terrible nightmare where evil Dodges deliberately smashed innocently superior Fords for fun.

"Deputy Lawson," that stupid female voice shattered his beautiful illusion. "There is not much time. Elise's life is in danger. If you will not help, I will find someone else."

He jerked his eyes open as the car's door slammed shut. "What?! And leave me in the middle of nowhere? Come on! You can't do that!"

"Good-bye." The Challenger began to back away.

"Aghh!" Lawson balled his hands into fists. "Wait!" he yelled. "Fine! I'm coming."

The car obediently pulled up next to him and reopened its door. "Quickly."

With a final glance at his now-pathetic dream car and internal voices screaming to run the other way, he gritted his teeth and stepped into the white Challenger that referred to itself as Carbon.

152

Chapter 21

Consciousness hit Elise like a four-ton dump truck. Everything hurt, and her mind was wrapped in a thick fog that refused to lift. Her eyes refused initial efforts to open, and when they finally complied, her world was still dark. Panic instantly shot through her core. Was she blind? Where was she? She tried to sort through what had happened, but could only call up shadowy images of fear.

She lay motionless for a few moments, focusing on her breathing, trying to fight through shrouded thoughts. A bed. She was tucked between soft sheets resting on a surprisingly comfortable mattress. Was she in Mesa Springs?

Slowly her eyes began to make out the pale walls of a medium sized room. There was a door directly in front of her.

This was not her bedroom. A pristine white dresser sat against the far wall, decorated by a transparent vase filled with fresh wildflowers. Light colored curtains were pulled across a large window, and on the small nightstand beside her bed sat a clear glass of water and a white porcelain lamp.

Everything about her surroundings emanated serenity and a sense of home, but her mind was baffled. Where was she? Her body felt heavy with sleep, and she gave in to the inviting sheets and pillows for an indefinite amount of time.

Her thoughts gradually increased in clarity, and as the fuzziness lifted the need for an explanation took its place. Allowing a wide and fulfilling yawn, Elise forced her body upright against the backboard.

Carbon. The word echoed in her mind like a revelation, the details of running away from school and any semblance of normal life returning so clearly that she wished they hadn't. She remembered the car's cool informative tone insisting on fleeing across the country to some place in Montana. A dark mountain and bright lights, then that same voice instructing her to willingly walk into the enemy's open arms, promising to come back for her.

A warning not to believe what they told her. She couldn't remember a rescue, but this didn't feel like the enemy.

Cautiously surveying the room a few more minutes, Elise decided to investigate further. This didn't make any sense, and staying put wasn't shedding any light on the situation. She moved slowly and quietly. If this was indeed the enemy, it couldn't hurt to have stealth on her side. She pulled aside a corner of the heavy drapes, spilling streams of daylight into the white room.

She cautiously peeked out the slit. Whoever put her here would almost certainly be watching. Judging by the distance from the ground, she was either on the second or third floor, and beneath her was a grassy meadow. A simple dirt drive led out into distant towering mountains. On every side were rolling hills of various shades of green.

Elise blinked to make sure it didn't disappear. The surroundings were wild, but truly beautiful. She couldn't detect any movement apart from the gently swaying branches, or a single person in sight. And it was quiet. Way too quiet.

The peaceful scene held her captive a few moments, but a noise from somewhere within the house forced her attention back to the problem at hand.

Given the car's insistence on getting to Montana, Elise doubted Carbon wouldn't deliver on her promise to come back for her. Furthermore, considering the unlocked door and her cozy abode, she judged that her life was not in immediate danger. If these people weren't going to hurt her, then she could certainly make it her aim to find some answers in the meantime.

A slight trembling of hesitation persisted within, but she resolved to venture past the looming closed white door. Glancing down, however, she noticed she was wearing a soft pink night gown and … she was clean? A brief investigation turned up her clothes on the dresser, washed and folded.

Who are these people? Elise wondered as she donned her jeans and T-shirt. Her sneakers were beside the dresser, so she put them on as well.

The door didn't squeak as she pushed it open, but she winced nonetheless. Outside was a long hallway with soft grey carpet bordered by ornate wooden railing that overlooked a spacious foyer.

Still there was not a human soul in sight. Elise inched gingerly to the left, senses peeled for the slightest movement. Surely they were watching her.

Trying to appear calm and collected, she followed the grey carpet until it stopped at the top of a staircase that curved down into the huge foyer. Sturdy looking oak doors stood at the center of the room beneath. A way out.

Stepping quietly down the stairs, Elise affirmed that no one else was in the room. As unreasonable as it seemed that these people would let her just get up and leave, she figured her best plan was to do just that.

Glancing around cautiously, her hand contacted the smooth brass door handle as a cheerful male voice echoed through the room.

"Ms. Perry! Welcome, how was your rest?"

Elise spun around to face a grey haired gentleman in pressed slacks and a light blue button down. His face was well tanned, and despite the grey hair he didn't look a day over fifty. He wasn't hard to recognize.

His handsome face smiled broadly, "I'm sorry, I haven't even introduced myself." His confident stride crossed the distance between them within seconds.

Elise was completely frozen to the ground.

"Dr. Rayford, at your service." He extended a hand with a mock bow. "Or just Geoffrey, if you prefer."

Her tongue was firmly stuck to the roof of her mouth, and she only stood and stared at his awaiting hand. He recovered quickly, patting her on the shoulder instead.

"Don't worry, little lady. I know you've been through quite a bit." His eyes looked at her with a strange intensity, but his face showed only kindness and concern. "Come on, let's chat over some breakfast."

Carbon's parting warning materialized in her mind. *Be careful, and do not believe what they tell you.* But looking into Dr. Rayford's face, she realized her options were nonexistent and cautiously headed in the direction he was pointing.

* * * *

Sheriff Deputy Shane Lawson had certainly had better days. This one would actually have rated pretty highly if a crazy Challenger named Carbon hadn't played demolition derby with his brand new Mustang GT. Even so, there were some perks, and the further that dreadful moment of impact receded into history, the faster this day improved.

Things didn't clear up very quickly, and he still wasn't sure that he believed 'Carbon's' story that she was indeed part of the car. His skepticism was reined in slightly by a lack of alternate explanation, but he wasn't ready to give in that easily. If there was someone holding the controls, they could be watching him. He imagined a little nerdy guy seated at a computer somewhere, holding his sides as he laughed nonstop at this cop's gullibility.

"So, *Carbon*," he felt simultaneously ridiculous and important talking to an empty car. He cleared his throat. "I'm not convinced that you're the car and all… this whole AI thing is pretty sketchy."

"Sketchy?"

"Yeah." See, now the person was pretending to not understand colloquial speech. Clever. "I don't believe you."

"Oh."

So they were playing dumb. "Yeah. And I may not know who you are or what you're doing, but I promise you I will find out."

Lawson settled back into the seat smugly, imagining the guy's face. He had called their bluff.

Given the lapse into silence, the person was probably still figuring out how to respond. "You can come clean now or later. Maybe I can even help you."

Again there was no response.

"Why don't we just start with your real name. Who do you work for?"

"Deputy Lawson, until you accept my previous answers, I will not offer any more."

So they were sticking to the original story. "Fine. If you're really a computer controlling this car, prove it to me. I'm listening."

"I do not need to prove anything to you. Whether or not you believe me is irrelevant."

Lawson felt his confidence waver. Either someone was really bent on lying to him, or the car was telling the truth. "Okay, granted. It's just that you don't meet talking cars every day, and it's a little hard to accept."

"That is understandable. Elise was surprised as well."

"She didn't even know?"

"Remember I am not answering any new questions yet."

One thing was for sure, dealing with this thing was every bit as annoying as any other computer. "Look, I believe you, okay? Your name is Carbon, and you are this car. I get it. Now will you talk?"

"As soon as you would like to know. Would you like to know?"

It was impossible not to roll his eyes. "Yes. Let's start at the beginning."

"Okay. Please pay close attention. I picked up Elise Perry from her school four days ago, sent by her father for her protection. Because of recent events I was forced to take action quickly and keep her in my care until we could reach a safe location. However, last night I was cornered on a cliff and they took her. Her life is in danger, Deputy Lawson, and I need your assistance to get her back."

"Wow, hold up." Lawson rubbed two fingers on his forehead. "Her father built you?"

"That is correct."

"To protect her?"

"Yes."

"Why?"

"I cannot give you that information until I am confident of your intentions."

"What the heck does that mean?"

"You could do more harm than good if you share that information with the FBI or other law enforcement."

Lawson stared at the car's instrument cluster. It seemed like just as good a place as any to direct conversation. "What are you, running from the law?"

"I cannot give you that …"

"Yeah, yeah, I know." He cut the car off, waving his hands dismissively. "Let's move on. Who are these people you say kidnapped her and how is her life in danger?"

"That is also sensitive information. However, I can assure you that her life truly is in danger. I am working only in her best interests. Please, Deputy Lawson, help her."

"You're not giving me much to work with here. I want to help, really."

"That is why I contacted you."

"But I need to know, why won't you go to law enforcement? The FBI? They would help her. You should call them."

Carbon's response left no room for argument. "No."

"Why not?"

The car paused as if debating how much to tell him. "What happened when you placed Elise in the FBI's protection?"

"I don't know, why don't you tell me?"

"They took her. *I* had to get her back."

"You?" Lawson was honestly surprised. The image of his Mustang came to mind, then a picture of the mangled Impala. It made sense now.

"The FBI and local law enforcement will not provide sufficient protection. The person after her has prominent positions and political connections. There is not enough evidence to bring him down. Elise being in his hands makes it nearly impossible. We must get to her quickly, she is in danger."

"Yeah, I got that part," he responded. "Why did you let her go in the first place? You were there at the diner, I saw you."

"Elise was not and will not ever be my prisoner. If she wants to leave, I will not stop her. She decided I was untrustworthy and contacted the police. Would you have preferred that I interfered?"

"Well, it would have saved us a whole lot of trouble, no?"

Carbon didn't respond.

Letting out a deep sigh, he said, "Yes, I'll help you."

How could he walk away and *not* feel guilty? His mustang's tragic ending must not be for nothing. And as suspicious as the whole situation sounded, he could tell something much deeper lay underneath, and he intended to find out what it was.

Chapter 22

Sprawled out over the table was the most beautiful spread of breakfast Elise had ever witnessed. Fresh pancakes, waffles, grits, eggs, sausage, fruit and juice; there was enough food for eight people at least. Dr. Rayford sat her down in front of it all, a servant waiting on hand for anything she might want. The woman had dark reddish hair in a loose bun, and clearly understood very little English. Rayford talked with her in a thick language Elise did not recognize.

Hungry as she was, she found herself in no mood to eat and only did so after much prodding by her host. However, it was absolutely delicious, and her stomach appreciated being filled.

Having chattered away about the weather and his latest hikes through the woods, Rayford abruptly shifted the conversation, motioning for the maid to clear the table. "Ms. Perry... may I just call you Elise?"

She nodded, and he smiled as if her friendship was a precious diamond among coals.

"Elise. Much of what I am going to tell you will be difficult to accept." His eyes bored into hers unflinchingly. "But I feel you're ready and can handle the truth." He stood up, and she felt like a minnow beside a shark. "Would you take a walk with me?"

How could she resist? Following him obediently through the front doors, he let out a long breath as sunlight washed over their faces. "Your father and I were good friends. This is ... not easy. So many things have changed." He stared wistfully off into the horizon and gave a deep sigh.

"You must be wondering why you've become so popular lately. First your father sends someone after you, then the FBI, and the police..." he shook his grey head gracefully. "I've got to hand it to you, little lady. You've taken a lot these past few days."

Not to mention being violently busted out of a prison as a hostage, being cornered on a cliff and dragged out against her will. She wasn't buying his Mr. Nice Guy act, but forced a pleasant smile anyway. "Yeah. It's been rough."

"Your father was a smart man. Resourceful, you know? Dr. Samuel Mathis, PhD. Oh, we were so close. He and I ran a health clinic at the Ceeling University." He continued walking in silence.

A doctor? "What happened?"

Rayford turned a grandfatherly eye upon her, "I believe I'm getting ahead of myself here."

"No, no," she rushed. "Please tell me."

"Heavens, child. You are an impatient one." His refined British accent was naturally condescending and mildly annoying.

"Please, Mr. Rayford. I want to know."

They walked on in silence a few minutes before he answered, "Elise, there is much to tell, and I'm confident you will know soon enough. But for now, just relax and try to enjoy yourself." She was about to protest further, but he interrupted, "Look, child. You have lived all this time without knowing. A few days, weeks, how much will it matter? What happened is in the past, it's done."

"But..."

"No buts. For now, I want you to focus ahead, not behind. You have a whole life in front of you! Why do you keep looking back for a past, a family that wasn't there for you? You're a big girl." He patted her on the shoulder.

"Now, I know you've been through a lot," he went on. "Sitting back and resting a day or two will likely do you more good than you could imagine." Gesturing around them at the rolling hills and towering mountains, he offered, "All this wilderness is yours to explore. There are beautiful trails through the mountains and maps inside. Just take care not to get lost. There are also games in the house and lovely places to sit by the fire. Now," he bowed slightly and backed away, "I have some matters to attend to, but if you need anything at all, just find one of my staff and ask. They're very helpful. I'll see you at dinner."

Elise watched him stride away in amazement. This really was an unexpected twist of events. She had to admit her attention was grabbed by what Rayford had said. But the first matter of business was finding a way out. Of course she would be careful, and exploring the woods a little seemed like a good place to start.

* * * *

A white Dodge Challenger headed south, weaving through foothills, around mountains and soaring down straightaways. As a cop, Lawson was unhappy about Carbon's ability to locate and evade law enforcement, speeding ridiculously fast in 'blind spots' as she called them. However, it was a little fun to have the upper hand technologically speaking, and the acceleration and speed of his new friend was nothing short of amazing.

Upon further prodding, Carbon had given a more detailed account of how these people had taken Elise, and how she was tracking her. According to the car's narration, they had first taken her to a local airport, flown out on a private jet, and landed somewhere in Colorado.

Twelve hours away, Lawson's mind was preoccupied with two main questions.

"Do you actually have a plan on how to get Elise back?"

"Yes. The first step is to assess the situation."

"And then…?"

"I will calculate what course of action is most likely to succeed."

As impressive as that sounded coming from a talking car, he had spent enough time arguing with his computer not to be too hopeful. "So, you don't really have a plan."

"If by 'plan' you mean a detailed set of actions ending with the safe rescue of Elise; no."

Well, that was good news. Going into a situation blind, the next natural step was to know all of your assets and liabilities. It didn't take long for Lawson to locate the touch screen display in the center console and begin exploring its capabilities.

He quickly discovered a collection of games, a strong internet connection, standard computer programs, and a myriad of databases. The data was mostly locked, but Lawson searched through it anyway.

"What are you doing?" Carbon asked.

He had expected the car to intervene at some point, but figured he had some leverage now that it wanted his assistance. "I'm just trying to see what's going on."

"You are trying to access classified information."

"Yeah. If you would unlock these, it would really help."

"I am not going to do that. Please desist in your efforts."

Lawson chuckled in amusement, "Not going to do that. You know, if you want my help, and you really want to get Elise back safely, you should tell me everything. How can I be any good if I don't know what's going on and what our options are?"

"I know what our options are. When it becomes necessary, I will inform you."

"I see. You just need a biped to walk around and pick the girl up."

"Yes."

That proved the car was honest. "Look," the young deputy pointed out, "I'm risking a lot here to help you get this girl back. You could be lying, and I could end up in jail the rest of my life. Trust goes both ways."

"You would not have agreed to help if I had not eliminated your means of escape."

Lawson snorted in derision. "Yeah. But I didn't *have* to come, and I'm still risking everything."

"I apologize, but the risk is too great of you sharing that information with the FBI or someone else."

"Okay," he held up both hands in surrender. "I promise not to tell anyone. It will be a secret."

"It *is* a secret," the car corrected him.

Gee, arguing with Carbon could give anyone a headache. Especially those who haven't slept in three days. He found himself yawning against his will.

"You should rest, Lawson. I need you to be alert when we arrive in Colorado."

"Yeah, yeah. Thanks for the concern. I'll sleep when I'm confident we can pull this off, and I know more of what we're dealing with." It was certainly a bluff; he doubted he could remain awake for another two hours.

There were a few moments of silence before Carbon compromised. "In gratitude for your assistance, I will unlock one of the files."

"Great. Can I choose which one?"

"No." The car fell silent again.

Using the touchscreen, Lawson navigated back to find that a file titled *Systems and Procedures* had indeed been unlocked. Soon he was surfing through folders of schematics, operations, and emergency protocols.

"Is there anything in particular I need to look at?" he asked.

"You requested knowledge of 'what we were dealing with'. This file is a detailed list of my systems that may be needed." The operations file was highlighted and replaced by dozens of subfolders. "Weapons systems may be a good place to start; it would be unrealistic to assume they will not be necessary."

A chill of excitement crept through Lawson's tired body. He let out a low whistle as the weapons folder opened further into a multitude of sub-files. How did a civilian get his hands on this kind of weaponry?

As far as he could tell, the car was built of reinforced carbon fiber panels coated with some type of shielding substance.

"Wow. What's up with this clear stuff?" The image depicted several molecular structures and a list of the chemicals involved.

"That is my protective outer layer. My carbon-fiber skin is coated in graphene and a specialized paint."

"Specialized?"

"The paint contains metallic particles that form reinforced webbing over the surface. In the event of an impact or strike, these particles can be flooded with an electrical current that deflects the force of the blow. Any remaining energy is spread evenly among the lattice and absorbed."

That sounded pretty cool. He moved on to offensive weapons systems.

After a brief search, he found schematics of the entire car. Carbon was equipped with four machine guns, two mounted behind the front headlights and two mounted on plates that lifted out of the trunk. These could apparently swivel and had full range of motion.

Furthermore, there were two missile-launchers that rolled out of each rear fender and were stored in the trunk compartment. The rotating wheels each held six projectiles.

He wasn't sure what to say to a car that was loaded up like a fighter jet. "Wow," he repeated again to himself. Whoever this girl's father was, he must have some serious connections, and Lawson sincerely hoped they were on the right side of the law.

Considering the deadly armament, it was beginning to dawn upon him how disastrous the implications would be if he caught with this vehicle. He could kiss his career in law enforcement goodbye and life in prison wasn't that far-fetched.

"You say you were built to protect the girl, right?"

"That is correct." Carbon responded.

If the weapons systems were any indication, this rescue was not going to be as easy as he had first thought. But he was already committed and set himself to memorizing the generous assets he had to work with.

Chapter 23

In an FBI Mobile Command Unit, Alan Stewart rested his head on a blue and white faux granite table. This case had slipped from hot to mild and was already bordering on freezing. The car had not been found, and by now it could be just about anywhere in the country. Besides, if these guys were as professional as they appeared, they would have long since ditched the car and it would likely never be discovered.

Several other agents were resting in similar fashion, scattered around the moving vehicle in various positions. They had been running through Samuel and Nancy Mathis' old files, desperate for some type of lead. None had surfaced and they were headed back to their base of operations in Chicago.

* * * *

When she stepped out of the shower, Elise found a simple blue dress neatly folded on the dresser. It fit her well and was quite comfortable, exactly the opposite of how she felt about her stay at the Rayford Manor.

There was nothing to complain about; she had spent hours wandering trails through the foothills and mountains, following streams and constantly looking out for any sign of where she was or how she could reach Carbon. The terrain was lush green meadows interspersed with small forest covered mountains, but that didn't help her locate herself. In addition, there was absolutely no sign of civilization nearby and she didn't have the faintest idea of where to go.

She wasn't alone, however. Every now and then she noticed people driving around on ATVs and in a small green truck. Maids were occasionally seen wandering through the house, and a woman who called herself Deana had given her an overview of the trails, a compass and a detailed map. Whenever Elise tried to communicate with any of them, they spoke in a strange language and could only understand the simplest English phrases. She desperately hoped she wasn't in another country; she had been unconscious for a long time and they could've brought her anywhere.

Nevertheless, she was being treated like royalty and had to admit it was enjoyable after spending most of her life unwanted, shuffled from home to home, but she was on her guard to discover the catch. Nothing was free.

Was Carbon on her way here now? Had the car lost her signal? She was growing more unsettled by the minute, and her stomach clenched as a maid appeared at her door and motioned for her to follow.

Falling in step compliantly, Elise wondered if these foreign people were also here against their will. But whenever she tried asking, they just smiled and repeated, "No understand," and Elise gave up after a few tries.

The real issue bugging her was why. She felt completely lost in a maze of towering walls, trying to find her way out when someone turned the lights off. Why would Rayford be nice to her?

Her host was already waiting at a table set for two, elaborately decorated with intricate silverware and glasses. She had only seen movies with this sort of thing.

He stood, "Make yourself comfortable, Elise. I'm so glad you could join me."

She mumbled her thanks and perched nervously on an expensive looking chair.

"What would you like to eat?"

A personal menu? "Uh, anything is fine," she stammered.

He gave a short but refined laugh, "Ah, Elise. Relax, you're making me nervous just watching you."

"Oh," she glanced down. Was it that obvious?

Her host exchanged strange words with a maid she hadn't noticed standing behind her, and the woman disappeared. Elise averted her eyes to the soft table cloth.

"Have you enjoyed your stay?" his grandfatherly baritone voice inquired.

"Yes, thank you." Elise wasn't sure why she was so afraid. She tried to convince herself it was the strange lighting, the fancy surroundings or Rayford's thick British accent, but deep inside she knew why. Deeper than her questionings into Rayford's behavior were doubts about the premise of all Carbon had told her. Whoever programmed the car could have intentionally tricked her. She had no proof the man in the videos really was her father, or that he was not a criminal as the FBI agents suggested. She really was operating in blind faith here.

The tiny voice of logic wasn't helping Elise's nerves and confidence. Carbon said they would lie, but what if Carbon was lying?

Rayford's chiseled face looked at her with concern. "I trust you've had a delightful day."

"Um, yes." She felt extremely plain between both his proper accent and the elaborate surroundings.

"Splendid."

Two maids materialized placing covered plates before them, vanishing with equal speed through a narrow door.

"Fresh Alaskan salmon. I hope you enjoy it." Rayford lifted the silver cover off his own plate, a great waft of steam escaping. "Did you get a chance to hike some of the trails?"

She nodded in response.

"Just beautiful, aren't they? The wildflowers are so pretty this time of year."

Not sure what to make of anything, Elise found herself simply staring at her plate in confusion. This guy was not what she expected, and she hardly knew what to do with it all.

"Mmmm," he was exclaiming, having tasted the fish. "That is positively delicious."

Fumbling with a fork she had randomly selected from a large array on her right, she delicately tasted a small bite. Maybe it was poisoned. But it was pretty tasty, and if Rayford wanted her dead, that didn't explain why she was eating this meal now.

"Do you like it?"

"Yes," she answered honestly. "Thanks."

His face lit up. "I'm glad."

They ate without speaking for a few minutes, questions buzzing around Elise's head like a million aggravating gnats. She wanted to demand a reason for him kidnapping her, an explanation of what happened with her father, and immediate release, but timidity and caution kept her mouth firmly shut. Except for eating, of course.

"So," he wiped his mouth with one of those fancy cloth napkins Elise had only heard about in expensive restaurants. "I know you're wondering what happened with your father, and what's been going on. As I said, I knew your father very well, rather much like a brother. But what I know is ancient history."

She stared at him, unsure of where this was going. "Excuse me?"

"It has been ten years since I saw Samuel, your father. You, my dear girl, were the last one to see him."

A hazy image flashed across her mind, but it was nothing clear.

"Yes, I'm afraid you're the only one who knows where he is."

"But I don't!" she exclaimed. Did he really believe that she knew?

He leaned forward, ignoring her interjection. "I would very much like to hear the story of what you *do* remember."

"My whole life?"

He shrugged, "Sure. Anything you can recall."

The idea caught her off-guard. She had never tried to just remember, and a stream of painful feelings rolled in unbidden. That was not somewhere she wanted to go.

But the pain made her momentarily bold. "Why don't you explain why you kidnapped me first?"

Rayford's jaw dropped. "Kidnapped?" he asked, incredulous. "Kidnapped? My dear girl, I call that a rescue."

169

"A rescue?!" She returned his expression with every ounce of shock, perhaps more. "You...you dragged me from my car, drugged me and brought me here unconscious. What do you call that?"

"Dear me," he looked down for a moment. "I see your point."

Duh, she thought angrily.

"I believe we have some... rather large misunderstandings."

She only continued to stare at him. Was this some kind of trick? How could she honestly believe that he meant to *rescue* her? "What exactly were you rescuing me from?"

Stroking his chin thoughtfully, Rayford cleared his throat. "I see we have more to cover than I first thought. I didn't want to do this, but it seems necessary now."

"Didn't want to do what?"

He stood up and slid his chair back under the table. "Come on, Elise. You wanted answers, and now you'll get some."

Following his motions, she followed behind him wondering what he could show her and why he was so reluctant to share. They traveled down two hallways, finally stopping at large double doors on the right.

"Here we are," Rayford withdrew a key from his pocket and unlocked one of the heavy wooden doors. He held it open for her, and she cautiously proceeded into a large room with thousands of books, several computers, and a small lab setup in the back.

"This is my study," the tall gentleman explained, leading the way to the back of the room. Stopping at a great big mahogany desk, he shuffled through a tidy pile of folders until triumphantly exclaiming, "Aha!"

He extended the overstuffed beige folder in her direction, "Here, take this."

Gingerly accepting the package, Elise tried to open the folder without spilling the contents all over the glossy wood floor.

"Inside you will find various articles and newspaper clippings about your father and our clinic. They run from the beginning of his career to the whole affair with..." he waved his hand dismissively, "Well, I thought you would appreciate reading some accounts first hand."

"Thanks," she mumbled, but her heart sank as she thumbed through the loose papers.

He watched her sadly, "Remember, Elise. The past is not what counts. The future is in your hands."

True to his word, they were hundreds of pages here, and she recognized the man in the pictures from the videos Carbon had shown her.

"I'll leave you to read. If you need anything, just call. Excuse me." With a graceful bow, he disappeared out the thick doors.

Returning her gaze to the folder in her hands, she sighed and braced herself mentally. Whatever the truth was, she needed to find out.

The first few articles were about her father as a graduate student at John Hopkins University. The authors gushed over his 'brilliance' and cited the many contributions this young scientist had already made to their field. The following pieces covered the installment of a new pregnancy clinic at the Ceeling University, with huge resources donated to the study and development of in vitro fertilization and genetic stuff. Slightly bored with those – they were written mostly in science speak – Elise only skimmed them to locate both the names Dr. Samuel Mathis, PhD, and Dr. Geoffrey Rayford, PhD.

It was the last pile of articles that chilled her to the core. The thickest by far, these clippings were a collection of everything from the New York Times to local newspapers to science magazines. And they all shared the same story.

The earliest piece was a front page headline, "Award-winning scientist accused of fraud and treason". There were pictures of her father, that kind face, and the lengthy article spoke of 'mountains of evidence' piled against him, as well as a conspiracy 'too atrocious to comprehend'.

The following day was no better. "MISSING!" the front page proclaimed, citing Dr. Mathis' sudden disappearance as 'highly suspicious and possibly incriminating'. Paper after paper repeated similar messages, and Elise felt that small flame of hope extinguish the more she read. Finally she came to a group of articles about her mother's death.

"Wife of Suspect Scientist Found Dead," was one title. The article described how the body of Nancy Mathis had been discovered in an old Ford truck several hundred feet off the roadway. Although the truck had been struck by another vehicle, the police did not think the impact had caused her death. Instead they listed it as a possible homicide/suicide with further investigation to follow. A later piece mentioned Dr. Mathis as the chief suspect, with fingerprints all over the truck and the body. He was never found, however, so the charges could not be made official and the case slid into the category of the cold and unsolved.

The article also stated that the whereabouts of the Mathis' children were unknown and that they were considered endangered. They supplied a picture of the six year old girl named Irene and her older brother Alexander.

She stared at the photograph. The young girl's face was smiling brightly, a childish giggle frozen in time. Was that really her? Shifting her gaze, she focused on the young boy. He looked to be about twelve, and his face… her heart froze. Alex. The recognition was stirring a tide of memories from somewhere within, and in a desperate effort to stem the rising flood, she slammed the folder shut and pushed it across the desk.

Backing away, Elise sank heavily into Dr. Rayford's soft leather chair. If this was true, and so far she had no real reason not to believe articles from sources like the New York Times, it explained why the FBI was looking for her. Could her father really be a criminal? A murderer? It didn't make sense no matter how she looked at it.

So she was really Irene Mathis, but how did she get here? Why would her father risk getting caught to come back for her? Then again, he only sent a car. He did not bother coming himself.

The knowledge was like an iron anchor weighed over her chest, but she steeled her resolve and opened the pile once more, determined to learn every detail no matter how horrible. She needed every piece of information available.

Chapter 24

"Are we there yet?"

"No."

It had been many years since Deputy Shane Lawson's last family car trip, but this one was becomingly strikingly similar. Releasing an exasperated sigh, he rearranged himself on the front seat. Even his rear end was growing weary.

"How much longer?"

Carbon had proved more enduringly patient than his mother on car trips of old, but somehow that only increased his frustration.

"Forty-seven minutes."

At least they were getting close. They had been in mountains for the past hour, somewhere deep in Colorado. If Lawson was a hermit, this is where he would live. The last real signs of civilization had disappeared a good while ago, and he wasn't sure how this affected their chances of getting the girl back.

"You said this guy Rayford is a scientist type, right?"

"Yes. He holds a Doctorate of Medicine from the University of Oxford as well as a Doctorate of Philosophy in Chemical Engineering. He has also won various awards for his discoveries in the…"

"Okay, I don't need a list of his accomplishments," Lawson interrupted curtly. "What kind of facilities do you think he has?"

"What do you mean?"

"I mean whatever we're about to run into here. Should I expect a shack, a cave, one crazy guy, an army…?"

"I do not know. We are not there yet."

That figured. Carbon had no insights, so for the next thirty minutes he attempted to memorize their location and direction of travel. The car had provided him with a GPS on the touch screen, and he wanted to make sure that if he needed to get out of here alone it would be possible. The only available sources of reference were road names and the occasional house, and soon even they disappeared.

Without warning, Carbon slowed and pulled into a clearing about five-hundred feet from the road. A thick grove of trees hid them from any passing traffic, and they stopped underneath foliage that would prevent any eyes in the sky from taking notice.

"Deputy Lawson, please go cover my tire tracks."

It had been a long time since boy scouts, but he did his best with a tree branch and a couple of sticks. When he had finished, he stood back to admire his work, feeling surprisingly accomplished. Getting out and moving around probably helped more than anything, and this untouched wilderness inspired adventure.

Walking back up to Carbon, he just hoped the trees really were thick enough. Black was definitely a better color to hide in a forest. It was a little uncanny to look at the slick white body with the knowledge that it was watching him and only God knew what else. The car's form was nothing short of magnificent, he begrudgingly admitted, with strong accents and a commanding front end. It was amazing how much a person could build into a car, but then again, it may have been just Lawson's imagination. He had always loved anything with a motor in it, especially cars.

The woods were silent, save for some chirping birds and miscellaneous scampering. Just the squirrels, he reassured himself, noting the lack of breeze and dropping temperature. He did remember to bring a jacket along, but it had never left his Mustang and likely never would.

"Okay, Carbon. What's our move?"

"I am assessing the situation."

"And…?" It was really hard to draw information out of this car.

"We seem to be on the edge of public property. The road ends in a half-mile, as do all other roads within fourteen miles."

He whistled, "And that's all this Rayford guy's property?"

"Not technically. It belongs to GeoForm, a subsidiary of a company in which Rayford holds over fifty percent of the stock."

"So yeah, he pretty much owns it."

No reply.

"How much land is there?"

"1500 acres."

"Wow. Where is Elise in all of that?"

"She is deep inside. There must be a building, though satellite imagery shows only undeveloped land. No power is supplied out this far, but it is feasible that they have their own power plant capable of generating enormous amounts of electricity."

"Wouldn't the government know about something like that?"

"Not necessarily. Rayford is a brilliant man, and he has many connections. This would not be too difficult for him."

Lawson rolled his eyes. Hearing about all these geniuses made him feel akin to a lump of coal. Sheriff deputies had to be smart too, he wanted to inform the car.

"So we're just going to sit here?"

"For now. Get inside," Carbon instructed him. "We have planning to do."

He did as he was told, and found a satellite picture waiting on the touch screen. "What is this? I thought the satellite images were useless!"

"They did not show a building, but I am now accessing different satellites to get a more accurate picture of the land."

"You have your own satellites?"

"No. They belong to the people of the United States."

"You're hacking military satellites?"

"The images are appearing on the screen, Lawson. You need to focus. Look for heat signatures or any signs of a structure."

"Yes, ma'am."

* * * *

Elise lay flat on her bed. Rayford had returned after an hour, and upon seeing her weary expression, insisted that she go straight to bed. "Past is past," he had reiterated, leading her back through the maze of hallway and up the stairs to her room. They could discuss more over breakfast, he had promised. Bidding her a good night, he had left her at the white door.

So far she had only stumbled in and collapsed on her stomach, her thoughts in too much chaos to consider. And her feelings… they weren't even allowed to speak yet.

It was true then. This explained why Carbon refused to tell her much about her father; why her father only spoke in vague statements. But why wouldn't the car have just lied? Surely that would've been easier.

The only reasons she had for trusting Carbon were her dad's videos, the freedom the car had given her, and general feelings of trust for the car itself. None of these were very solid arguments. They were all based on the underlying hope that her dad was good and loved her enough to come back for her. Foolish.

Her heart fought violently against this logic. The car had saved her life and this man was the one who had kidnapped her violently. Twice.

However, it appeared she was comfortable and safe here for the time being. Even if Rayford had more up his sleeve, at least he was playing nice.

This reality was not the one she wanted, and closing her eyes she wished for nothing more than to wake up in Mesa Springs in an ordinary, simple day.

* * * *

Lawson was not an architecture guy, but even he could appreciate the planning that had gone into this compound. Using Carbon's sources of questionable legality and high resolution zooming, they had located a structure built right into a mountain. All that was visible was about three feet of dark green metal roofing, and most of it was obscured by trees and shrubbery.

176

He had pointed out his discovery to Carbon, who had remained silent for most of the time.

"What are you thinking?" he asked, having determined than any desired information had to be extracted from the car manually.

"I am examining the building you located, as well as surrounding areas."

"Okay. All I see is the tiny little patch of roof. Mind sharing what you found?"

"It is difficult for my sensors to penetrate the mountain. However, I was able to focus through the front face of the building and lay out the most exposed area."

"A diagram would be nice. Can you do that?"

"Of course." Within moments, Carbon had drawn an outline of the structure on the screen.

Lawson hadn't actually expected his request to be possible, but this was pretty cool. The image was only black and white, but gave a nice visual for strategizing.

"There are two floors, and this is the first. An additional wing is attached on each side of the house, but I cannot get an accurate read of them."

He scrutinized the image on the screen, noting the layout of hallways, rooms, and closets. "What is this?" He pointed to the back wall, which was colored in a deeper black than the others.

"That wall is solid steel lined with lead. My sensors cannot penetrate it."

"That's where the house ends?"

"Unlikely. House walls are not usually constructed with lead, and there are no wires or power supplies running out in any direction. At the very least, there must be generators or some type of power supply behind there. Conveniently, the heat signatures are completely hidden by the mountain on top."

"Wow. So this is like a perfect fortress for an evil scientist to run experiments and other diabolical things."

"What?"

"Never mind." He couldn't help it if the car couldn't appreciate his sense of humor. "Where is Elise now?"

"She just returned to a room on the second story, and her phone's signal is also coming from that location."

"They didn't even take her phone away? Why don't you call her and tell her to meet us somewhere?"

"Rayford returned the phone, but it is bugged. He is probably hoping to find out what Elise's father is planning and who is working for him."

"Oh." Lawson felt a little dumb for not figuring that one out earlier. "But why hasn't she called you? Doesn't she want to be rescued?"

"I do not know why she has not called or what she is thinking."

"But you could still call her, right? Just don't say anything important."

"She will call if and when she wants to talk with me," the car stated simply. "Until then, it is better to stay in the background and wait for Rayford to lower his guard. I have already taken Elise from him twice, and he will not let it happen easily again."

"How much does this guy know about you?"

"Not much. He only has a name and the description of my hologram. Unless Elise has told him more." Carbon added the last part as an afterthought.

Lawson shifted restlessly, "So we're just going to sit here for now?"

"Yes. I am monitoring the activity near the house and searching for signs of defense systems."

That did sound important, but he had other things on his mind. "Well, I'm going to need to stock up on some supplies. You know, food and water?"

"Yes, I know. It may not take that long."

"And if it does?"

"Early tomorrow morning, when it is still dark, we can drive to a nearby town. I do not want to risk anyone identifying me in the daylight."

"Okay, okay."

In the meantime Lawson just had to occupy his mind, and fortunately Carbon had a bountiful spread of video games. He could get used to a car like this.

Chapter 26

Elise was up with the sun the next morning. Sleep had been sparse and most of the night had been spent tossing miserably with indecision. It was one thing to be in an undesirable situation with clear goals in mind. But here she was walking on flimsy ground in the dark surrounded by quicksand.

There were two sides at odds here: Rayford and Carbon. The former had done little for her but show gracious hospitality and share information, while the latter had not only rescued her from the black-suited people at school but also from the wayward FBI agents, a crisis that had been Elise's own making by not following the car's advice.

She felt loyalty toward Carbon and apprehension toward Rayford, but her British host had several things going for him. For starters, he actually treated her like an adult and gave her some solid information. So far he had been nothing but kind and understanding. And he had been right; the day off was refreshing and gave her a new perspective she couldn't see from trapped inside Carbon's cab.

It all boiled down to who her father was and what he wanted with her. What if he really was a murderous criminal? Everything he programmed into Carbon could be a lie. The car was sure that Rayford was evil, and if that was false …

Rayford's advice to forget the past and move on was tempting, but how could she possibly proceed without knowing who to trust?

Relieved that the sun had finally risen, she again donned her jeans and t-shirt. The only thing that was clear was the need for more information, which she intended to get soon.

Heading out of her room, Elise remembered Carbon's vow to come back for her. There was no doubt that the car would deliver on its promise; just thinking of the car's single-minded determination to get her to Montana made her smile.

But what will be waiting in Montana? A small voice whispered inside her head. That thought worried her deeply.

She proceeded back down the curving staircase and found another beautiful breakfast prepared in the kitchen. This time, however, there was no sign of Rayford, only a hand written note on her plate.

Dear Miss Elise,

Sorry I can't join you for breakfast. Work has kept me busy, but please feel free to come into my office when you would like. All my books and computers are at your disposal; maybe you can find some of those answers you were looking for!

Geoffrey Rayford

Elise set the note down with a sigh. This guy was strange, but maybe he wasn't all bad. Regardless, the French toast waiting under a silver cover was delicious enough to slide her suspicions into the background. It was amazingly nice to have meals prepared for you.

After polishing off her plate and downing both the glass of water and orange juice, there was little else to think of besides the next step. She could wander around outside, relax in her room – she had discovered a television hidden in a tall piece of furniture – and wait for Carbon to come get her, but that didn't seem like a very productive use of time. Besides, Carbon had been less than forthcoming with information, and here Rayford had given permission for her to do endless research at her convenience.

Wasting her life away just waiting for the car wouldn't accomplish anything.

At any rate, it would be unwise to automatically dismiss all of Rayford's claims. Fairness and logic demanded at least a short investigation.

With a final sigh, she stood and pushed her chair back under the table. She felt a small twang of guilt looking at the now messy spread. She had always cleaned up after herself and it didn't seem right to expect someone else to do all the work. An image of the dark haired maid from yesterday came to mind. The woman had been careful not to look at anyone in the eye, busily doing all the chores in silence.

Deciding she could at least take the dishes into the kitchen, Elise carefully gathered them in her arms and walked over to the white swinging door she had observed the maids using earlier.

To her surprise, however, the door was locked. That was strange, but she still deserved points for trying. With a shrug, she replaced her load on the table and headed back out to the foyer.

She hadn't really gotten a good map of the place yesterday, and now that she was paying more attention, she noticed that this house was oddly constructed. Of all the homes she'd been through in foster care, she had never seen one built like this.

The spacious foyer had one staircase leading up to a hallway of bedrooms, a semi-normal breakfast room off to the side with presumably a kitchen behind it, a large dining room down the hall, and then another elongated hallway leading back to a large office. She couldn't remember how many other doors they had passed, but she made a mental note to check.

Rayford had said she could go wherever she wanted, and figuring a morning walk would do her good, she slipped outside and surveyed her surroundings again.

The horizon still revealed only wilderness: some rolling hills, some towering mountains, the occasional meadow. She tried to recall what the scenery was like on the cliff where they took her, but her efforts were unfruitful. It had been night and all she could remember were bright lights, a roadblock, and panic. They might not have taken her very far at all.

Maybe she could find out in Rayford's office. He must have some type of geographical charts of the area. Besides, if she ever needed to escape, it would certainly help to know where she was and what her options were. At this point, they appeared pretty minimal. Choices: wander out into the wild and risk starvation or being eaten, or stay in Rayford's house safely until Carbon could get here.

The latter definitely appealed to her as the more sensible option. After all, the car was limited to roads, and if she wandered too far into the wilderness it would have no means of finding her, and neither would anyone else.

Turning to face the house, she noticed for the first time that it was actually built *into* the mountain. Was this one of those new schemes to save on heating and electricity? Somehow, Rayford just didn't seem like the kind of guy who worried about such costs.

The house's face appeared much like a lodge or ski resort, composed of the sturdy round timber of a log cabin but arranged with the elegance of a modern home. There was not much to see behind a front porch that ran the length of the front, because it simply disappeared into solid mountain. And it wasn't a very small mountain either.

Elise squinted trying to see up over the roof of the house, deciding that it was built on the very edge of a range of tall peaks. Climbing up that way looked nigh impossible and promised little but more wilderness for miles.

This was certainly a strange place to build a house. Rayford had to have good reasons for locating himself in the middle of nowhere, and she only hoped those reasons weren't as treacherous as Carbon and common sense alluded.

Making a mental note to pay more attention and keep her eyes peeled, Elise headed back in the house to find Rayford's study and attempt to learn what she could.

As she quietly closed the front door, it occurred to her that staying by a window might be wise. Conducting research in Rayford's back room, she would never know if Carbon pulled up.

But as long she came back and checked every thirty minutes or so, it probably would be fine. She would just have to be careful.

The house remained still as she headed back to the office, wondering why she was walking as stealthily as possible and jumping at every small noise.

* * * *

The leaves covering the forest floor were damp from the cold night, but the sun was beginning to warm things back to life. Through a pair of binoculars a log-type structure was barely visible, and the details remained fuzzy.

"We need to move closer."

A tall, brown-haired man wearing dark jeans and a plain brown jacket stood on an outcropping to get a better view. Trees were both excellent for hiding and irritating for spying, especially when you're traveling around in the wilds with a big white car.

"Yeah. I can barely see the house from here." With a sigh, Lawson lowered the binoculars and slipped back through the shrubbery into the forest.

The white Challenger was parked behind dense brush, and Lawson had covered the back with branches to be sure no one spotted it from the road.

He had always liked the outdoors and adventure, and felt much more confident after stocking up last night. Carbon had driven to the nearest twenty-four hour Wal-Mart, which had proven to be quite a drive. As Lawson had slept through most of the trip, it wasn't that bad.

The only thing he had been unable to purchase was a firearm. It seemed imprudent at best to use his ID out here. Carbon had supplied the cash – a fact which had improved their relationship considerably – and he bought the necessary food and water, a hunting knife, binoculars, several electronic things Carbon demanded, and clothing better suited for the rugged outdoors.

And this was certainly rugged. Whoever this Rayford guy was, he picked one of the most genius places to set up base.

The roads were narrow and dangerous, even those that were on the map, and there simply wasn't much of anything else around.

This place was virtually undetectable, and he doubted his fancy new car friend would ever have found it without the girl's locater device.

Not to say he wasn't impressed with the car's abilities. To the contrary, he was thoroughly impressed with Carbon's resourcefulness. She had even instructed him to make a tiny earwig out of a Bluetooth device and other miscellaneous parts she had ordered him to purchase.

And that was certainly a miracle. Lawson knew as much about computers as he did nuclear engineering: absolutely nothing. He had grown up an outdoors kid and stayed that way, proudly ignorant of most technologies, with the exception of a few manly toys. Like cool phones and cars.

At this point, he counted himself lucky for being considered the best candidate for Elise's rescue. However, he kept it well in mind that this opinion could change rapidly if things went downhill.

The door opened for him, he really liked that feature, and he slid into the black leather interior.

"How much closer do you need to be?"

"Um," no scientific answer came to mind. "Just a little bit, I suppose."

"A little bit?"

Lawson nodded. "Yep."

"That is not very helpful."

"Ok." He cleared his throat, attempting to determine a solid number. "Half a mile."

"Are you guessing?"

There was no point in lying. "Yes. But it'll work, trust me."

Carbon made no further comments as they backed onto the road. Lawson had given up wondering how the car was able to drive itself and know where it was in relation to, for example, the sheer cliff on the other side of the road. This had been a particularly troubling factor the previous night when Carbon had begun driving without headlights to avoid detection.

However, the car had proven more than able, and had declined Lawson's offer to drive not once, but twice. So he kept quiet and made sure his seat belt was securely fastened.

"The facility is well guarded. I am ninety percent certain that most of the structure is behind the main house where my sensors cannot reach. There is a way to gather more data, however."

"I'm listening."

"Of course you are. There is nothing else to do."

Lawson sighed. In one short day he had learned that this car had a proclivity for stating the obvious in a slightly obnoxious way. "So, what's this plan involve?"

"You."

"Oh, that's great. Otherwise I might think you kidnapped me for no reason at all."

"I did not kidnap you."

"However you want to look at it, Carbon. Now, does this plan leave me with a reasonable chance of survival?"

"A fairly good chance, yes."

Lawson swallowed. He had been kidding about the whole chances thing. Good guys always win, right?

Carbon continued, "As I told you last night, there are routine patrols around the perimeter. They only come by every four to six hours, and so far have consisted of two ATVs and a small truck. Each time they appear from beneath the house, run a basic course and return to where they came."

"Hold on. So there's some kind of garage thing under the house?"

"Yes. However, the only vehicles parked inside the detectable structure are the small truck and an SUV. The ATVs keep disappearing toward the back. There must be a room behind the lead wall, but I cannot determine dimensions or what else may be inside."

"Wow." Lawson whistled quietly. "This guy went and built himself a bat cave."

"A bat cave?"

"Yeah, you know, a secret hideout. A base thingy. Like Batman."

"Batman?"

"The movie! Come on Carbon, do your research. You've got to know about Batman."

"The fictional vigilante of Gotham City?"

"Very good. See, now you are a smart car."

"I do not find this relevant."

It was true, even Lawson had forgotten his original point here. "Okay, okay. So what were you saying about this plan of yours?"

"You will need to slip past the patrol, which should not be difficult, but of greater concern are the surveillance devices located on all the access roads as well as spread throughout the area."

"Oh. How many are there?"

"563."

"So that's not too many, right?"

The screen in the center console flickered to life. "I have mapped out their positions, and you should be able to avoid them. There is a blind spot near the house itself where you can descend from above."

Carbon had superimposed little white dots over a satellite map of the area. There was a great concentration close to the house. Lawson attempted to trace a path avoiding the little dots with his finger. It was fairly easy, until he reached the structure and dozens of little lights.

"I have to climb up the mountain?"

"Approximately 1400 feet above the house."

Lawson released his breath slowly. The car had high expectations. It was a good thing he had invested in sturdy hiking shoes.

"Each of the patrols has been armed. It would be wise to assume that any person you see here will be likewise."

"Great." He glanced over at his new hunting knife, wisdom from Indiana Jones flowing into his mind. Never bring a sword to a gun fight. Never mind his little four inch blade.

"There is a 9mm HK semi-automatic pistol under the passenger seat." The glove compartment opened, revealing a package of ammunition.

"How do you do that?" Lawson retrieved the box, inspecting the open compartment. It must be some sort of vending machine.

"That is irrelevant at this time. Conserve ammunition, I do not have much."

Feeling under the seat, his fingers touched the cold steel of a short barrel. It wasn't his .45 Taurus that he fully regretted leaving inside his Mustang, but this was certainly better than nothing.

"Why am I doing this again?"

"To rescue Elise. Geoffrey Rayford is both willing and capable of killing her or worse. We need to move quickly."

"You're indestructible, right? Why don't you just bust through the front door, I'll grab the girl, and then we get out of here." He prided himself on his bravery, but risking life and limb when it wasn't necessary was just stupid.

"I have considered something similar. However, the chances of success are dismal. It is unlikely that I can puncture very deep inside, and such an attempt would place Elise at even greater risk."

Lawson let out a heavy sigh.

"I have every confidence in you, deputy. Your training is sufficient for this type of operation."

He couldn't help a short laugh. Being a sheriff in Gad City, Iowa was not exactly the height of excitement. And the training requirements weren't quite that of the Navy SEALs. But this was why he became a cop, was it not?

"Okay, Carbon. You better be right about this. Now, what am I supposed to do exactly?"

"Do not worry, Lawson. Your life is of concern to me as well. I do not wish for you to fail in this mission."

Well, that was sure comforting.

"Elise's signal has moved mainly between a second-story room in the front, and a large room bordering the lead barrier."

"Why not just call her on the phone?"

"Her phone is bugged, remember?"

"Oh, yeah."

"The house's phones are also under surveillance. It would be impossible to alert her without alerting Rayford as well. My plan is to first disable the house's systems by destroying the power generators."

"Oh." It sounded good, but Lawson wasn't sure what to say. Planning had never been his strong point.

"At night when they open the garage doors, I will destroy the power sources, eliminating them without damaging the building's structure. Elise must be in her room at this time, and I will call her cell phone and tell her to run outside. Without power, Rayford's surveillance and lighting will be down and we should have enough time to pick up Elise and escape."

He thought through the plan a moment. "Then why do I have to sneak in there?"

"I need a precise layout of the structure. Since my sensors cannot penetrate the wall, you will need to do so and scan the building from the inside."

"With what? Did you steal a tricorder from Star Trek?"

"I have not stolen anything." The magical glove compartment opened again. "This device works much like a camera, except it records in three dimensions."

Picking up the small silver device, Lawson shrugged. If cars could talk and drive themselves, he supposed anything was possible.

"We are a half mile from the house now. There is an outcropping a hundred and twenty feet ahead suitable for you to use for surveillance."

"Thanks." He hadn't even noticed they were no longer moving.

Slinging his binoculars around his neck, he stepped out into the woods and hoped Carbon's faith in his abilities was not misplaced.

Chapter 25

Elise had been searching through old books and files for an hour now, and had very little to show for it. There were two computers, but they were both locked by passwords. Truth be told, she was getting more than a little frustrated with the whole research idea.

"Ms. Elise!" The door swung open at the hands of a cheery looking Rayford. "I apologize for not meeting you for breakfast. Something urgent came up and… oh, never mind." He surveyed her modest stack of books and magazines. "How is your search going?"

Not having time to think of a proper response, Elise's face apparently told the whole story for her.

"I'm sorry, my dear. As a scientist, I will be the first to tell you that gathering data is a most miserable and prolonged process."

Striding over to the wall, he slung his coat onto a protruding hook. What had made him so happy?

"Have you given up?"

She was taken aback by the bluntness of his question.

"Really, most all of the pertinent information was collected in this folder." Rayford walked to the desk and placed a hand atop the cardboard folder exploding with newspaper clippings.

"Um…" she began, but he raised his hand to silence her.

"I can see that you're not satisfied yet, and that's quite all right, the past is most difficult to forget. But," he glanced at a shiny platinum watch on his wrist, "I have about an hour's free time before..." he trailed off in calculations. "Mm-hm. That should do."

Reaching behind, he grabbed a wooden chair and brought it up to the desk, arranging himself carefully across from Elise. She felt slightly guilty resting instead in his plush swiveling office chair. "Okay, little lady. An hour of question and answer. I am at your service."

Looking at his smiling grandfatherly face, Elise was finding it increasingly difficult to hold him in a negative light. Could this man be her archenemy?

"Really?" she asked, not sure of his openness.

"Really." He folded his arms across the table and sat at attention.

"Okay." Where to start? She had so many questions. "What about my dad? You worked with him, so what was he like?"

"Ah, Samuel." Rayford stroked his chin thoughtfully. "You would've liked him, that's for sure. Very amiable sort; got along with everybody. As I said before, positively brilliant. He contributed much to the world of science, and..."

"What exactly?" Elise interrupted him.

"What?"

"His contributions. What did he do?"

"Remember we ran a health clinic together, and he specialized in..." he launched into a detailed explanation, but most of the words were lost on Elise as he delved into a technical description of their jobs. She did gather that he researched genetics and something about in vitro fertilization. Rayford paused and observed her blank expression. "Don't worry about that too much. It's really not very important right now."

"Oh. So what happened?"

"Your father was a great success story; a prize of modern science. The technology he was developing, however, was quite sensitive in nature and his work was partly funded and overseen by the government. Just making sure the data didn't leak out into the wrong hands.

"Your father seemed to welcome the new procedures, and all appeared to be running smoothly. Years passed, and evidence began to surface that he had been willfully keeping crucial information from the review board, even from the other members of his research team. This was upsetting, warranting a clandestine investigation into his activities." Rayford leaned back in his chair and sighed.

"What they discovered was awful. I could not believe that it was true. I mean, I had known your father for so long and... you just don't expect this sort of thing. I decided to confront him about it; get to the bottom of all this. There had to be a good reason."

There was a pause as he stared vacantly into space as if remembering. "I ran into your father in the lab. I had learned of the accusations before the investigators even got a warrant, so I arrived before the police or anyone else. At this point, I was convinced the information was fabricated or just mistaken in some way.

"But when I saw Samuel in the lab," his blue eyes hardened, "...*our* lab, he waved a gun in my face." Rayford spit out the word *gun* as if it was poison, "He said he'd have to pull the trigger if I followed him. Completely shocked, I really had no choice but to wait for the police and point them in the direction he went. It would seem he had learned of the investigation beforehand and returned to the lab to steal all the papers and research."

"Everything." This time when Rayford's eyes met hers, there was nothing in them but pure fury. "Not only did he steal the data, but he deleted every electronic file we had and destroyed what papers he didn't take with him. My life's work... gone."

The thick British accent combined with the ferocity with which he spat out the words had Elise cowering somewhat in the depth of the chair. The grandfatherly image was momentarily swallowed by this raging monster. But almost as suddenly as the rage had swelled it subsided, leaving the grey haired gentleman rearranging his necktie.

Talk about Dr. Jekyll and Mr. Hyde. Then again, she could almost sympathize with his cause. If someone had stolen everything she ever worked for, maybe she would be just as angry. Especially if it was someone she trusted. That's why it was better to trust no one.

"It is still painful," Rayford offered, clearly as close to an apology for his outburst as he was going to come. "I have spent my efforts here reconstructing the data as best I can, but there are simply too many missing puzzle pieces. I honestly don't know what took over your father. Perhaps as it is with many brilliant men, he became too ambitious. I simply don't know. One could speculate for a lifetime."

Elise was almost afraid to ask another question, but it just kind of spilled out anyway. "What then? He just disappeared?"

"As far as anyone can tell. His wife's body was found several months later. The articles provide detail if you want, but the bottom line was that your father was the chief suspect. That was the last time I heard anything about him."

His eyes met hers meaningfully, though he fell silent. Surely he didn't think she had anything to do with this.

She tried to change the subject. "So, what about me? How do I fit into all of this? And why are the FBI involved?"

Rayford gave a short laugh. "Slow down, lady. So many questions! I'll start with the easiest. The FBI are involved because the information that Dr. Mathis stole has the potential to threaten national security, and they want it back. Or at least they want it destroyed. You, Ms. Elise, are his daughter, Irene Mathis."

She wasn't stupid. That part she had already figured out. "But why all of a sudden? I barely remember my father, why do they think I know something now?"

Studying her carefully, he shrugged. "I cannot be completely certain, but it is likely they just now learned of your identity. Your father was a genius, and when he tried to hide you he was almost successful. He *was* successful for ten years. Now, the real question is: why are you here now? Who were you with before I found you?"

She stared back at him in confusion.

"You weren't with the FBI, or the police, and their attempts to bring you into protective custody failed. Someone else had to be involved."

There were no questions in his statement, but Elise didn't like the way this was going. He was the one supposed to be giving answers here, not her.

"No," he continued. "Someone else was watching you. And when the officials got close, they got to you first."

She broke his gaze and looked down. The accusations were pretty obvious.

"I have an important conference call soon, so I'll leave you to think by yourself. Tonight I will be happy to answer some more questions, but I suspect you have more answers than you know. Just think about that."

Standing, he eyed her quietly for a moment. "Miss Elise, I really do want to help you, and I understand your delicate situation. But please consider that there are more people than yourself involved here, and sometimes doing the right thing is extremely difficult and costly."

The next time she glanced upward, he had retrieved his coat and was opening the sturdy oak door. "Of course, you are still free to do whatever you feel is right and make use of anything you find here." He gave her a comforting smile. "Good bye for now."

Echoing footsteps continued down the hall even after the heavy door fell back into place. Elise allowed her head to sink on top of her arms on the hard desk. Instead of making things clearer, Rayford's answers had only further muddled her mind.

Frustrated, she closed her eyes and moaned. Why couldn't she be back in Mesa Springs, enjoying life as a normal teenager?

Chapter 27

Lawson huddled behind a prickly tree.

"Move straight ahead twenty feet and stop out of sight."

Carbon had directed him through most of the wilderness, and now he was on top of the house itself. Pipes of varying sizes protruded from the earth in the most random places, but apart from that, there was absolutely no sign that either a house or a mysterious evil compound lay hidden below.

Carefully crossing the twenty feet or so, Lawson was grateful that he was no longer climbing sheer cliff walls with Carbon's approximate measurements.

"You do not know how far twenty feet is?" the car had inquired innocently.

"Well, roughly, but not exactly. I'm not a computer."

But despite his complaining, Carbon insisted this was the only way and it would have to suffice. And she was right. His only problem thus far was that the volume on the earwig was a little too loud and his ears had taken to a dull ringing.

"Remain still until I say."

The only thing that kept him from likening his current adventure to a high school game of paintball was the pistol at his hip, the voice in his ear, and the lack of opponent. Carbon said there were surveillance cameras and the occasional person, but so far, he had not seen or heard anything except a few birds and a confused looking chipmunk.

The plan was pretty simple, in a manner of speaking. Even Lawson could understand it, without his secret agent training and all. Get in, map the place, get out. Basic recon.

But he was about to embark upon the most difficult part; actually getting inside the evil lair. *Right into the belly of the beast*, his mind kept reminding him.

Truth be told, he had no idea what he would say if they caught him. 'Hi, I'm a lost hiker' seemed like the best bet, or maybe he could claim to be a wayward pizza guy. Who ran out of gas four miles back and for some reason left the road and decided to go on a nature walk. Okay, that explanation wasn't going to work. Definitely the hiker thing.

"Lawson. There is a large boulder against a cliff face to your right. Do you see it?"

"Yes," he whispered. It was sprouting green fuzz all over, but it really did seem half the size of Texas. 'Large' didn't do it justice.

"Get behind the boulder. From there you should have an adequate line of sight to plot a course down around the side of the structure. Satellite imagery shows dense foliage that should conceal you completely until you step through the garage door. The motion sensors should be too far to be activated.

"Remember that you have to wait for them to open the door, as the control is located past the barrier, and that I will lose contact with you once it closes again. Good luck."

Letting out a deep breath, Lawson steeled himself and fought his way into the green mess of trees and shrubs. Carbon hadn't been kidding about dense.

The ground was moderately steep here, and he tried carefully to not send any rocks or twigs careening towards the bottom. Cars didn't think about little details like that.

Fortunately he reached the ground level of the garage without incident, and found himself with a pretty good view of the entrance to the structure. It appeared much as it had through the binoculars; a cozy little mountain cabin.

What if the car was wrong? What if he was actually sneaking up on some little old lady or a couple on their honeymoon?

But his thoughts froze as a tall, dark haired man walked in front of the brown garage door. Dressed in blue jeans and a plaid button down, the man paused in front of the door, scanning the area.

Lawson stopped breathing. The guy was only about fifteen feet from his position, and in the stillness of the morning was bound to hear even the slightest crunch. But fortunately the guy didn't stop for long, and the door began opening.

It was actually a little disappointing; the thing creaked and groaned and opened meanderingly just like an ordinary garage door opener. Not much diabolical here.

Then another sound punctured the air. It was a crisp snap followed by a high-powered whine. That was more like it.

The black haired main issued some smooth commands into the opening before stepping inside.

"Now," came Carbon's voice. "They are turned away and there is a vehicle you can hide behind."

Why was he doing this again? But for the sake of the blood rushing in his ears, he did as he was told.

Ducking behind a beat-up green Toyota Tacoma, it was all he could do to keep his jaw from dropping open. There were no more doubts to Carbon's story.

The section he was now hiding in was just like a standard garage complete with the Tacoma and also an impressive new Nissan XTerra, fully loaded with a bull bar, winch, snorkel and roll cage. But behind the vehicles, the brown block wall had also slid open, revealing a much larger room with silver walls. It *was* like Batman!

This Tacoma did not provide much to hide behind. *Carbon!* He thought angrily, desperately searching for a new and improved hiding place.

But before he could risk a glance under the truck, an engine sputtered to life somewhere within the silver room. Crouching behind the rear tire, he waited for the noise to move out. Resting purely on the hope that no one stayed behind in the room, his plan was to dart inside as soon as the vehicle passed his position.

196

The decision came quickly, and he tried to think invisible thoughts as he slipped out of the garage and out of sight into the second room. The doors began sliding shut in the next instant, and Lawson jumped behind the nearest object he could find.

His first impression was the sheer space in here. In his initial survey, the silver walls seemed to go back for miles.

Glancing more closely at the nearest wall, all he could deduce was that it was a metal of some sort, and the object he was hiding behind was a very large crate.

This would be much cooler if he was watching from the safety of his living room. Then again, it *was* pretty awesome.

Only silence echoed in the room, and Lawson figured it was safe to assume he was alone. Cameras, however, were another matter. If they had not already picked up his dash into here, they would almost certainly capture him wandering around on a grand tour. Too bad Carbon couldn't tell him where they were anymore.

Oh, well. Nothing ventured, nothing gained. Carbon estimated he would have forty minutes until the scout returned, and then another five hours or so until the doors would open again. Not counting the inconvenience of no bathroom breaks, Lawson didn't figure he could last that long in here without being discovered. So whatever he was going to do, he needed to do now.

Staying low, he tried his best to remain behind various objects lining the walls, holding out the little silver tricorder thing Carbon had given him. She said it worked like a camera, but he still felt special holding it. Definitely a Bond toy.

This worked for a few minutes until he came to an option of two doors. To his pleasure, neither was locked, or had secret thumbprint access points, which would have presented a major problem, and he chose the one on the left. As he proceeded down an empty hallway, the noisy hum of generators met his ears. Sweet music.

This hallway was narrow and did not contain any objects whatsoever, much less anything worth hiding behind. If anyone came down here, there would be no way around a face to face confrontation.

And so Lawson moved quickly, hoping no one showed up. The air was growing considerably warmer, and as he rounded a corner he saw what was sure to be the power-supply room, and it conveniently had a large plexiglass window to prove this point.

There was only one problem. There was a man on the other side, and this man was looking straight at him.

Lost hiker, Lawson told himself, waving at the man with a grin. The guy was big, 6'6 at least and built like Schwarzenegger, and he only returned Lawson's grin slightly. Boldness could take people by surprise, and so Lawson heartily pushed the door open and slapped Mr. Big on the back. "Hey, man. I'm just checking to make sure everything's good down here. You need anything?"

The man stared at him with dark eyes, but they seemed more confused than anything. Lawson pointed at the silver thing Carbon had given him. "This is my checking thing, so I'm just going to check real quick, okay?"

A short string of utterances came from the man's mouth, none of them intelligible. They didn't even speak English? But the man seemed agitated, so Lawson did his best to reassure him.

"It's okay, it's okay. Just relax." Holding up a finger, Lawson spun his 'tricorder' in a semi-circle, double checking that the record button was activated. That should be more than enough for Carbon.

Turning back to his new friend, Lawson patted the man's solid shoulder. "Thanks. Let's just keep this between us, okay? Ciao."

With that, Lawson spun on his heels and fought to walk calmly back down the hallway. He had what he needed, and every part of him wanted to run as fast as possible out of this place and retreat deep into the woods.

But that would be highly suspicious, and if there were cameras, his best bet was to keep his head low and his gait unconcerned. A little whistling tune came to mind, but that seemed rather ludicrous, so he kept quiet.

The large silver room couldn't come fast enough, and by the time he sank down behind his crate, he was drenched in sweat. Checking his watch, he had fifteen minutes for the surveillance party to return. Fifteen minutes for the generator guy to keep their little visit to himself.

* * * *

Elise had relocated herself to her bedroom. The study contained all the information she wanted to erase, and she was beginning to wish she had never asked. Right now, she just wished Carbon would show up. Maybe it was taking so long because the car had gone to pick up her father first. Maybe he would come and rescue her.

A deep sense of logic scoffed at the very idea. Sure, the father who didn't even want to keep her as a child would come back and 'rescue' her from this nice warm house with food and water, and bring her into his life of crime.

But she really had no reason to believe Rayford, either.

The confusion had sapped her of all strength, and lying on the soft bed, she only stared out the window at the serene mountain landscape.

* * * *

FBI Agent Alan Stewart was fast asleep in his bed for the first time in over a week when the annoying chirping of his cell phone startled him awake.

Still mostly unconscious, he mumbled some form of greeting into the mouthpiece.

"Agent Stewart," a female voice responded. "We need to talk."

His mind conjured up fuzzy thoughts and images, but couldn't place the tone. "Who is this?" he asked groggily, willing his tired mind to wake up.

"My name is Carbon."

That was enough to snap him to full attention. Carbon. The woman from the Elise Perry case, the one who had kidnapped the girl from her school. He jumped into action to trace the call.

"Do not bother trying to trace the call, it will not work."

"What do you want?" he fumbled around his nightstand searching for something to write on.

"I have information regarding Elise Perry."

"Yeah," he snorted. "You should. Where is she?"

"I have sent the coordinates to your email. The place belongs to a company named GeoForm, held by Dr. Geoffrey Rayford, a former colleague of Dr. Mathis."

"I know who he is," Stewart interjected impatiently. "What's at these coordinates?"

"Miss Perry, and she is in grave danger. I cannot supply sufficient information for a warrant to search the location, but I would recommend sending in several agents as soon as possible."

"Yeah, a nice setup for an ambush. If it wasn't for you, Elise would be safe in our custody as we speak."

"I can assure you, Agent Stewart, that my only priority is Miss Perry's safety."

"You work for Dr. Mathis?"

"That is all, Agent. Thank you for your time."

"Wait, Carbon…"

But it was too late. His phone flashed *Call ended: 1:24*.

"Agh," he growled, running his hands down his face. Sleep would have to wait.

Chapter 28

Lawson was sure he had counted over twenty thousand seconds when the heavy doors finally slid open. Freedom was so close.

He crouched like a loaded spring, hoping there was a better way out than in. His hand instinctively drew his gun, but then replaced it. Could he really justify shooting someone here? After all, *he* was the one trespassing. There was no real legality to protect him from any rash actions.

The hum of the small truck's engine drew closer, and Lawson risked a peek around the open door. All appeared clear and empty, and with the sound still a fair distance away, he sprinted to his previous hiding place behind the Tacoma with his back braced against the outer wall.

When the truck drove past, all he needed to do was slip around the corner, dive into the brush and scramble up the mountain. Piece of cake, he told himself. His shaky hands told another story.

And so it came, the small green truck driving past him, and so he jumped out through the opening, headed straight for the dense thicket to his right. He saw a figure standing out of the corner of his eye, but it wasn't until midair that Lawson began rethinking his blind leap.

When gravity reminded him of its influence, the tall stranger had already placed himself squarely between the deputy and his point of landing, broad shoulders creating a solid buffer.

Lawson barely pulled up to keep from colliding with the man, and in his attempt to alter his trajectory mid-leap he twisted his body hard the left. Which would not have been a problem in and of itself, but combined with his continued forward momentum resulted in a hard and sudden plop on his rear end.

His tailbone screamed a loud protest, and in the shock of it all, he apparently forgot to leap up and run away. Instead he just sat there like a fool, staring at the dark-haired figure before him. This never happened to James Bond. What had gone wrong?

"Hi there." The man with the plaid checkered shirt and jeans stood with crossed arms regarding him with a look of amusement.

Unable to find any words, Lawson only stared back blankly.

Footsteps pattered up from inside the garage, and two more men emerged on either side of him. This was definitely not good.

"Um, hi." He had finally found his tongue, even if nothing intelligible to say had come to mind yet.

"Hitchens," one of the guys wheezed, breathing hard from his little run. "This is the guy."

Lawson only looked back up at the black-haired man innocently. *Lost hiker.* Clear blue eyes didn't reveal much, but Lawson got the impression of a spider determining whether it was hungry enough to eat the poor little fly that just got caught or wait until later. Either way, it was a bad feeling.

"You got a name, son?"

"Uh, Joe." It was the first thing that came to mind.

"Just Joe?"

"Joe… Steamer." Great thinking, Lawson. Related to Stanley, no doubt?

Hitchens only continued to stare thoughtfully. "I see. Well, Mr. Steamer," the name rolled off his tongue like he wasn't convinced. "Do you mind telling me what you were doing in there?"

Lawson rubbed his hands together and glanced at each of the men beside him. "Can I get up please?" Not only had his graceful landing proved him an imbecile, but he felt like a child sitting at the three mens' boots.

"Of course." Hitchens grinned, which made him look more like Tom Cruise than anything, and stretched out a hand to Lawson. "That was quite a nasty fall."

"Yeah." Lawson accepted the hand and attempted a short laugh. The man's grasp was like being caught in a bear trap, for goodness sake. He would really hate to cross this guy. Yet here he was.

Brushing the dirt off his back, he noticed no one else looked very amused. Clearing his throat, he began as practiced. "Well, I was backpacking through these mountains and got kind of lost."

The black haired man raised an eyebrow.

"Backpacking without a backpack?"

Lawson chuckled nervously. "Yeah, you noticed that."

He had always been good at making up stories for skipping school, and he prayed his finely-honed senses would not fail him now. "You see, I started out from my aunt's house – I'm just visiting – and I really packed carefully for this trip. I even brought along the old GPS, my water filter, boy-scout compass as a back-up, maps of the area; the whole nine yards."

His audience appeared pretty skeptical, but he gushed on, animating every sentence with sweeping arm movements and dramatic facial expressions. "If I wasn't such an idiot," the three men definitely needed no convincing there, "I would still have my pack. But I sat down for a break somewhere... oh, it was an amazing view, and after I had gone on for a while and it was dark, I went to get a flashlight and realized," Lawson slapped his hands to his cheeks in feigned horror, "I had set my pack down and totally forgotten to pick it back up! Crazy, right?"

Again, they all seemed to be in agreement.

"And I'm really sorry for trespassing and all, but you see, I was just looking for some water and maybe a phone. It's only been a day, but you know, a person can't go long without water." He offered another apologetic smile.

"I see." Hitchens' expression really didn't change much. It was quite unnerving. "Why didn't you just ask for help? Knock on the door?"

Lawson looked sheepishly at his feet. "Um, I was... well, some people around here aren't the nicest and... I just thought it would be best to avoid disturbing anyone. Sorry."

The taller version of Tom Cruise put a hand on Lawson's shoulder. "Well, I guess you learned your lesson." Glancing up, the deputy saw a friendly smile on the man's face. Somehow, he wasn't convinced. "Why don't we go inside, get you some water, let you call your aunt, and point you toward the nearest road. Maybe even drive you there."

It was hard to look extremely happy at the offer while his hopes of escape sank like the Titanic. "Really? Thanks! I'm sorry, it was stupid to sneak around like that. It won't happen again, I promise."

Hitchens released his shoulder. "I believe you. Now, Mr. Steamer, just follow these two gentlemen upstairs and they'll get what you need."

"Thanks," Lawson mumbled again, with a brief glance up before staring back at the ground subserviently.

"Let's go," the blonde man to his right pointed to the wide stairs in front of the house. This guy wasn't smiling.

Without many options, he went obediently. Where was Carbon? The car had to be listening, so why didn't it do something?

Once inside, Lawson took in the simple but undoubtedly expensive and overly large foyer, from the curved staircase up the side to the large oak door he passed through. His mind screamed to run outside, just run anywhere that wasn't here, but the presence of Curly and Moe provided suitable deterrent. He doubted he could make it more than five feet without being tackled.

Sitting atop a marble counter was a white corded phone, talk about the dark ages, which Moe picked up and handed to him.

"Call your aunt, Joe. My friend will go get you a glass of water."

Sure enough, Curly disappeared into a door at the back and Lawson gingerly accepted the phone. This presented a fairly major problem. Carbon had said all the phones were bugged; his phone call couldn't be faked. Worse yet, he didn't even know a single local number.

Moe continued staring at him. Offering a weak smile, he turned to the phone hitting seven random digits. With any luck, it would be a real number and he would get an answering machine. Or better yet, no answer at all.

He put the phone up to his ear, his mind racing through options when the call fell through. With Curly gone, he might be able to ditch Moe and make it out of the house. The dense brush wasn't that far away.

To his surprise, however, the phone rang twice before an old lady answered.

"Hello?"

"Uh, yeah. You see, I..."

But before he finished trying to explain, the old woman's voice cackled, "Joe? Is that you?"

Lawson nearly dropped the phone. Fortunately had had a good grasp, although it took him a moment to recover. Carbon. This wasn't the first time she had talked to him in another person's voice.

"Yeah, Aunt Jemima, it's me."

"Thank heavens!"

Jemima sounded extremely relieved, and Lawson couldn't resist the opportunity to smirk at Moe.

"I was so worried when you didn't call me to check in this morning! These mountains are a dangerous place. You never know what could happen. I was beginning to think a grizzly had gotten you. Heavens, whatever would I tell your mother?"

"It's okay, Auntie. I'm fine, just a long story. These nice people let me use their phone, and gave me some water. Do you think you can come pick me up?"

"Well, your uncle Herb's got the truck right now, but I'll be over as soon as possible. It might be faster to walk, though. Those people got a map?"

Lawson gave Moe a questioning glance, noting that Curly had reappeared with a glass of water, and the blonde man nodded in affirmation. "Yeah. You know what, don't worry about me. I'll just follow the road back, and maybe be home for dinner."

It took a moment for Aunt Jemima to respond. "Well, I guess that'd be best. Just be sure nothing happens to you. I don't know what I would tell your mother."

Lawson reassured his concerned aunt that all would be well and hung up. He had to give Carbon points here; that was downright creative.

Accepting the glass of water from Curly, it was easy to drink in one gulp. He had been very thirsty.

Moe spoke up. "Well, Joe, you can just wait in here and I'll go get you a map."

"Thanks." Lawson smiled brightly. Surely they would let him go now, or maybe he could just walk out the door. To his displeasure, however, he noted that this time Curly stayed behind.

A few minutes of awkward silence ensued, and Lawson cautiously looked around the room. Was the girl nearby? According to Carbon's map, she had been somewhere in the front of the house, at least a few hours ago.

Smiling at Curly – the man was watching him like a hawk, though the animosity was lessened since the phone call – Lawson stole a glance upward. The stairs ascended to a hallway that overlooked the foyer, wood colored railing running the length of it.

The lighting was such that he almost missed the slender form staring at him from behind said railing. A side glance at Curly said the big man had seen her as well, so in an effort to act natural Lawson turned and continued glancing around nonchalantly.

Don't do anything, Lawson begged her silently, hoping Curly would reemerge soon with a map and send him on his way.

But apparently the girl had not received his telepathic memo, and she walked slowly down the stairs with confusion etched on her face.

Please be quiet, please be quiet.

Lawson glanced at Curly. "Is this your daughter?"

The big man's gaze flickered from the girl to Lawson, and he shifted uncomfortably, "No." He offered no further information, but grew increasingly agitated.

Erratic thoughts darted through Lawson's mind. If he pulled the gun on Curly, maybe he could grab Elise and run. But he knew they wouldn't make it far. Not with this security.

Their chances were better waiting. That is, if she didn't do something stupid. But as Lawson watched her approach him hesitantly, he saw his chances dwindling.

"Hi," he stuck out his hand. "Name's Joe. The lost hiker." He rolled his eyes toward the door. "Moral of the story; don't leave the GPS sitting on a log somewhere."

She only stared at him, recognition getting clearer and confusion deepening.

She glanced at Curly and back at him, and walked even closer. "Joe…" she repeated slowly. But she seemed to reach a decision and brightened her tone. "You're a hiker?"

He grinned nervously, "Yeah. Nothing like nature at its best."

Nodding in agreement, she turned to Curly. "Is this your friend?"

Watch it, girl, Lawson pleaded silently. "Well, he is now. Just helping me get back home."

Elise shifted her gaze back to Lawson, her green eyes holding a zillion questions. Those eyes were actually quite striking, the honest confusion and fear spilling out. He couldn't help but feel compassion for her, and he wasn't a very emotional guy.

He wanted to tell her Carbon had sent him, that it would be okay. And looking into her open face he almost did.

But just as he decided to try and escape, Moe reappeared from the kitchen, and he wasn't alone. Hitchens was beside him as well as a grey haired gentleman Lawson recognized as Dr. Geoffrey Rayford from Carbon's pictures.

"Whoa!" Lawson backed away from Curly, placing himself between Elise and the rest of them. "What's going on? Do you have my map?"

Rayford shook his head, "Joe, Joe… I think we have some matters to discuss first."

Lawson backed closer to the door hoping Elise would as well. But she had frozen and was now beholding the situation in bewilderment.

"Dr. Rayford?" she asked. "Who are these people?"

"Don't worry about it, dear. These are friends, and that," he pointed at Lawson, "may be a very dangerous man."

"Hey!" the deputy held up his hands innocently. *Please run, girl.* "I'm just lost! I said I was sorry for trespassing, okay?"

It was Hitchens who stepped forward. "Come on, Joe. Let's just go clear up some matters, and we'll send you on your way with that map."

"Um, thanks, but I think I'll be okay on my own. Thanks for the water, sorry for intruding." He knew better than to turn his back on this type of situation, and finally his fingers met the doorknob behind him.

Anyway he looked at this, it just wasn't good. Elise was standing not two feet from him, Hitchens eight feet further and flanked by Curly and Moe. He only saw one chance.

The girl was still looking at Rayford, and started to speak when Lawson seized the opportunity. Flinging the door open, he simultaneously yanked Elise in front of him and put his gun to her head.

"Move any closer, and she dies."

She gasped in his arm lock, grabbing his forearm with her fingernails. But his concentration was on the four men who had jumped to instant attention. Carbon had said they wanted the girl alive.

"Look," he said. "I just want to get home. I don't want to hurt anybody. Just back away, and I'll release her once I pass the meadow. I don't want any trouble."

"It's too late for that," Rayford hissed, and Hitchens began to move forward.

"Hold it!" Lawson shouted, digging the gun into Elise's temple.

She cried out in pain, and he struggled not to loosen his grasp.

It seemed to work, however, as each man froze in his tracks. If looks could kill, though, Lawson would've been dead on four counts.

"You don't know what you're dealing with," Rayford continued as Lawson began backing down the steps. Elise was struggling more now.

"Let me go!"

"Don't move!" Lawson cautioned again. There, they finally reached the bottom step. Now would be a good time for his bullet-proof friend to appear.

The girl was proving quite a fighter, however, and bit down hard on his arm.

208

"Ow!" he hissed in her ear. "Stop it! Please, Elise. I'm not going to hurt you. Carbon sent me."

She froze, but it was too late. Lawson didn't feel anything, but he heard a solid crack as he dropped to the ground, his thoughts fading to black.

Chapter 29

Elise felt herself dragged down as the deputy's body collapsed backward.

"Elise! Are you all right?!" Rayford's voice sounded from somewhere above, but as she rolled onto her stomach off the limp form, her thoughts were elsewhere. She couldn't remember his name, but she definitely remembered this deputy's face. What was he doing here?

A trickle of red blood appeared on the side of his head, and she glanced up to see a dark-skinned man standing triumphantly with a gun in hand.

"Good work, Leonard!" Rayford's voice congratulated the man as he and the three men from inside gathered around where she now knelt.

"Ms. Elise, that was terrifying! I'm so glad you're okay." One of them pulled her up to her feet while another two lifted 'Joe' off the ground.

"Is he dead?" she blurted.

"Oh, heavens no. Leonard here just conked him good on the head. Don't worry, dear, we'll call the police and get this matter all sorted out." Rayford shook his head emphatically. "Just crazy the people out there."

She stared as they carried him back into the house. Was he really here with Carbon? Lawson. That was his name.

"Come on, Elise. Let's get you back inside." Rayford ushered her up the steps. "I'm so sorry you had to go through that."

He went on complaining about the state of society and the amount of dangerous criminals that wandered the streets, but her mind kept running through what Lawson had said. *Carbon sent me.* If Carbon sent him, where was she?

Elise stopped in the middle of the foyer, interrupting Rayford's chatter. "What was he doing here?"

The dignified gentleman paused and regarded her with an even look. "You heard him. He said he was a lost hiker."

"But you didn't believe him," she pressed. "And who were all those other guys in here?"

Rayford gave a small laugh, "As always, so many questions. And that's why you're going places, my dear."

Compliments weren't going to throw her off that easily. "I mean it. What's going on?"

Her host walked a few steps farther and opened the door to the hallway. "Why don't we discuss this over lunch?"

"Can't you just answer my question now?"

Rayford's eyes narrowed. Taking a deep breath, he let it out slowly. "You're right. More is going on here, and that man was much more dangerous than a crazy murderer. I will tell you what you want to know, but please, let's move somewhere more private. This is quite a sensitive matter, as you can see."

She watched his face skeptically. How much of a choice did she really have?

"I know that was frightening," he continued gently, "but you have to trust someone. I promise to keep you safe."

Reluctantly she began to walk down the hallway. Judging by Lawson's condition, if he was here with Carbon, his plan had not gone very well. She was probably on her own for a while, and considering the four henchmen that had materialized from nowhere, her best bet for any kind of escape was cooperation.

If Carbon was waiting out there, she sure hoped the car would do something soon.

* * * *

"You want us to drop everything and head there *now*?" FBI Agent Liz Kerry stood in front of her boss, hand casually propped in protest.

"Yes, that's exactly what I'm saying." Could he be any clearer?

"Because of a phone call from this 'Carbon', kindly giving us a hint to go out to the middle of nowhere and look for the girl?"

He just stared at her. There was no need to repeat himself. His coworker had a right to be tired, but she was walking a thin line here. "Look, Liz. If you're that exhausted, go home and get some sleep. I'll send someone else."

"Come on, Stewart. I'm not being bull-headed, I'm just trying to do my job and make sure we don't run into a trap."

"I appreciate your concern, and can assure you I have a carefully thought out plan. May I remind you that I have been doing this longer than you and am capable of managing my assets." He was being overly hard, but if she could be insolent, he could surely be cranky.

Liz wasn't very ruffled, she only sighed and cleared her throat. "Of course, sir. I'm sorry."

"Now," Stewart waved as Agents Rico Guerrez and Phil Masters arrived in the room. Both had coffee in hand, and both looked like they needed it. These three together were the best of his undercover ops team.

A glance at his wristwatch he was reminded of what precious little time they had. At least according to Carbon.

"Okay, people. Sorry to disturb your beauty rest," he glared meaningfully at Liz, who only shrugged, "but we have some work to do."

* * * *

Elise had followed Rayford into his study, where he closed the door and paused. "It may be difficult, Elise, for you to accept what I'm about to tell you." He put his fingers together against pursed lips as if determining what to say. "But I believe you can handle it.

Certainly, with the way you're asking questions, you're bound to find out sooner or later."

She glanced around the room, uncomfortable. Was he going to confess to everything?

But he only smiled in an odd way and walked over to the bookshelf on the back wall. "I think you will like this."

Moving uncharacteristically fast, the grey haired man rearranged the books and typed into something she couldn't see. He motioned for her to join him, and she gasped in shock as an entryway appeared where there had been solid wall.

Sturdy steel doors clicked and whined after Rayford pressed his fingerprint into a lock on the side. She had suspected he was up to more than just mountain rest out here, but somehow it had never occurred to her that he might have a lair hidden behind his house.

The doors slid open to reveal a silver hallway lined with fluorescent lighting that emanated from somewhere near the ground.

"Neat, huh?" With another chuckle, he started down a narrow walkway. Its sides and walls were a shiny metal, the floor unpainted concrete. "Remember I am a scientist."

She glanced at him, unsure of how to react.

"Well, this is my laboratory."

They passed several closed doors, but finally took a left into a short hallway, followed by another right. Elise hoped she didn't have to find her way out alone.

Stepping into Rayford's 'laboratory' was like stepping into a futuristic science fiction movie.

"I'm glad you like it," the scientist had evidently picked up on her awe. Touchscreen computers and clear glass lined the walls, the latter covered with chemical equations written haphazardly in white. There was plenty of empty silver counter space in the center and a large closet of presumably chemicals to her left. "I find it easy to work here," he explained. "I have this all to myself. This is what I wanted to show you."

He began typing at a computer, backing away for her to see the screen as he spoke. "I know this science stuff can be boring, but bear with me. Here is a picture of a normal strand of DNA. Your father and I were working on genetic therapies and intentional genetic mutations, initially in an effort to improve livestock. We could cut out traits from sickly animals and so forth, making them stronger and healthier."

"That wasn't so difficult, and we eventually turned to not only targeting stronger genes, but actually enhancing them. At first our attempts were met with very little success, but your father had a brilliant idea. Instead of directly modifying the DNA, which too often destabilized the entire structure, he suggested attaching a type of converter, a 'middle-man' if you will. This chemical bonded with the traditional A, T, C, and G in the DNA without interfering with normal functions. It had virtually no effect on the subject's genetics at all. We called it a freerider.

"The purpose was that this Chemical, let's call it X, could act as a translator for other compounds introduced to the body."

If Elise's expression was as blank as her mind there was no way Rayford could miss the confusion.

He frowned, "It's a catalyst. For instance, let's say Compound Y contains inputs necessary for increased physical strength. Without the converter chemical X already in place, it would float around the bloodstream and eventually be destroyed by your body's defenses. But with the converter already attached to the DNA strand, your body can read the information and conform to its instructions."

She stared at him in silence, struggling to comprehend what he just told her. "So... my dad developed a way to, uh, enhance animals?"

"Precisely. His research was going amazingly well, and the animals we tested exhibited all the traits desired. However," he made an ugly face. "Once we moved up in the experimental stages, the university shut down our research for 'ethical' reasons. All of your father's work was lost, the experiments never fully completed."

Rayford sighed deeply, "There was really so much promise in the research. The possibility of countering cancer, or any genetic disease..." he trailed off.

"So my dad did genetic research. What does this have to do with me?"

"Remember I told you about the clinic your father and I ran together. One side was for research, the other was a private clinic for In Vitro Fertilization. It was quite a setup, you know, as the means of integrating this converter X could only be done at the time of fertilization. A compound was added that introduced the chemical at precisely the right time, allowing the freerider to be built into the forming zygote."

Elise nodded slightly, afraid of where this was going.

"You see, my dear. Your father and mother wanted another child, but were unable. Naturally, they tried IVF at the clinic, and after a few tries..." he waved his hands in her direction. "Well, here you are."

She could easily see what he was hinting at, but refused to draw vague connections. "What are you saying?"

"You progressed normally in development; you really were such a delightful child." His grandfatherly smile appeared again. "But that's how the freerider gene was designed to work. There is no evidence of the converter unless you add the other half, so to speak."

Drawing in a deep sigh, Rayford clasped his hands before him. "It was only in the investigation of your father that anyone found out what he had done. You see, human testing was and is strictly forbidden, mostly due to the ethical reasons and potential human rights violations of the person carrying the gene.

"However, this all happened at the same time as the accusations of fraud and treason, charges which your father never publically faced. As you already know, when he disappeared, he took you with him. Until now, that was the last anyone heard of Irene Mathis."

Elise just stared at Rayford's face, searching for a hint of playfulness or lying. This had to be a joke. Or just not true. She didn't feel any different. Then again, if she was different, she wouldn't know what normal felt like. Could this explain why so many people were looking for her, why they were willing to spend so much time and resources over her?

Rayford pulled a chair over. "Here, have a seat. I realize this is a lot to take in at once."

Accepting his offer, she sank warily into the chair. "So, I have this chemical in my DNA?" He nodded, and she continued to sort through the implications. "What does this have to do with... with me, and the FBI, and you and… everything?" She felt like it should be obvious, but her mind had not come up with any logical solutions.

Rayford leaned over to look her squarely in the eyes. "Our research was shut down initially because of ethical reasons. As I said, we tested using animals with amazing degrees of success; all sorts of animals. Keep in mind there is a good reason tests like this can be run for decades before conclusive results are ascertained.

"What we discovered as years went by was that…" He seemed reluctant to go on. "While there were no initial effects of the freerider gene, eventually the animals suffered severe side effects."

Her heart skipped a beat. "Like what?"

When he continued, his voice was quiet. "Eventually the DNA strand destabilized, causing debilitating sickness leading to death. It was too complex for the body to copy correctly again and again. Errors inevitably arose."

Eying him suspiciously, she honestly didn't know what to think. Carbon said he would lie, but this seemed too elaborate, even for Rayford.

Was she really terminally ill? She felt fine, and was rarely sick.

"But there is a bright side, Elise," Rayford stood and pointed to the flat screen monitor. "I think there may be a way to fix the problem. If I can study your DNA, I believe I can engineer a system to stabilize it."

Somehow she doubted his motives could be that pure. "But I feel fine."

"Yes, right now that is true. In the animals there was a high level of variance over the amount of time it took for the genetic code to destabilize. The pattern seemed to operate in proportion to body weight, but there wasn't a solid trend. Really, you should expect at least a few more years without any symptoms, maybe more. It is impossible to tell precisely."

Elise averted her eyes to the monitor where he had drawn up scientific gibberish. Her father had really done this to her? Is this why Carbon wouldn't tell her anything?

"So, I have a proposition for you. I am offering you a safe place to stay, my legal team to work with the FBI, and my services to develop a cure. In return I only request the ability to further my research; the research your father started."

Her expression didn't change, and he continued softly in his crisp British accent, "The situation is truly terrible, and I wish there was a way to undo what your father has done. However, we need to face reality and make the best we can out of what we have."

Silence ensued. Elise couldn't think of anything to say.

"I'm truly sorry. I'll give you some time to yourself, I understand this is very difficult. Come, let me show you a nice room back here. It's too dangerous to stay in the main part of the house. But I'm sure you won't need any convincing after our friend Joe's little stunt out there. There are a lot of people out there who would like to get their hands on you."

Lawson. Elise briefly wondered what they'd done with him, but her mind was too overwhelmed to give it much thought.

Allowing Rayford to steer her into a simple white room with a cot, she sank down heavily as he disappeared with a sympathetic smile. She definitely needed a time out.

Chapter 30

When Rayford stepped into his study, Hitchens was waiting patiently at his desk.

"Sir," the tall man stood. "I found something you'll want to see."

"Has our lost hiker come to?"

"No, he's still out cold. But it does concern him. I sent his mug to our friend, who identified him immediately. You won't believe who this guy is."

"Do tell, Hitchens. I can't stay in suspense forever."

"Joe Steamer is a Deputy Shane Lawson of the Simoa County Sheriff Department."

Rayford cocked an eyebrow. "I've never heard of the place."

"He's the deputy who responded to Elise Perry's 911 call and brought her to the federal prison in Iowa."

"Hm." Rayford gave Hitchens a puzzled glance. "That is very interesting. You think he works for Mathis?"

The younger man only shrugged. "I'm sure we'll find out soon enough. My only concern is who else was working with him. There's at least one other; our 'Aunt Jemima', and then this Carbon that was never found. Remember that when we got the girl out of the car, we never found anyone else. And then the guys turned up dead. Someone had to have been nearby, and they must have more resources than we first thought."

"And you think they're going to try something."

"Almost certainly. We should be very careful."

"I agree. Do what is necessary to awaken our deputy; I think he'll have the information you need. And send Miles up here. It's time for a real talk with Miss Perry."

* * * *

Three FBI agents sat quietly on a private jet. For all official purposes, they were headed to Colorado on business, and nothing was to be discussed here. Stewart had given them a fifteen minute briefing before sending them on their way.

He had stressed that this mission was purely reconnaissance, but of course if any opportunities arose…

Each one was studying a folder of information Stewart had provided, enjoying the rest of sitting still while preparing mentally for what lay ahead.

* * * *

Elise shot up from her cot as the door was thrown open. Rayford stormed in with one of the henchmen from earlier close behind.

"Miss Perry," his tone was tight, his eyes disturbingly angry. "I think it's time we be honest with each other."

"Wha..?"

But he held up a hand and interrupted, "You lied to me."

The accusation was simple, and his eyes bored into hers with a dangerous fury. "After all I've done for you… I just don't understand."

This was a dramatic change from twenty minutes ago, and one Elise was not prepared to handle.

"You said that you didn't know Mr. Steamer, or should I say Deputy Shane Lawson."

Elise blinked. How had he figured that out?

"I want to help you here, Elise. But you need to level with me. Let's begin with something basic. How about Carbon?"

He knew about Carbon? She looked up at him questioningly. "Who?"

His lip curled into a sneer. "Don't play with me, girl. We know she was the one who picked you up in Mesa Springs and that she grabbed you again outside the LaDache Prison."

But Elise only stared at him blankly. During her brief twenty-minutes of silence, she had decided that even if Rayford was telling the truth, her only solution was to find her father and ask him personally. And given the British gentleman's fit of rage, her decision was well founded.

"She drives a black car, claims to work for your father... come on, Elise. I know you know what I'm talking about."

Anger swelled up like a torrent. How could this man be so two-faced? Did he really expect her to trust him? Maintaining her silence, she only met his gaze defiantly.

"What? Do you want to die a slow, horrible death as your DNA rips itself apart?" he taunted. "I'm the only one capable of finding a cure, and you know it. I'm just asking for simple cooperation."

Elise couldn't believe that this was the same man she had spoken with earlier. Her heart took joy in the fact that he didn't actually know who Carbon was. Far be it from her to inform him.

"Fine," he snapped. "I didn't want to do this, but you leave me no choice." Rayford made an effort to collect himself and backed away purposefully. The big man behind him stepped into his place, and grabbed Elise by the shoulders.

She winced at the pain, but refused to speak.

When she glanced back at Rayford, he had drawn a needle from somewhere and was grinning at her wickedly. "This won't hurt at all."

* * * *

Dark. Everything was dark. Stars? No, fireflies! But the fuzzy lights expanded, then contracted back into a singular point of light. A dim light bulb was somewhere overhead. Gradually it grew brighter and a pale white wall came into focus.

He was in a small room. At first it appeared to be spinning, but eventually slowed to a decent level of perception that lent to the knowledge that he was indeed sitting still. And he couldn't move.

His vision was foggy, and as he attempted to lift an arm, the only response was a cry of agony at the base of his skull.

"Welcome back." A figure seemed to materialize from thin air, its form distorted as though moving waves ran through its length like TV static.

"Shall we first dispense with the bull?" The person came closer, but it may have been an optical illusion. Why wouldn't the world hold still?

"First, I don't believe we've had a proper introduction. Let's start with your name."

Name? What name?

"If that's too hard, I'll start for you." The form was very close now, and finally a tanned face came into view. "Your name is Shane Lawson."

Was it?

"Let's go a little further. You trespassed onto my property, recorded data with this," a small, shiny object was shoved in his face, "lied about your identity, and then put a gun to the head of a certain girl."

Really? Had he done that?

"You don't seem all here yet, so we'll start with something simple. Who do you work for?"

Trying to speak, sparks of pain reignited in his head, and his tongue seemed glued to the roof of his mouth.

The person in front was muttering something unintelligible, and another attempt to focus revealed at least one other person in the room. He barely noticed as that person stepped forward and pricked his arm with something. Thoughts were as elusive as clear vision.

The two ignored him for an indefinite amount of time, talking in low voices, and unwillingly Lawson's senses began returning to him. The first sensation to hit fully was a high-pitched ringing and searing pain in his head. Soon after that, the two shadowy figures standing in front of him resolved into two men, both of whom appeared vaguely familiar.

Slowly he began to feel his feet and hands again, and the reason why he was unable to move became apparent. Someone had tied him to this chair. Why would anyone do that?

Looking back up at the men, he simply couldn't recall what he was doing here.

"There, you're looking better already." The taller one stepped closer. "We'll start at the beginning again. What's your name?"

Lawson. They had said his name was Shane Lawson. It seemed correct. Finally unsticking his tongue, he mumbled a garbled reply.

"What was that?"

"Lawson. My name is Lawson." Maybe.

"Good. Now, who do you work for?"

Images of a police cruiser and the police training academy came to mind. Oh, yeah. "The Sheriff Department of Simoa County."

His interrogator seemed amused. "That's true. Let me try again. What are you doing here?"

Funny, Lawson had been wondering the same thing. "I don't know."

"Of course. Let's see if I can help jog your memory. Elise Perry?"

The name sounded familiar. Important.

"Dr. Samuel Mathis? Are we ringing any bells here?"

But Lawson only drew a blank.

"Let's try another name. Carbon."

Carbon. He knew Carbon. She was his friend. Wait... Elise. Carbon was Elise's friend.

It all fell together at once. He remembered the car, the girl, why he was here, and another thing. He needed to get out.

Looking around, it became immediately evident that escape was unlikely at best. The small block room was like a prison cell, his bonds were strong and tight, and even if his two interrogators just stood aside and watched, he doubted he could move at all.

He now recognized the tall man as Hitchens from outside, but the other one he had never seen before.

They would kill him. Looking into Hitchens' eyes, it was plainly clear that he wanted information, and once he got it that would be the end of the road.

"Come on, buddy, don't be shy. We can move to more persuasive measures if you don't want to cooperate."

Why didn't Carbon do something? He hadn't signed up for torture, just a quick and easy rescue.

"Look. I'm going to give you five minutes to think about this. You can start talking, and we'll get you some pain pills for that headache and a free ride home. Otherwise… well. You can probably figure it out for yourself."

That was for sure. The two disappeared through the door, leaving Lawson alone. It was cold, he realized for the first time. Freezing.

"Deputy Lawson, do not move." Carbon. They hadn't removed his earwig? Some bad guys.

"Do not speak or acknowledge my voice. They are watching you."

He sure wished he could speak. A thousand complaints filed through his head, but he realized it was a moot point.

"I was able to wirelessly gather the data you collected while you were outside. The information reveals a weakness in Rayford's lead shielding, allowing me to sketch the compound and communicate with you. I have acquired three targets. Because of your situation, I may have to act before nightfall, so be alert. Once their power supply is gone, the facility will be in absolute dark as there are no windows."

Thanks for the reminder.

"I have pinpointed your location to somewhere on the second story, a thousand feet past the barrier. Elise's trace has ceased to function, so I will be unable to locate her precisely until I create a larger opening in the lead shielding."

Lawson wasn't sure, but that sounded like a euphemism for blasting the wall into oblivion.

"At that time I will guide you to her location and meet you both as close as I can. Stay alert."

With that last warning, the cold room fell silent again. Carbon had overlooked a crucial detail in her plans. How was he supposed to go rescue Elise when he was stuck tied to this chair?

His mind posed a helpful question: *What would Bond do?*

The hero had faced many challenges like this, and always lived to make another movie. Surely there was a way out.

First matter of business, he determined that his chair was not bolted to the floor. That was good.

Secondly, he needed something sharp to try to cut loose these ropes. This was a little harder. The room was absolutely empty apart from the light bulb on the ceiling and the door's round knob.

But as he stared at the knob for any potential weakness or sharp edge, it twisted open to reveal Hitchens smiling amiably. But not really so amiably, just happy. This was the kind of man who liked to hit things.

Lawson prayed that Carbon acted soon instead of waiting to see how much he could survive. Judging from the car's general attitude, however, he held no great faith that this would be the case. He'd have to talk with his attorneys about that later.

"So, Mr. Lawson. What have you decided?"

What would Bond do?

Chapter 31

Hitchens was sure this man would crack. It was just taking longer than expected. So far he had not uttered a word, and Hitchens could respect him for at least taking his blows admirably. However, this was business, and it was vital that Hitchens got the information he needed.

Placing his hands on Lawson's wrists, he leaned heavily on them to stare directly into the man's bloody face. Really, Hitchens had been quite humane so far. All of the damage was superficial except for the broken nose, and that was minor considering what he could do.

His victim's face contorted with pain as Hitchens felt fragile wrist bones under his palms. "Okay, sheriff. Let's just get this over with. How many people are you working with?"

But before he had fully finished his sentence, a deep rumbling cracked through the air. Hitchens struggled to steady himself as a tremendous explosion shook the ground under his feet and knocked him off balance.

The lights flickered, then died.

* * * *

This was his only chance, and Lawson knew it. Flinging his body around, he threw his weight to land the chair's legs in the direction

Hitchens' body had disappeared, grateful for the distraction of several more loud explosions.

He landed on target, and the man struggled underneath him for minutes before growing still. It was not an experience Lawson enjoyed.

Despite that he held less than kind feelings toward this man who had spent the last ten minutes as his tormentor, the sensation of smothering the life out of anybody was not something he ever wanted to experience again.

Especially since now he was stuck. He rocked his feet violently, but only managed to bring the chair halfway to upright before it toppled over again.

The air was growing warm, and Lawson wondered how much of the building was on fire. There couldn't be much oxygen back here under a mountain and all, but surely blowing up generators involved burning a fair amount of fuel.

He froze his efforts as the door creaked open. A small light beam swept across his face, and footsteps brought the flashlight closer.

Great. He couldn't even move, much less defend himself. But the light paused as it was set on the floor, and soon a knife was cutting away at his bonds. The person's face was hidden in the darkness, but the hands were rough and dark.

Who the heck was that? "Hello?"

"Ah-lo," the voice responded with a thick accent, the man working deftly with his knife.

"Who are you?" Lawson asked as he shrugged the ropes off his right hand and then the left.

But the man remained silent, and helped Lawson to his feet. His new friend stretched out a hand offering a pistol and a flashlight.

"Um, thanks," he stammered in surprise.

The man pointed out the door, and in the dim light Lawson recognized him as the man from the generator room. "Go quickly," the man instructed in his heavy accent before flicking off his flashlight and vanishing into the dark.

"Deputy Lawson, are you all right?" Carbon's voice asked from inside his ear.

Everything hurt. "Yeah. Peachy."

"We have a problem, and you need to move fast. Exit to your left."

A problem? Shocking.

But Lawson did as he was told, flicking on his flashlight he sprinted to the left, ignoring the strange desire to look back at what remained of Hitchens.

"Now take another left. It is a narrow corridor with nine doors on each side. Elise is in the fifth one on the right."

Sure enough, Lawson headed down the claustrophobic hallway lined with doors. Some had oddly shaped slots, all of them were locked.

Counting twice to be sure he was at the correct door, Lawson swung his flashlight beam up and down to find a way inside.

"Carbon," he whispered. "How do I get in?"

"You could find the key or destroy the lock."

Oh, like it was that easy. He had already seen the Mythbusters' failed attempts to shoot off locks. "What? Can't you open it remotely?"

"No. It is not an electronic lock."

For such a high-tech setup, this guy was really backward in his lock security. Sighing in disgust, Lawson tried to inspect the lock closer. There was a deadbolt as well as a basic lock on the door handle. These things weren't usually a problem on television.

Unfortunately, however, Lawson didn't have a lock-picking kit, and even if he did, he did not have the skills to use it. "I need some help here."

"One of the guards likely has a key."

As much as Lawson didn't like where this was going, based on his very limited ammunition and fairly limited time, he decided that it would have to do.

"Do you know where the guards are?" he whispered.

"Yes. In fact, there are two men headed your way."

Splendid. Glancing around, he saw that if he was going to confront two armed men in this hallway, it probably wasn't going to end well.

"The door to the right is unlocked, and the room is empty." Carbon informed him. What was hiding behind all the other doors?

Footsteps began to echo closer, but when he pulled the next door handle, it was locked as well.

"Your other right, Lawson."

Right. This door was unlocked, and Lawson thought he saw the swath of a high-powered flashlight just as it clicked shut behind him.

"Hurry," a British voice whisper over the noise of jangling keys. Should he jump out now and surprise them, or wait until they enter the room?

"Hold still," Carbon's voice sounded in his ear. "There is another man with a gun at the end of the hallway."

Every fiber of his aching being froze in the pitch black, one hand resting on the doorknob. He heard Elise's door swing open, though no voices were audible.

Why didn't the girl complain? But the dark was dead silent except for the sound of fire crackling below, and the sound of shuffling in the room. Heavy steps began receding in the other direction.

"They have Elise, and their backs are turned. Act quickly."

It was about time. Throwing his door open, Lawson first tossed his lit flashlight onto the floor and trained his pistol down the hallway at three fleeing figures. They were barely visible, and the first one appeared to be carrying the girl over his shoulder. He took aim at the one in the back, who had just turned around with his own weapon.

Gunshots ricocheted in the hallway as they exchanged fire, and Lawson's small flashlight shattered to darkness as it was obliterated in a million pieces. Lawson himself had managed to get off three shots before retreating back into his room, and based on the heavy thud and quickly retreating footsteps, he figured he had indeed hit his target and the other two had not stuck around to find out.

"Carbon," he whispered. "Where are they?"

"One is down at the end of the hallway, the others are still running with Elise."

Darn. Jumping out of the room, Lawson sprinted after them. His face stung terribly in pain, along with most other parts of his body, but adrenaline masked the effects as his feet pounded the floor.

"Which way?"

He paused at the end of the hallway to retrieve his victim's flashlight, grimacing at the crumpled form and vacant eyes. *Survive!* his mind screamed.

"Left, then your next left, then turn right into a wide hallway."

All these corridors looked the same, especially in the thin beam of a flashlight, and he only hoped Carbon knew where they led.

Lawson could hear voices from somewhere ahead of him, and ducked behind a wall just as a spray of bullets came his way. "Carbon," he whispered angrily. "What now?"

"Wait one moment. They are taking Elise; you cannot catch them in time. You need to hurry. Several timed explosive detonators have been activated within the structure."

The structure. Where he was.

"Proceed as quickly as you can." The car was continuing, "Rayford is headed to a vehicle, and he is likely attempting to escape with Elise and destroy any evidence left behind.

"Now. They are out of range. Run."

He needed no further encouragement.

"Continue straight, but proceed with caution. There is a hole in the wall large enough for you to pass through, but there is much debris lying around."

Sure enough, as Lawson sped toward a very solid appearing wall, the ground around him was strewn with metal, wood, and glass like some sort of battlefield, and the wall itself... There was a jagged hole where explosives had blown through, and he was forced to slow down to carefully slip between the shards without slitting himself open.

He hissed in pain as his shoulder scraped a knife-like obtrusion despite his efforts.

"Rayford is starting a vehicle and Elise is with him. You do not have much time."

Shut up! He wanted to scream. Tell me something I don't know! But all his effort was spent running as he found himself in another hallway. Some of the walls were beginning to burn or maybe just finishing burning, he didn't stop to investigate.

"There is a door ten feet in front of you. It is unlocked."

There was some good news. Throwing the door open, Lawson recognized the spacious foyer even in the thin light. Almost there.

Blood was pounding like a thousand drummers in his ears. He couldn't discern any other noise as he flung the front door open and burst into the night. A white car reflected the moonlight in front of him as he bounded down the staircase in two giant leaps. His second jump was swallowed in an eerie lull before a tremendous force slammed him forward.

He was airborne, caught in a shockwave. Brilliant light engulfed him, and his head exploded with sound.

Tumbling into something, he couldn't remember landing. Maybe his senses were gone. Maybe he was dead.

Silence swallowed the world, but as he lifted his head, a fiery explosion was just receding. He blinked in the darkness that followed, but his shocked eyes refused to focus.

A far away voice sounded in the shadows. "Hang on, Lawson. Do you hear me? Are you all right?"

He blinked, and blinked again. Carbon? He wasn't dead. He was moving.

"Deputy Lawson? Please respond."

"Hi." It was the only thing that came to mind. What was he supposed to say?

"Are you all right?"

"Carbon."

"Yes. I am here. You are inside, you are safe."

Safe? Inside?

"The explosion has temporarily blinded you. It will not take long to pass."

How had he landed inside? But sure enough, he felt soft leather under his aching fingertips, and reaching out he patted down on the solid dashboard. What a catch.

"What's happening?" Dim lights were beginning to creep back into his vision, but it wasn't fast enough.

"Rayford remotely detonated explosives that were strategically placed to collapse the structure."

"Self-destruct?"

"Precisely. He is attempting to escape with Elise in a green Nissan Xterra. We are in pursuit."

"Oh." That explained why they were moving, although he was fairly confident his head was swimming on its own. Never before had he felt so close to passing out.

The effort was agony, but he managed to pull himself to upright and squint out the windshield. The blazing inferno behind them became a small speck in the rearview mirror as they flew through the flat grassland.

After crossing the prairie, the road began twisting and curving back into foothills. At first Lawson concluded he must still be mostly blind, but he recalled Carbon's propensity for driving without headlights and realized he could now see stars out the window and even the vague outline of trees against the moon's pale light.

"How far are they?"

"About one-third of a mile, but we are gaining on them rapidly. That SUV was not built for speed."

Through the pain, Lawson managed a short grimacing chuckle as they raced through the night. This car was not humble.

Chapter 32

Rayford alternated from slamming his foot on the gas pedal and the brake. He knew his driving was erratic, and although he had not seen any headlights following, he had also not forseen the attack on his house. Where had Mathis gotten resources like that?

Gritting his teeth, he braked hard as he threw the Xterra around another corner. Someone would pay for this. The girl was strapped into the passenger seat, out cold. She was lucky she was so valuable.

His breathing was growing regular again, and he checked back in his mirrors less obsessively. There was no way anyone survived that explosion, and no emergency crews were close enough to get there for another twenty minutes at a minimum.

The steering wheel remained clenched in a steely grasp, but the silence of the forest night over the Xterra's engine was comfortingly still. Except for a peculiar noise.

Rayford strained his ears, listening to the strange humming in the distance. His thoughts were diverted as a large object crashed onto the roadway a few hundred feet ahead.

There was barely enough time to slam on the brakes, and the SUV came to a screeching halt. A large tree had fallen, and he knew this was no coincidence. Executing a rapid three-point turn on the narrow road, he stopped to see a vehicle blocking his path.

He reached for his Glock as his lips turned up into an angry sneer. The Xterra's headlights illuminated the white nose of a Dodge

Challenger. Carbon. So she was here. Hopefully Mathis was with her.

Yanking Elise's seatbelt off, he grabbed the girl's limp form and dragged her out of the vehicle. How the seasons change. Burying the gun into her head, he found it surprisingly difficult to support the motionless body as a shield.

"One move and she's dead!" he screamed, staring in rage at the rumbling car. He couldn't see past the glare of the windshield, but if a door opened it would be unmistakable. "Just stay in the car!"

He inched toward the side of the road. If he could just get into the woods, it was unlikely these people could follow.

Another pair of headlights had just appeared behind the white sedan when a soft hiss sounded in the night. Rayford screamed as his hand exploded into nothing, his right shoulder catching shards of metal and bone.

A spread of automatic weapon-fire punctured the air next, and he was surprised to find himself still standing. The headlights that had been approaching were now backing away in a hasty retreat.

"Don't move!" A male voice commanded as Rayford clutched his arm in shock, the girl having slid to the pavement at his feet.

It was that accursed deputy. What, was he here to do all Mathis' dirty work? "How dare you..." Rayford hissed in furious rage. He could feel his body slipping into shock, and he fought it desperately, wishing the man before him to die a hundred painful deaths a thousand different ways.

"I mean it," the deputy warned as he neared with a pistol trained at Rayford's chest. "Carbon there has another aimed right between your eyes. I wouldn't suggest moving." The man tucked his firearm in his belt before scooping up the girl's form gingerly. Rayford really hoped it hurt.

It wasn't long before the deputy disappeared with Elise into the white vehicle, and the car executed a deft turn on the narrow roadway before rocketing off into the dark.

He had begun to stumble back into his Xterra when the second pair of headlights emerged yet again, headed toward him. A lean Hispanic man jumped out, concern evident on his face.

"FBI!" he yelled. "Sir, are you all right?"

Obscene phrases passed through Rayford's mind, but he stifled them. "Ah!" he moaned in pain, an effect that wasn't necessary to fake. "Please help..." he cried piteously, holding out his injured arm.

"Oh my gosh!" the man exclaimed. "Sit down, sir. We'll have an ambulance here in no time."

Rayford did as he was told while the agent took off his jacket and used it to slow the bleeding. But as the color drained from his face, a tiny smile crossed his lips. They had made a serious mistake in leaving him alive.

Chapter 33

Thirty minutes had passed since confronting Rayford on the cliff side, and Lawson's gasping breaths had finally returned to some degree of normalcy. Granted, it was more like wheezing, and he tried not to think about any permanent damage his body had undergone.

In the passenger seat, the girl stirred.

"Elise?" Carbon asked.

She moaned, curling as best she could into a fetal position. In the dim light from the car's softly glowing instruments, her forehead was visibly soaked and water dripped down her face. Carbon had explained to him that Rayford had injected her with some sort of drug that was wreaking havoc with her DNA. He had been lost in the scientific jargon, but was able to grasp that her life was very much in danger if she didn't get help soon, and that the only suitable antidote was waiting in Montana.

Which required a trip Carbon counseled would take ten hours at best, depending on traffic and law enforcement. Touching the girl's forehead he found it to be burning hot.

"Is she going to make it?"

"She has a favorable chance, but her body temperature is excessively high. There is cold water in the glove compartment. Use a piece of cloth and try to cool her face."

Lawson did as he was told, pleading quietly with the girl to hang on. They couldn't have gone through all of that for her to die here. But besides his prayers and the cooling water, there was nothing to do but wait as Carbon sped through the mountains.

* * * *

The sun rose slowly the next morning, and Elise looked closer to death every hour. She had stopped shifting and moaning thirty minutes ago, and Lawson would have pronounced her dead except for the weak pulse in her neck. Her skin was white and clammy, and her fingers were cold.

Watching her, Lawson's considerable pity for his own injured state was somewhat lessened, but he couldn't keep himself from fading in and out of consciousness as time wore on.

It was like a dream. He occasionally awoke to the middle of a busy highway or to a rising peak. He had lost all concept of time when a hand tapped him gently on the shoulder.

"Mr. Lawson," a kind voice said near his ear. "Sir? Are you awake?"

He groggily opened his eyes, struggling to focus on a smiling wrinkled face.

"Mr. Lawson?" the woman asked again.

"Yes?" he fumbled for words. Who was that? He shook his head to clear his thoughts, glancing over at the empty seat beside him. "Where am I?"

"We have reached Montana." Carbon informed him. "Elise is safe, and her condition has been stabilized."

He again tried to focus on the woman's face, without much success. "Come here," she ordered as a grandmotherly hand wrapped around his arm. "Let's get you inside. I think you've had enough for one day."

They had done it. He wasn't dead. The girl was alive, Carbon was in one piece, and the bad guy was... well, at least he wasn't here.

Lawson was all but extracted from the car in the old lady's surprisingly strong grasp. She was saying something, but relief had

236

already flooded his system and he realized how weak and weary his body felt.

"Deputy Lawson," Carbon's voice came in his head again. He would have to remove that earwig later. "You do not need to respond, just rest. You are in good hands here. They will take care of you."

Allowing the grey haired woman to lead him into a house, he was grateful for a shoulder to lean on. To his delight, their short trek ended with a heavenly bed. Maybe it was all perception, but rest had never appeared so wonderful.

"One more thing," Carbon added. "Thank you."

But Lawson barely registered the words as he drifted off into a dreamless sleep.

AFTERWORD

This book was written upon the premise that there is nothing new under the Sun. Every story ever told has been told before; albeit in many different forms and many different ways. This story is much the same; a tale woven to incorporate what I believe is the Creator's loving longing to bring all people to know Himself, and to return every child – no matter how broken, no matter how rejected – to Himself for healing, restoration, and that amazing thing that is Love itself.

Now available in the "Carbon: Resurrection" series:

The Trilogy
    Carbon I: Salvation
    Carbon II: Redemption
    Carbon III: Revelation

The Last Four
    Restoration (Book I of IV)

Available soon…
    Retaliation (Book II of IV)
    Reformation (Book III of IV)
    Reconciliation (Book IV of IV)

Also by Carrie Yonge…
    Soar (Book I: Wings of Eagles)

Email the author:

    carbonthebook@gmail.com

Visit us online at www.carbonresurrection.com

Like Carbon on Facebook
and
Follow Carrie Yonge on Twitter

www.ingramcontent.com/pod-product-compliance
Lightning Source LLC
Chambersburg PA
CBHW070559130626
46556CB00001B/222